THAT WOMAN
NEXT DOOR

HARPER BLISS

That Woman Next Door

ladylit_ publishing

OTHER HARPER BLISS NOVELS

About That Kiss
At Your Most Beautiful
A Breathless Place
If You Kiss Me Like That
Two Hearts Trilogy
Next in Line for Love
A Lesson in Love
Life in Bits (with T.B. Markinson)
A Swing at Love (with Caroline Bliss)
Once Upon a Princess (with Clare Lydon)
In the Distance There Is Light
The Road to You
Far from the World We Know
Seasons of Love
Release the Stars
At the Water's Edge
High Rise (The Complete Collection)

THE PINK BEAN SERIES
THE FRENCH KISSING SERIES

Copyright © 2021 by Harper Bliss
Published by Ladylit Publishing – an imprint of First Page V.O.F., Belgium
ISBN-13 9789464339062
D/2021/15201/06
NUR 340
Edited by Cheyenne Blue
Proofread by Claire Jarrett
Cover design by Caroline Manchoulas

To the glorious, restorative wilds of Brittany

JANUARY

CHAPTER 1

MARIE

I kill the engine and stare at the house. It looks so desolate in the middle of winter. Maybe depressing is a better way to describe it. After all, there's a reason we call it a summer house. Why couldn't my family have bought a place in Provence, I wonder for the umpteenth time since I started the drive down from Brussels this morning. Along grey road after grey road, with no prospect of any new growth, for months to come. But I didn't come here for fun. I came to cold, wet, rural Brittany on the first day of the new year with the single purpose of punishing myself. Of looking inside myself to find out if I still have it in me to continue doing what I do after what happened.

I suck in a deep breath and get out of the car. As I lift my suitcase out of the boot, a gust of wind whips up my hair, which I had cut a few days ago to look my best for my self-inflicted exile. To what end? There's no one here to see me. My mother warned me the internet might be too spotty for a successful Skype connection, after she asked me, again, whether I, a purebred city person, was absolutely certain I wanted to sequester myself in Brittany.

I could have escaped to an exotic beach. Or ventured on a coast-to-coast road trip through the United States. Or embarked on a Scottish castle tour. But I chose wintery Brittany because, for the first time in my life, I'm not choosing excitement. I have to say no to anything thrilling. I have to create the time and space I need to evaluate what has occurred. I need to find out how it could have happened and if it will again.

I know myself. Put me anywhere amongst a group of people and I will pick out the most attractive woman and have her in my bed in no time. Or maybe I've lost that skill as well.

It doesn't matter here. There are no people around. Our house is the only one on this road, although, through the barren trees, I can spot another house around the corner, about a hundred metres away. Distant enough to not have to see or hear the people living there, if anyone lives there at all at this time of year.

I unlock the door and am greeted by a cold blast almost as harsh as the temperature outside. I quickly close the door behind me. At least it looks the way I like—renovated to today's standards, at my insistence.

I think of my warm, gorgeous apartment overlooking the Ixelles Ponds in Brussels. The light that streams in through the large windows even in winter. I shiver. Up until a few years ago, this house's only means of heating was a fireplace, which may sound romantic, but is anything but when you run out of logs in the middle of the night. Or when you wake up in the morning and your buttocks nearly freeze to the toilet seat.

But I couldn't do the kind of penance I'm after in

Brussels, surrounded by the luxury of my daily life and the convenience of a city. Something had to be stripped away. Something major had to give. The house in Brittany was the first place that came to mind and here I am, trembling inside my coat, on the dreariest winter day. For some reason, I felt like I needed to arrive on the first day of the new year. As though it matters. As though I have to start an actual prison sentence mandated by the courts instead of this self-inflicted punishment I have chosen.

I switch on the thermostat but keep my coat on. It will take a while before it's warm enough for me to relax. I transfer the rest of my stuff from the car into the house and unload the groceries I brought. I'll have oceans of time to dedicate to cooking because there are no food delivery services to the middle of nowhere.

After I've dragged my suitcase upstairs and unpacked most of my clothes, I stand in front of the bedroom window. When there are no leaves on the trees, the house around the corner is visible from here. Because I'm already starting to feel like the only person left on the planet, even though I've only just arrived, I desperately search for a sign of life inside the house. I don't see any lights glowing behind the windows, but there's smoke coming from the chimney. Even though I've been coming to Brittany on and off for decades, I have no idea who lives in that house.

I've always considered my family's holiday home a house without neighbours. In summer, it kind of is. When the days are long and the nights warm, and you can sit outside in the lush garden until well after dark, neighbours are of no importance. And I've never come here on my own. It's always been with either family or a short-term love interest—the longer-term kind has never interested me until…

I take a moment to remember the last woman I was with. It was the night before the day everything went wrong. I shake off the memory of Véronique—again—although I know I will have to deal with it at some point. After the investigation into what happened in the operating theatre cleared me, the hospital administrator advised me to see someone to help me process the incident. I chose to take a leave of absence instead. I don't want anyone's help. I want to solve this crisis of conscience—and confidence—that's waging a filthy war inside me by myself. It didn't feel fair to accept any kind of assistance because for the woman who died on my operating table, there is no more help. For her, it's all over forever. So why should I deserve any kind of help in dealing with what I did?

The lights in the cottage beyond the trees flickers on. For an instant, I consider switching the bedroom lamp on and off to signal my presence. Instead, I think I might take a walk over there tomorrow.

CHAPTER 2
OLIVIA

M y feet hit the treadmill in such a satisfying way today. This is why I run, I think, while my fists pump the air in a rhythmic motion. To feel like I'm flying. To feel strong. To feel like I can do anything. I increase the speed so I can go a little faster, so I can empty my tank. Even though I've already run more than seven kilometres, my feet can still easily keep up.

My treadmill sits in front of a window with a view out over the fields at the back of my house. I only ever see animals. Mostly birds and cows. Or my cats, who like to wait for me to open the door for them instead of squeezing through the cat flap—they're princesses like that.

What the—? Something much larger than Deneuve and Huppert's furry bodies darkens the window. My already elevated heart rate shoots up a notch. What the hell is happening? I press the red emergency button on the treadmill to make it stop. Who on earth is this person with the audacity to trespass on my property and walk around my house? I'm not expecting any deliveries today. I prefer to group them as much as I can and have them delivered to the supermarket in town, where I can pick them up at my own convenience instead of having my day disturbed by someone showing up at my door.

A woman wrapped in one of those long puffy coats stares at me through the window. She waves as though I'm supposed to know her. I don't recognise her from the village and I'm certain I'm not related to her—not that any member of my family would show up at my house in the middle of any given Wednesday afternoon.

I wipe the sweat from my forehead. I feel cornered. My first instinct is to leave the room and hide upstairs. She doesn't look like she's in distress, although I guess her car could have broken down, her mobile phone might have died, and my house might have been the first one she came across. Maybe she does need help. I take a deep, shuddering breath to pull myself together.

The woman tilts her head. She's probably wondering why I haven't opened the door yet. I suppose I no longer have a choice—as if I ever had one. I drape a towel over my shoulders because I'm dripping with sweat. That's an excellent run ruined. I'm supposed to be in the delightful throes of runner's high right about now, but thanks to this intruder, I've been robbed of the highlight of my day.

I open the door and greet her with an unwelcoming glare. I'm not the type to give strangers a hearty welcome. A fact that's been held against me many times, yet I haven't changed.

"*Bonjour,*" she says. "I'm so sorry to interrupt your run." She hardly comes across as very apologetic. She looks Parisian with her expensive haircut and cashmere pashmina, but her accent is different. "I arrived at the house around the corner yesterday and I noticed signs of life here."

"Yes?" This is not making any sense to me at all. The only other house in a five-kilometre radius is a holiday home owned by some rich Belgians who visit a few times over the summer. I've never had any dealings with them and none of them have previously bothered me before.

"I just wanted to introduce myself." The woman extends her hand. "Marie Dievart. *Enchantée.*"

"Hello." I give her hand the quickest shake I can. My palms are still sweaty. My body is cooling off too quickly standing in the door like this. None of this is ideal. Least of all this woman who wants something from me that I'm unable to figure out. "Olivia." As I wipe my sweaty hand on my leggings, a visible shiver runs up my spine. I pull the towel around my shoulders ostentatiously.

"You'll catch a cold if you don't cover up," Marie Dievart says matter-of-factly.

Duh! All I want is to close the door in her face. Wait? Is she expecting me to invite her inside my house?

"Don't worry. I'm a doctor," she says, as if that makes any difference.

"Look, I'm sorry, but I need to shower."

"Oh, okay." She studies me with an unnerving intensity. "Would you like to come round to my house later for coffee or a glass of wine?"

"What?" Why would she even think that's what I want? "Who are you again and what are you doing here?"

"I'm so sorry, Olivia." She has a very personable manner. She looks like she wants to grab my hand again but has decided against it last-minute—thank goodness. "I'll be staying at my family's holiday home for a few months, so I figured that would make us neighbours. I thought it only polite to introduce myself formally."

"A few months? In the middle of winter?" I shiver again. My sweat-drenched top is ice cold against my skin.

Marie nods. "I need the time away from… my life," she says.

"Okay, well, have a good stay." I attempt to close the door hoping she'll get the hint.

"You don't want to have that glass of wine? I have an amazing Nuits-Saint-Georges waiting to be uncorked."

A wine snob on top of an abrasive trespasser. I shake my head. "No, but thanks for asking."

I'm about to close the door on this woman entirely, but she regards me so intently, it's as though she wants to undo my wish to shut her out just by looking at me. Her eyes are a peculiar kind of green. Her cheekbones are alpine. Oh, I get it. She's one of those women who is so attractive they're used to always getting exactly what they want. She probably can't fathom that I'm not interested in sharing a posh bottle of wine with her.

"I'd hate to have to drink it alone." Her voice is sweet as honey.

"Shouldn't have come here on your own then." I feel something furry rub against my legs. Huppert slips outside and then just sits there, attracting attention—her favourite activity apart from sleeping.

"What a cutie." Marie crouches down to make Huppert's acquaintance.

If only Deneuve had decided to come to my rescue. She wouldn't have any of this. She probably would have swatted Marie Dievart's perfectly manicured hand away if she'd tried to pet her. But not Huppert, who can't get enough of the attention. She's purring, for heaven's sake.

"What's your name then?" the woman asks my cat, as though she can reply to that question with anything other than a meow.

I need to cut this short. If I stay exposed much longer, I'll be out with a cold for days, or even worse, bronchitis. Heaven forbid I need to see a doctor. I wouldn't want to have to call on my new neighbour, while she was the one who made me sick in the first place. That would be too ironic.

"I'll leave you to it then," I say, trying to add a polite smile. I can't help but, very briefly, wonder what I look like to this stranger, with my sweat-drenched clothes and my hair matted against my head. She must be very lonely to be inviting the likes of me to her place.

"Okay. Sure." She looks like she's about to admit defeat. She turns to walk away, but before I can close the door properly, she turns to me, and asks, "Is this how everyone here is? Is it a Breton thing, this unwelcoming attitude? Just so I know what to expect for the rest of my stay."

"You're asking the wrong person." As I say it, I'm aware of how utterly rude I'm sounding—and being.

"Clearly." She does walk away now.

I guess that, once again, I failed to make a new friend. I couldn't care less.

CHAPTER 3
MARIE

I've been in Brittany for five days and I'm already bored out of my skull. I've called my mother every day and my sister every other day, making them worried about me because I can go weeks without talking to them.

The only company I've had is from my antisocial neighbour's cat, which has clearly taken much more of a shine to me than its owner. There are the birds in the sky and the occasional cow in the surrounding fields. The other day, a tractor rumbled past and the noise was a welcome relief from all the silence. Traffic is so scant that every car that drives down the road is almost an event. Yesterday, zero cars drove past.

If Cranky Olivia goes anywhere, she doesn't drive past my house to get there. While I understand I interrupted her run, she could have been a touch more friendly. She could not have been any ruder. There goes my so far only hope for any human contact. On the way back from her house, I had to remind myself that human contact is not what I came here for. If that's what I'd wanted, I'd have travelled to the south, where people spend winter in the sun and might be more up for a chat.

The problem is that I'm not used to having so much time alone with my thoughts and I have to remind myself that I came here for that very reason. To no longer hide from myself. But I've had to resort to taking a sleeping pill every night since I've arrived, otherwise I wouldn't sleep at all. I keep seeing the devastation on the husband's face when I had to tell him his wife had died on my watch. It's etched into my brain and his inconsolable grief shows up every time I close my eyes.

Even so, the days have taken on a certain rhythm. I sleep until the effect of the pill has worn off, which is usually well past nine—another new experience for me. When I open the bedroom curtains, I can't help but see Cranky Olivia's house and wonder what her deal is. After a leisurely breakfast and shower, I like to drive into Bonneau to buy groceries and go for a little stroll. I spend my afternoons reading, walking if the weather permits, watching excruciating daytime TV and cooking, until I declare wine o'clock at the ridiculous time of five in the afternoon.

Evenings are long and lonely. I often find myself toying with my phone, scrolling through my contacts, daydreaming about what would happen if I called someone and asked them to join me. I haven't called anyone yet so far, but I'm not sure how much longer I'll be able to stop myself.

A rustling noise captures my attention—the smallest sounds do, which is why I often let the TV play in the background. It's probably Olivia's cat again, scurrying through the bushes to the side of the house. She didn't even give me its name. I don't even know if it's male or female. Although friendly, the cat hasn't let me come close enough to figure that out. Maybe today it will. To my surprise, there's a knock at the front door. That can't possibly be the cat. My heart leaps into my throat at the prospect of another human calling at my house.

I rush to open the door. To my even greater astonishment, it's my inhospitable neighbour with a bottle in her hands.

"I hope I'm not interrupting anything," she says. "I was going to leave this at your door, but, um, then I figured I'd give it to you in person." She thrusts the bottle in my direction. "It's a locally fermented cider. The distillery that produces it is just outside of Bonneau. You can visit and take a tour of the premises."

I open the door wide so she can't possibly mistake my invitation. "Come in." I make it obvious I won't take no for an answer. "And thank you."

"Only if you're not doing anything important," Olivia says, but enters anyway.

"You're very welcome here." I hold out my hands to take her coat. She peers at them with a puzzled look in her eyes.

"It's nice and warm in here. Best take off that outer layer."

"Are those doctor's orders?" A tiny grin appears on her lips.

"Correct." I forgot I mentioned I'm a doctor. I've never been shy about announcing my profession. The number of women I've been able to talk into bed just by using that line is vast. I take Olivia's coat and hang it up before escorting her into the living room.

"Wow." She takes in the room. "Those renovations

took forever, but they were worth it. I've been curious to see the inside of this house ever since."

"Feel free to have a look around."

She casts me a wide-eyed glance, as if I've given her the keys to a long-lost kingdom.

"I—I actually wanted to apologise for the other day. You caught me at a bad time. I'm sorry I was so impolite."

"Thank goodness." I heave an audible sigh of relief. "That's not who you really are." I briefly touch her shoulder and she all but flinches. Not the touchy-feely type then. "I'm so glad you came over. I've been going a bit stir-crazy." I lead her to the lounge and invite her to sit.

"Why?" she asks matter-of-factly after she has taken a seat.

"Because there's no one around. It's just me." I study the bottle she's brought. "Do you want to drink this or would you prefer a glass of wine?"

"Whatever you have open is fine."

At least she's not asking for coffee. It's only four in the afternoon but it's Saturday and on Saturday wine o'clock comes early.

"Your cat came to visit me a few times." I go into the kitchen to fetch a bottle of red.

"Huppert likes to wander," Olivia says, as I return with a bottle and two glasses.

"Huppert?" I cock an eyebrow. "After Isabelle?"

Olivia nods and I get a vibe. *That* kind of vibe—the kind I'd previously always have acted upon. I take my time pouring the wine. I study her face when I give her the glass, but it doesn't give much else away.

"My other cat's called Deneuve, after you-know-who. She's not as sociable. She's more like me." Olivia chuckles as she holds up her glass.

"You're plenty sociable now," I say, "I'll drink to that." I don't tell her that I would have invited the postman in for a drink if he ever had any mail for this address.

"*Santé.*" Olivia takes a sip and nods approvingly. "Not bad."

"Do you live here permanently?" I look her in the eyes. They're brown and intelligent.

Olivia nods, but doesn't hold my gaze.

"Did you grow up around here?" I ask.

"My family are from Normandy, so not too far away. About a two-hour drive."

"Any particular reason you ended up in Bonneau of all places?"

"Probably the same as you."

Olivia's going to make me work for it. Even though chatting is not that big a part of my job, I'm missing the contact enough to put some effort into getting this conversation flowing. "It's gorgeous here in spring and summer. My family's been coming down for a long time." I send her a warm smile.

"Yeah." She rests her gaze on me for a split second. "This house is usually empty this time of year. Why does a doctor need to get away from her life?" For someone so reluctant to listen, she seems to have remembered all the details of what I said.

"That's a long story." I need to do some more soul-searching before I can share my error with an uninitiated party.

"Okay." She gazes into her wine glass. "Are you expecting any other people or will it just be you?"

"Just me." At least that's the plan.

"I've always appreciated that you don't rent out your house to god-knows-who in summer." She narrows her eyes. Olivia is quite fond of her privacy, that much is obvious. "Where are you from?" she asks.

"Brussels." The vibrant memory of the life I'm used to stings less now that I have company.

"Ah, the city the wealthy French love to flock to in droves," she says. "Or so I hear. I've actually never been."

"You've heard correctly. Brussels is full of French people. It's like a much cheaper version of Paris, minus a lot of the charm, of course." I give a quick nod. "I lived in Paris for a while, but things didn't really work out for me there."

"What kind of doctor are you exactly?"

"I'm a neurosurgeon." For the first time since I qualified, it feels strange to say it. Of course, I *am* still a surgeon. I'm still qualified. I wasn't even suspended. I could go back to work tomorrow if I wanted to—if I hadn't suspended myself.

"Oh, wow." Olivia's eyes grow wide—the usual reaction. "Cutting into people's brains?"

"If you want to put it like that." I'm keen to change the subject—also a new sensation for me. I've never been the humble kind of surgeon, if one even exists. It takes a lot of confidence to, as Olivia just put it, cut into another human's brain. "What do you do?"

"I'm a translator. English to French. I do a lot of crime."

I chuckle at how she expresses herself.

Olivia looks at me funnily.

"It sounded like you're the one committing the crimes," I clarify.

"Oh, uh, right—" She seems a bit thrown. "No, I don't commit them. I just translate novels about them into French."

Perhaps our senses of humour are not exactly the same. Maybe because she's French and I'm Belgian. Or maybe she doesn't think a lot of things are funny.

"Working on anything gruesome at the moment?" I ask.

She pulls her lips into a tight smile. Good heavens. Even if *that* vibe I briefly caught earlier is correct, I'm not sure she's someone I want to deploy my charm on. She seems like she would be far too much hard work. Before, I might have risen to the challenge, I might have even relished it, but part of my mojo seems to have died along with the woman on my operating table.

"I'm actually working on a romance at the moment. After ten years of almost exclusively translating crime fiction, I thought I'd try my hand at a lighter genre."

"And? Is it raunchy?" Ha. I surprise myself. Maybe the incorrigible part of me simply can't help it. I perk up even more.

Olivia's cheeks redden. Because she comes across as so guarded, it's definitely the most adorable sight I've seen this year so far. "Quite. It's an adjustment. Some words… I have to look them up because I've never heard of them." She takes a sip of wine and hides her face behind her glass as best she can.

"Straight romance?" I might as well take the opportunity to see if my earlier hunch was correct.

"Gay. Two men." She gives a full-blown chuckle now. "It's kind of funny, actually, because I spent the better part of last week working on a chapter that involved a lot more penises than I like to deal with in my life." Her gaze skitters away, then returns. "I'm a lesbian and, um, not very well acquainted with the male, um, organ."

I hadn't expected her to just come out and say it, but

why the hell not? Maybe this wouldn't be so much work after all. Maybe I can have some fun with Olivia. It feels like the clouds have opened and cleared a huge patch of blue sky, especially for me. I've seduced many straight women in my life, but put a lesbian in front of me—or better yet, in my lounge, in this remote house in Brittany —and it's like a red flag to a bull.

CHAPTER 4
OLIVIA

For reasons I will spend the rest of the weekend analysing, I want to make an impression on this woman. Perhaps my subconscious flagged her as very attractive when she showed up on my doorstep unannounced the other day. Admittedly, right now, it's not just my subconscious anymore. Marie Dievart is hot in that glamorous, outgoing, chic way I've always had a soft spot for because, to me, it's all so utterly unattainable—both for me to be like that and to ever be with a woman like that.

Granted, I haven't spoken to another person since I chased her away from my property and it's about time I fulfilled my weekly quota of chit-chat, but it's not just that. Otherwise, I wouldn't have just told her I'm a lesbian. I wouldn't have made a penis joke—but I guess there's a first for everything.

I gulp back some wine, nearly emptying my glass, to settle myself. I came to apologise for my manners the other day, not to ogle my new temporary neighbour. Although, I guess, in the grand scheme of things, and the tiny scheme I've devised for my life, there's nothing wrong with some innocent ogling. I usually only encounter women like Marie on television in glossy shows about high-powered lawyers.

A wide smile plastered on her face, Marie reaches for the bottle. "Refill?" It sounds more like a command than a question so I hold out my glass. I get the distinct impression not many people ever say no to this woman. And she's a bloody brain surgeon. I should give up all hope of ever impressing the glitzy doctor right about now—it was fun while it lasted.

"Full disclosure." She leans back and slings one leg over the other. "I'm a lesbian as well. Just so you know." She rests her intense green gaze on me.

"Really?" I couldn't sound more uncool if I tried.

She nods slowly as though drawing a conclusion in her head already. This visit has taken a turn I find hard to process.

"Are you in a relationship?" Marie asks.

"No." It comes out a little abrupt because I'm trying to sound defiant, which is hard to accomplish when you only have one short word to work with.

"Me neither," she says, turning this conversation into a spectacle of innuendo—and making me very uncomfortable. The silence that follows is unusually deafening to my ears.

She's the first one to speak again. Maybe I didn't respond to her statement the way she expected me to—it's the story of my life. It's why I live on my own in the middle of nowhere. "So, it's just you in that house?" Marie asks.

"And Huppert and Deneuve."

"Of course." She sucks her bottom lip between her teeth. "You don't get lonely?"

I shake my head. "I prefer my own company. It's how I want things to be."

"Whereas I've been going nuts after five days by myself."

"You're probably not used to it."

"You can say that again."

"You live with someone in Brussels?" Some of the earlier tension has melted away and I feel like I can breathe normally again.

"I don't, but let's just say I don't spend a lot of time alone. I work long hours and I'm never starved for company, if you know what I mean."

I have no idea what she means, but I nod anyway.

"I welcome any tips for living a life of solitude." She regards me over the rim of her glass as she drinks.

"You have to want it. People shouldn't be alone against their will. That's what makes you lonely." I tilt my head. "You clearly came here to be on your own, but you don't really want it yet. It will take some time to get used to. Especially because it's really quiet here this time of year."

"So I've noticed."

"There's a bar in Bonneau, but…" I try to make my shrug casual. "I'm pretty sure it won't be your scene."

"Do you sometimes go there?"

I shake my head. "Never."

"As long as I can enjoy a glass of wine in your lovely company." She drinks again, then puts her glass down. "I should be just fine."

I don't know what to say to that. I don't know how to say she shouldn't expect me to come round every other day and share a bottle of wine with her. That's not how I live my life. I only came here to apologise. And, maybe— but the jury is still out on that—to check if she was really as attractive as I remembered her in my flustered post-run state. Now that I know she is, I definitely won't be calling round much anymore. I'm staying well away from that kind of temptation. Although, now that I'm here already, I think I'll stay a while longer.

"But what do you do all day?" Marie asks. "To fill the time? Before I arrived here, I never realised a day could feel so long." She has opened another bottle of wine. She seems to be able to hold her alcohol well.

I haven't eaten anything since my run earlier and the wine is starting to go to my head. But I'm still here and I'm not going to stop drinking now.

"I have a routine and plenty of activities," I say.

"Examples, please?"

"It's different for me. I live here. This is my life. For you… being here in this house that isn't your home, away from your regular life, everything will feel different."

She arches up her eyebrows as if to scold me for dodging her question and stating the obvious.

"I run. I work. I cook. I write. I play the piano. I watch TV. I work in the garden. I read." Summed up like that, it sounds a little dull, even though that's the opposite of what my life feels like.

"Maybe you'll cook for me some day?" Marie says. That's her reply to what I just said? I thought she was after practical tips, not that I offered many of those. I just drily listed my daily activities, but still.

"Maybe." I don't want to make any promises I can't keep.

"Did you say you write? Or do you mean as part of your work?"

"I, uh…" In hindsight, I shouldn't have included that particular activity in my list. "Yes, I do some writing on the side."

"What do you write?" Maybe it's because I'm the only other person in a five-kilometre radius, but Marie's interest in me seems heart-warmingly genuine.

"Just some poetry." I try to sound aloof. "Nothing fancy."

"Are you published?"

"God, no." My writing is not something I ever talk about. Never. With anyone. I'm not about to change that now.

"So, you're saying that there's nowhere I can read my intriguing new neighbour's poetry?" She juts out her bottom lip in a faux-sulk.

Intriguing? Is that what I am to her? I'm about to shake my head but even more than being extremely shy about my poetry, I suck at lying. I have zero talent for it—even for the little white lies. I can't knowingly claim a falsehood. My life would have been so much easier if I had found a way to be better at lying, but the capacity to do so successfully has forever remained elusive to me.

"I do post it online. Instagram poetry is an actual thing these days."

"Instagram." She nods as though that's an app only her much younger nieces and nephews—or her children, who knows?—would use. "I've never really had time to explore social media. Maybe that's what I'll do now that I'm here."

My cheeks start burning again. The thought of her

reading my poetry is unbearable. Another reason to stay away.

"I guess I'll need your username." She reaches for her phone. "Actually, maybe we should exchange numbers, in case there's an emergency." Again, it sounds more like a command than a suggestion. "You can text me the link to your poetry later."

Fat chance of that happening. And how do I get out of giving her my number?

She hands me her phone. "Here. Put in your number. I'll give you a buzz later so you'll have mine as well."

There's no way out except typing in a wrong number, but that's not something I'm capable of either. It won't be too much of a nuisance though since I never pick up my phone, unless it's my mother calling—and even then, I have to think about it.

I give her my number, and a few seconds later my phone beeps from my coat pocket in the hallway. I guess, on some level, it can't hurt to have a direct line to a hot doctor.

"I look forward to discovering your poetry on Instagram," Marie says. "I'm curious."

"What are your hobbies?" I ask, keen to change the subject.

"That's the problem. I don't really have any hobbies apart from…" A mischievous smile appears on her face.

"What?" I cock my head.

"Women, I guess." She catches my gaze but it's not possible for me to return her confident stare. I have to look away. Wait. What did she just say? Women are her hobby?

"What do you mean?" I ask.

"I like to date. Show my date a good time. Flirt. See where it goes. Not get enough sleep for a woman my age."

She grins. "Spending the night with a woman has always given me more energy than an extra hour of sleep."

What the hell? Have I been beamed to a different universe in which people actually say outrageous things like this? Did she spike the wine before she poured it? Heat creeps up my neck and settles on my cheeks. "Your hobby is… sleeping with women?"

"I guess. If you wanted, that could very well become one of your hobbies, too, Olivia." Did she just waggle her eyebrows? Is she coming on to me now? I need to get out of here pronto. But there's still something I need to tell her. Although I guess I could text her later now that I have her number.

"It couldn't," I say drily.

"Not much action around here, I gather."

"No." I shuffle to the edge of my seat. What will she think of me if I get up now? Does it even matter? Maybe a little, but I'm not sure I can stay. Maybe Marie finds this amusing—this is her hobby, after all—but I don't. "I should go. The cats will want their dinner." I realise how utterly ridiculous that sounds. But that's what I am—the perfect example of the proverbial cat lady.

"What? No, no, no!" Marie straightens her posture. "Don't go yet. I'm sorry if I was being too forward. It's just how I am, but it doesn't mean anything. I wasn't…" She gives a quick shake of the head. "Trying anything."

I'm glad that's settled then.

"I promise," Marie continues. "I am enjoying your company so much. Please, stay." She acts as though I'm leaving her alone to freeze in the Arctic instead of sip the rest of her expensive wine in this deluxe cottage in Brittany.

Despite her desperate plea, I've reached my limit.

She's a lot to handle. I've become too ill at ease to enjoy staying any longer. I get up and say, "I'll text you later." Although what I will send her will not be what she's expecting. "Thank you for the wine."

She stands and walks towards me. "Stop by any time." She briefly touches her hand to my shoulder and my muscles tense.

I head into the hallway to fetch my coat. I say a quick goodbye and practically flee her house. I hurry home, needing the safety of my own space, of my cats meowing at me as though I've been gone for days instead of an hour, of not being around someone as direct and brazen as my new temporary neighbour.

As I shut the door behind me and double-lock it, I consider that Marie Dievart won't last very long here in the middle of winter. It's too cold, too grey, too boring, and too lonely for someone like her. I can't see her relishing the beauty of it any time soon.

After I've fed my ravenous cats, I send her a text.

Thanks again for the wine. I forgot to ask that you don't show up on my doorstep out of the blue again. I'm not very good with that. Thanks. Olivia.

FEBRUARY

CHAPTER 5

MARIE

"D o you know Olivia?" I ask Yvette.

Yvette shakes her head and points at my empty wine glass.

"Sure. I'll have another."

She promptly refills my glass because she doesn't have a whole lot else to do. At the other end of the bar, two men are perched on stools drinking beer as though their lives depend on it.

"I don't know her either, to be honest," I say. "About as much as you can know about another person from a few texts." Thank goodness for Yvette and this bar, which Olivia claimed wouldn't be my scene. Not that I would normally frequent a bar like this, but nothing about my current situation is normal. That's the whole point. And it's actually quite cosy in here, with the rain lashing the windows outside.

"Actually," Yvette says. "If you mean Olivia Chevalier, the translator, I do know of her. She's lived on the outskirts of Bonneau for years, but no one ever sees her. It's like she's not real."

I nod vigorously. I seem to have downed most of a bottle already. "That's exactly right. I can see her house from my bedroom window, yet I never see her. How is that possible?"

"She's a very private person, I suppose." Yvette shrugs as though it's perfectly normal to hardly ever leave your house. "Have you read any of the books she's translated?" Yvette asks. "She did this detective series set in Ireland. It's very gripping."

Because I'm tipsy, I can't keep my mirth to myself. I was already picturing Yvette reading a gay male romance behind the bar. Yvette just rolls her eyes at me. She's used to much more rowdy crowds than little old me.

"I haven't read any of her translations because up until a few minutes ago, I didn't even know her last name." The only piece of additional information I managed to squeeze out of Olivia via text is her Instagram handle. "I've been her neighbour for more than a month now, Yvette, and she's never even given me her full name." Every morning when I wake up, I check Olivia's Instagram to see if she has shared anything new. She only posts a new poem once a week, I have learned, interspersed with the occasional picture of one of her cats or the rugged landscape behind her house.

"What's with this Olivia? What do you want with her?" Yvette is the kind of bar-owner who has seen it all, dealt with every kind of person, and has the gruff attitude to show for it. She doesn't take any nonsense, not from any drunkards, nor from me.

"I don't want anything from her. Or not that much, anyway. Maybe that she pick up the phone when I call. That would be nice. Or that she stop by my house once in a while, because heaven forbid I drop by hers unannounced." I huff out some air. This cheap wine is going to give me a headache in the morning, but I have nothing better to do than to nurse a hangover. "She's always busy when I text her. How is that even possible? How can a woman who lives alone with just two cats always be busy, Yvette?" I address her directly because I don't think she's actually listening to me.

"Beats me." Yvette polishes some glasses, as if any of the men I've seen here care one bit about how shiny the receptacle for their beverage is.

One of the guys at the other end of the bar bursts into raucous laughter, making me wish I had someone to laugh with like that. Yvette isn't going to help with that. Nor is Olivia, whom I've been thinking about a disproportionate amount because there's nothing else to think of—except the one thing I don't want to think about, even though it's the main reason for me being in this godforsaken village in the first place.

"Maybe I should just leave," I say, even though Yvette has just disappeared from behind the bar.

"What was that?" she asks when she returns.

"What am I even doing here?"

"I've been asking myself the same question since the first time you walked into this bar," Yvette says, not a smidgen of irony in her tone.

"I don't mean in your bar, specifically. I mean in this village."

"You're good for business, so you won't hear me complain." She grins at me. "Sometimes, you're even mildly entertaining."

I burst into a chuckle. "Oh, Yvette. You do crack me up."

"Hm." She goes back to polishing glasses.

"Maybe I will get out of here," I say, even though I don't mean it. I'm just trying out the words. Even though I've been in my self-imposed exile for over a month now, my hands still shake whenever I imagine scrubbing in for surgery. My breath catches in my throat. My brain—the organ I'm supposed to specialise in—shuts down, sending me into a state of utter panic.

"Don't forget to settle your tab before you go," Yvette says.

I finish the last of my wine and get out my purse. The first few times I came here I never had enough cash on me and Yvette doesn't take card payments.

I pay for my drinks and include a large tip. Yvette thanks me with a quick nod of the head.

"You're not driving, are you?" she says.

I look out of the window and sigh. "I suppose I'll have to walk."

"You're out of your mind." She hurries from behind the bar as though I'm about to pass out. "I'd drive you home myself but I have these two." She points at the men at the bar. "Can you wait until they've gone?"

"It's not that far, Yvette."

"It's at least five kilometres. It's pouring with rain. Have you seen the shoes you're wearing?" She shakes her head vehemently. "I can call someone, but it might be a while before he's available."

"How about some coffee then?" Rain drums against the window.

"Coming right up." Yvette leaves me to find my seat at the bar again. "You could call your neighbour. Olivia Chevalier to the rescue."

"That will be the day." I shrug. "She never picks up when I call."

"Give me her number. I'll give it a go."

"Try your man first before we resort to that."

She nods and makes a phone call. I imagine Olivia coming to pick me up in my tipsy state. The thought has a soft edge of comfort to it. I'd even be happy with Yvette taking me home and tucking me into bed. A smidgen of human warmth would go a long way. But I must deprive myself of that as well. I need to take more time to get back to myself, by not being myself for a while. How did this ever make sense to me?

Yvette pulls me from my tipsy reverie. "Best call Olivia," she says. "Alain is in no state to drive anyone tonight."

I dig my phone from my purse and give Yvette Olivia's number.

CHAPTER 6
OLIVIA

T he cats barely flick up an ear when my phone rings. Huppert is purring on my belly. Deneuve is pressed against my side as I watch TV.

It's after nine in the evening. I check the screen to see if it's one of my family. They know only to call this late if it's an emergency. It's an unknown number so I happily press the red button to decline the call. If it's in any way important, which I doubt, they'll leave a message. If not, I'll never hear from whoever that is again.

A minute later my phone beeps, announcing a voice message. Huppert is not happy with my shuffling around and hops off my lap. I call my voicemail.

"*Bonsoir* Olivia, this is Yvette from Chez Yvette. Your neighbour, Marie, has had a bit too much to drink and shouldn't drive herself home. Could you pick her up, please? Thanks."

What the hell? I've never been to Chez Yvette and now the owner's calling me out of the blue? How did she get my number? And when did I become responsible for picking up a drunk Marie from the bar? I don't see how this is any of my business. Marie is a bloody neurosurgeon. She's supposed to be much smarter than the rest of us—at least I hope she is. If she was going out drinking, couldn't she have had the foresight to arrange transport back home? She's probably used to catching a taxi and there are none in Bonneau. I heave a sigh. It doesn't feel like I have a choice. What is Marie doing at Chez Yvette, anyway? Looking for company, I suppose. If I pick her up, I can ask her. But I'm already in my pyjamas. *Bordel de merde.* I won't be able to enjoy the rest of my evening anymore, knowing that Marie might do something stupid like walk home in the torrential downpour I saw coming hours ago. It was announced by the kind of menacing, dark clouds that would urge any clear-headed person to stay home and wait for them to pass.

I scratch Deneuve behind the ear, assure her I'll be back in a jiffy, and change into outdoor clothes.

"I'm so sorry, Olivia." Marie doesn't look that tipsy, but I'm no judge as to whether anyone is fit to drive or not. I do know it's much better to be safe than sorry. "I wasn't thinking. I just nipped in for a quick drink, and…" She pauses, then stops, as though she has decided that's enough of an apology for dragging me out of my sofa on an evening like this. The windshield wipers go up and down furiously and I have to focus on the wet, black road ahead.

"It's fine," I say curtly.

"I hope I didn't drag you away from the composition of a poetic masterpiece." Marie sounds more teasing than apologetic. "I've been following your Instagram. If I didn't see the lights in your house go on and off once in a while, Instagram would be the only way for me to know that you're okay."

"Why wouldn't I be okay?"

"You look cute with those glasses on, by the way," she says out of the blue. "They're kind of nerd chic."

I cast her a quick glance. I can't believe she's sitting there grinning. But what did I expect? I've only seen the woman twice and neither time did she strike me as the repentant type—quite the contrary.

"Hm." I'm not sure whether I really don't know how to react to that compliment or whether I just don't want to. "I suppose I'll have to drive you back tomorrow to pick up your car?" I change the subject.

"That would be absolutely amazing. I mean it." I can feel her gaze on me. "I'll cook you a feast to thank you. What do you say? Come over this weekend?"

"I need to check my calendar." I don't have anything on this weekend, but she doesn't know that. I'm not about to just say yes. I need to consider the implications of accepting her invitation. "But you don't have to cook me a feast. That's really not necessary."

"Trust me, it wouldn't only be for you."

I'm well aware that I haven't been the most jovial nor welcoming of neighbours. That's not my style and I'm no longer in the habit of adjusting myself to others—of accommodating others at my own expense.

"Honestly, I thought you would have left by now." I cast her another quick glance.

"I've considered it. I was just talking about it with Yvette."

"What's the conclusion?"

"I don't know, Olivia, but I get the distinct impression

you would much prefer it if I fucked back off to Brussels and left you in peace," she says matter-of-factly.

"It would save me from after-dark phone calls demanding I pick you up at the bar because you drank too much."

Marie chuckles. "Fair enough."

I turn into her road. "Here we are. Olivia's taxi at your service."

"Will you come in for a minute?"

"It's late. I'm tired. Maybe another time."

"I feel if I don't get you inside my house, now that you're right outside of it, I might never get the opportunity again."

"Oh, please." I roll my eyes.

"I'll give you plenty of time to pretend I don't exist again afterwards." She cocks her head.

"If you put it like that." I'm only joking. It was never my deliberate intention to ignore Marie's presence in my neighbourhood. It's simply how I live my life—on my own, no matter who moves into the house closest to mine.

She hurries out of the car as though I might change my mind if she doesn't usher me inside quickly enough. I follow her, admiring the lack of puddles on the path to her front door and the workmanship required to lay such precise paving slabs.

Once again, I'm taken aback by the elegance of the Dievart cottage. From the outside, it looks like a typical Breton house, but inside it resembles the pictures on the interior design websites I like to visit. Large windows at the back. An extension housing a modern kitchen with bifold doors that open into the garden. Plush sofas and tasteful art on the walls. Built-in bookcases on either side of the fireplace with books organised by spine colour, interspersed with all sorts of fashionable trinkets.

"Sit, please. Let me wait on you hand and foot. Night-cap? Coffee? Wine? Anything else you might fancy?"

While I think about what to drink, Marie lights a few candles, making me feel even more like I've gone on holiday and ended up at a swanky but cosy resort—minus the sunny weather.

"I'll just have some water. I have a difficult scene to tackle tomorrow."

"More words you've never heard of?" she asks from behind the kitchen island.

I should ask who did the renovations on her house. I'd like mine to look exactly like this, although I'm pretty sure I can't afford it. "A break-up scene. Lots of dialogue. Not always easy to translate."

"The gays are at odds?" She brings over two glasses and a bottle of sparkling water.

"Yeah. Don't worry, they'll make up, though."

"I'm going to have to read this book when it comes out in French. Will you let me know?"

"Uh, sure."

She fills our glasses and after handing me one, holds up hers. "Thank you for coming to my rescue tonight, neighbour. I really appreciate it."

"You're welcome. Just don't make a habit out of it."

"What were you doing when you got the call?" Marie doesn't seem mortified by any of this at all. If the tables were turned, I'd be bending over backwards to make it up to the person I inconvenienced. Not that something like that would ever happen to me.

"Watching TV."

She nods. "At home in Brussels, I don't even have a TV. I never watch it."

"Hm, that figures."

"Why?"

"You're a highbrow neurosurgeon with a very time-consuming hobby."

She erupts into a giggle. "Is that why you couldn't get out of here fast enough last time? And you chose to forget I existed? Because I told you about that?"

"Yeah, kind of."

"Did you feel threatened by it? Because that was not my intention."

"It made me feel uncomfortable."

"Sorry. I can be too forward for my own good." Once again there's not a hint of contrition in her tone.

"I take it you haven't been able to practise your favourite hobby since you arrived?" I rest my gaze on her briefly. It's never a hardship to look at her.

"No, but that's one of the reasons I'm here. I needed a break from that as well."

"May I ask why?" Maybe it's because of the time we spent in the car together. Or maybe this is how Marie shows she's sorry. There's a more mellow edge to her tonight. She doesn't come across as abrasive as she was last time. And I'm curious why she's here.

She puffs out some air. "I guess I've come here hoping I can somehow reset myself. Things happened at work that…" She drums a finger against the side of her glass. "Someone died during a routine surgery. Someone who really was not supposed to die. I was only putting in an intracranial pressure monitor, a thirty-minute procedure I've performed hundreds of times, only this time, I made a fatal error. The kind I can't forgive myself for."

"I'm sorry." What else can I say? But at least now I know.

"I'm the one who should be sorry. And I am. I know I'm only human and even highly trained and experienced doctors like myself are not immune to making mistakes. Neuro is a very complex field, but…" Her voice cracks on the last word. "This simply shouldn't have happened. It was utterly avoidable. *I* was the one and only weak link. And… well, I guess I'm also here to figure out why this particular death has hit me so damn hard." She stares into her glass.

"I hope you've made some progress."

"I haven't because… my mind refuses to go there. This is the first time I've talked about it since I left Brussels. Before she finally retired, my mother was a ground-breaking thoracic surgeon and my sister is a plastic surgeon. You'd think I would be able to discuss this with my family, but they can't see it the way I do. I know why— because I'm exactly like them." She waves a hand in front of her face. "They draw the curtain on their emotions because that's the only way to do this job. There's no room for sentiment in the operating theatre, I agree. But… I haven't been able to connect with either one of them about this. It's not that they don't understand. We know we can't save everyone. And it's not them. It's me. Something's changed inside me and I've been feeling out of sorts ever since." Her eyebrows are high arches on her forehead. "That's why I'm here."

"Okay." I lean back in the sofa, indicating that I'm willing to stay well past my bedtime if she wants to talk more.

"I didn't mean to burden you with this." She scoffs. "I guess I was more than ready for it to come out." Her lips tilt into a grin. "Some days, I feel like I've gone into a monastery and taken a vow of silence as well as... abstinence."

"Maybe that's why you ended up at the bar. You needed conversation."

She pulls up her shoulders then lets them droop in a dramatic fashion. "I'm not sure coming here was the right thing to do. I'm not sure of anything. But I needed a change of scenery. I needed a break from my life. And... I guess, for the first time ever, I felt the need to turn inwards. Not that I've been doing a lot of that. It's hard to look inside yourself, especially if... you've lived the way I have." She finds my eyes. "I haven't always been the most considerate person. I've taken a lot for granted, my privileges as a doctor included." She scoffs again. "If only I were Catholic. I could do with a confession." She puts her glass down and the thud it makes seems to pull her out of her current mood. "Damn, Olivia, either you are the world's best listener or... I don't know." Her gaze is back on me. "There's something very calming about you."

"It's how I live so I guess it's also how I come across." I try a smile. "Except when you have the audacity to interrupt my run."

"I'm never doing that again." She squares her shoulders. "Thank you for listening to me. I'm not sure what Yvette put in that wine, and I may regret this in the morning, but I feel a sense of relief."

"I'm glad. It must be so hard, what you do. To hold someone's life in your hands. To have to make split-second decisions. To not feel anything. All of it is inconceivable to me."

"You get used to the pressure. I think my problem might be that I got too used to it, until something inside me snapped… It doesn't help that my entire family is made up of high-achieving surgeons."

That explains the luxury renovations then. And the fact that they don't visit their holiday home very often—they have no time.

"How long have you been a surgeon?"

"Twenty-five years, not counting internships."

"Twenty-five years of that kind of pressure is going to take a toll eventually."

"It didn't on my mother and it doesn't seem to be affecting my sister. Or so they claim."

"Not everyone's the same. You may all be surgeons and share genetic material, but that doesn't make you identical."

"I'm the only lesbian in the family. Well, as far as I know." She bursts into a chuckle. "Let's not go there." She crunches up her lips. "This is also something I tend to do: monopolise the conversation."

"You're not. You're sharing. It's not the same."

"Well… I'll share this as well." She shoots me a quick smile. "I really like your poetry."

Instant cheek flush. "Thanks," I manage to say. "And that from a highbrow neurosurgeon who never watches television."

"Correction: I've been watching a lot of really bad French TV since I arrived here. Your poetry is a welcome distraction, although 'distraction' is not the right word. Maybe it's because I met you before I started reading it. It's very sparse yet evocative. There's something special about it. Like I can hear a melody in the way the words are lined up."

I've never received face-to-face praise for my poetry before. I have no clue how to take the compliment. My first instinct is to flee her house again so I can process what she said in private, but this is not the kind of conversation I can run away from, no matter what my instincts tell me. Marie opened up to me. I owe it to her to stay.

"Thanks," I mutter under my breath, and the heat in my cheeks turns up another notch.

CHAPTER 7

MARIE

Do not hit on this woman. Do not hit on this woman. It takes every ounce of my willpower not to let my flirty side get the better of me. Olivia hasn't only been kind enough to pick me up—surprising me greatly in the process—but she's also the best listener I've come across in a long time, and she's adorable when she blushes like that. It's almost too tempting an opportunity. The situation seems set for seduction and fooling around. After showing Olivia my most vulnerable side, I sure could do with another kind of distraction than Olivia's poetry. A far less cerebral one.

"When can I expect the next poem?" I refill our water glasses.

"Soon," she says enigmatically. She doesn't appear very comfortable discussing her poetry. "Are you going to be okay?"

"Of course."

"If you don't wither away from boredom first."

"This place has been growing on me." I draw up my legs and tuck them underneath me. "When I first arrived,

I was probably in adrenaline and cortisol withdrawal. But I think the detox is almost complete, what with the utter lack of excitement here."

The small wrinkle I've noticed above her left eye deepens.

"Thank goodness you're here," I say, even though, up until an hour ago, Olivia's house might as well have been empty. "I promise not to abuse this knowledge, but it's good to know that I can call you in case of an emergency."

She shuffles in her seat. "I'm sorry I didn't answer when you called before. Unless it's my family, I never answer my phone."

"Earlier you said certain aspects of my life are inconceivable to you. Not answering my phone is inconceivable to me. It's second nature. Someone might die if I don't answer." Here I go again, making it all about me. I blame the scant conversation I've had the past few weeks. "Is there any particular reason you don't answer your phone?"

"It's not personal. I just hate talking on the phone."

"Yet you gave me your number."

"I didn't feel like I had much choice at the time."

"So… I can't come around unannounced and I can't call you. In that case, let me formally invite you to dinner this weekend right now."

"Okay."

"Does that mean you'll come?" Olivia doesn't make it easy for me not to bring the conversation back to me. She's hardly forthcoming with information about herself.

"I'll let you know by tomorrow. I need to drive you to your car, anyway."

"Oh, yes. I could also walk, of course. There's a

certain charm to a rainy windswept trek through the barren fields of Brittany."

"The rain is here to stay for the next few days, but it's your choice."

"I would love for you to drive me." I shake my head. "Look at me. I might as well have 'princess' tattooed across my forehead."

Finally, she laughs. Or maybe she just agrees with me. "Princesses don't usually go drinking at Yvette's. It's not a very regal environment."

"It's better than nothing."

"Have you explored any other establishments in the area?"

"I've been to every restaurant that's open this time of year. Most of them twice."

Olivia nods as she suppresses a yawn. "Sorry."

"It's time for bed." I rarely sleep before midnight but I feel like I should pretend that I do for Olivia's sake.

"Busy day tomorrow?" She sends me a smile.

"I'll be using all my energy thinking about what I'm going to cook for you."

"I'm not difficult." Olivia rises.

"I am," I say truthfully.

"Yeah," she replies, as though she hadn't expected me to say anything else. "I'll see you tomorrow. I'll text you before I come over."

"There's no need. You're welcome anytime. Thank you so much for picking me up." I escort her to the door where I keep myself from hugging her goodbye, even though, more than anything, I've missed another human's touch. My skin hungers for it, but this is not the time. I silently applaud myself for recognising this—it hasn't always been the case. Maybe I am making some progress on my journey inwards.

"Goodnight." She looks at me funnily for an instant, then disappears into the darkness of the night.

The next day, I have the pleasure of Olivia's company again. It's late in the afternoon when she finally shows up to drive me to my car, but I can hardly complain about that.

I'm just happy to see her. Although I'm used to a lot more attention from fellow lesbians, it doesn't bother me that Olivia doesn't appear the least bit interested in me in that way. Some may call me an acquired taste, but experience has taught me differently. Plenty of women have wanted to come back for seconds, and sometimes I've allowed them. Most of the time, I haven't. Except for Véronique.

Instead of coming to the door, she has texted that she's waiting in the car. As though hers isn't the only car I've seen all day, and I might have forgotten that she was coming, she honks upon arrival.

"How was the break-up scene?" I ask, once we're on the road. Rain is coming down in sheets. Olivia's wearing her glasses again, her gaze focused on nothing but the road.

"I will need a few more passes before I get it totally right," she says. "Jesus, this weather."

I let her drive in silence for a while. Although starved for conversation as well as touch, just being near her, near another person, is enough for a few minutes. Until I can't help myself any longer.

"Have you thought about my dinner invitation?" I glance at her sideways.

"Yeah, sure. I'll come." She casts me a quick glance. "You've raised my expectations with your mention of a feast."

"I'm not as good a cook as I am a surgeon, but I'm not bad." And at least my cooking has never killed anyone.

Closer to the village, the rain lets up a bit and Olivia chuckles. "I wonder what it's like to go through life with your level of confidence."

"What do you mean?"

"You're good at everything and you have no qualms saying that you are. Most people are not like that."

"I'm hardly good at everything." Is that really how I come across?

"I'll be the judge of your cooking skills this weekend. I'll let you know how good you actually are." Is that amusement in her tone? She sounds as though she's looking forward to it. "All the rest, I can't judge, although if you've had any say in the renovation and decoration of your house, you're very good at that as well."

"Thank you." Talking to Olivia is so different than talking to any of the women I usually end up in conversation with. I want more from her than she wants from me. I crave her company to combat my loneliness. She doesn't appear to need anyone or anything she doesn't yet have. "I did have a say in it." I wish I could invite her to my penthouse in Brussels. If she likes what I've done to the house here, she'll go nuts for that.

She nods her approval. "How about Saturday evening?"

"Come early for a long and luxurious aperitif." I can hardly wait, although I'll need to give myself a stern talking-to. My female Casanova instinct must not be allowed free reign. Not only because I can't fall into my old ways of trying to bed every woman I like. Even more so because if I'm going to be here for a while, I'd like Olivia as my friend, although friendship might be too high an aim with her. For now, I'd settle for having her as more than just a casual acquaintance—or an occasional dinner guest. But perhaps the main reason I need to keep my flirting antics at bay is because Olivia doesn't appear to be the least bit responsive to the mild flirting I've already deployed on her.

"What should I bring?" she asks.

"Nothing at all except your wonderful self." It's so easy to make her blush. I must not get too addicted to it and remember that it's probably pretty awkward for her. "Or, actually, if you'd have any of the books you've translated lying about, I'd love to read one of them. Yvette mentioned an Irish crime series?"

"Yvette?" As she speaks her name, we pull up outside Chez Yvette. Lights glow inside.

"I asked her about you. She said she enjoyed reading the books you've translated although I don't know if she's read the new genre you're trying your hand at." I glance at the door of the bar wistfully. How lovely would it be for Olivia and I to go in and have a quick drink? Just a coffee. Just the comforting sensation of sharing a beverage with another person I'm growing fond of.

"Who knows?" Olivia looks at me. "You can never tell what people really like if you don't know them."

"True." I reach for the door handle and, again, I can't help myself. "I don't suppose you fancy a cup of coffee?" I nod towards the bar.

I see her hesitate. She drums her fingers onto the

steering wheel. "I have some errands to run before the shops close."

Of course, it wasn't going to be that easy with her.

"All right. I'll see you on Saturday then. Seven? Six? Stop by whenever you want. I'll be expecting you."

She shakes her head. "Give me a time, please. It's your dinner, your rules."

I examine her face. She's not joking. "Six-thirty."

"Okay."

"I can't thank you enough for this, Olivia. See you soon." As I exit her car, I wonder if I should be the one playing coy—not my strong suit, but maybe it's worth a try. Maybe on Saturday. I have a few days to prepare.

CHAPTER 8

OLIVIA

I can't remember the last time I went to someone's house for dinner. Surprisingly, the prospect is quite thrilling. I'm carrying a heavy bag of books for Marie to choose from because I don't know what she likes to read. I've translated cosy mysteries, dark detective novels, and some pretty terrifying thrillers I wouldn't recommend anyone read in the middle of nowhere when it gets dark early.

When she opens the door, she plants a kiss on each of my cheeks. Her being from Belgium, I was prepared for one—or three, which is such a funny number of kisses to exchange as a way of greeting. Then again, Belgians are known to be quite peculiar. I googled her before I came over. She did some of her training in the US, worked there for a few years before returning home. As she mentioned, she did a short stint as head of neurosurgery in a hospital in Paris, after which she returned to Brussels. And now she's here. So am I.

She escorts me into the living room and makes a performance of opening a bottle of champagne. Not for the first time, it strikes me that she might be the kind of woman to make a spectacle of the smallest acts. She has that air about her as though every little thing she does has importance to it. The air of people who adore the spotlight. Who need to be in charge. Who need to make a difference. The air of someone who is the polar opposite of me.

The coffee table is filled with all kinds of fancy looking bites. She hands me a glass and urges me to sit and eat and drink. Soon she'll instruct me to be merry as well, although it's not hard when you get a welcome like you're the Queen of Sheba.

After she has calmed a bit and settled into a chair, she says, "I'm usually not one to entertain like this, but look at me now."

"I imagine you don't have much time for elaborate cooking in your everyday life."

"I make the time once or twice a week. It relaxes me."

"So, you do have other hobbies." I point at the bag of books I brought. "In case you want another, here's plenty of entertainment."

"I'll go through those with great interest tomorrow, but tonight, I just want to focus on you."

The thing with Marie is that I can't really read her that well—not that I'm an expert at reading anyone. I don't know if she means focusing on me because it's me, or simply because I'm the first person she's had over for dinner since she arrived. It's not the kind of thing you can just inquire about, I've learned the hard way. As my ex used to say—or maybe instruct is a better word—you must learn to get a feel for these things.

"In that spirit"—another thing I like about Marie is that she's a natural at making conversation—"I would like to pry into your life a bit. But please, have some more champagne first." She flashes me a grin.

I have no idea why anyone would bring clothes like the ones she's wearing to a place like this, although it is nice to set eyes on a dressed-up woman—especially one as attractive as Marie. Her top is cream cashmere, for warmth, I presume, although her shoulders are bare, so, in my view, it's the kind of garment that makes no sense at all. But for me, dressing up is wearing a denim shirt instead of a flannel one. If you're really lucky, which Marie is tonight, I will even iron out most of the wrinkles.

"There's really not that much to pry into." I take another sip. "I've told you what my life is made up of."

"Your current life here in Bonneau, yes." She fixes her light-green gaze on me. It's slightly mesmerising. "But what about before? How long have you lived in your house?"

"Eight years this summer."

Her eyes widen. "Don't tell me you've lived here all alone for eight years."

I shake my head. "I moved here with my ex. We lived in Le Havre before."

"Ah." Something lights up in her eyes. "There's an ex."

"We broke up a long time ago. Living in the middle of nowhere wasn't really her jam." As if that was the only—or even the real—reason we broke up.

"She wanted to move back to the city and you wanted to stay here?"

I puff up my cheeks with air. I don't like talking about this—about me and all the things that, according to my ex-girlfriend, make me so difficult to live with. "That wasn't really the crux of the issue, but..." I pause, hoping

Marie will go back to what she clearly loves doing most: talking about herself.

"How long ago did you break up?" She rests her elbows on her knees and regards me intently. She was serious about prying into my life.

"About five and a half years ago now, I think."

"How old are you?" She sounds slightly alarmed.

"Forty-four."

"You're in the very prime of your life."

"Yeah." I nod my agreement. "I guess."

"I'm just trying to understand why you would choose to spend the best years of your life hidden away in Bonneau with only a holiday home as a distant neighbour."

"I'm not hiding. I'm just not like you, or like most people. I like peace and quiet above all else and I've always preferred my own company."

"How long were you and your ex together?" She looks like she might consider operating on my brain next.

"About six years."

She whistles through her teeth. "That's a long time." She inserts a mirthful chuckle. "I think my longest relationship was about six months."

It's my turn to do a double take. "Six months?"

"Give or take. I'm not really one to keep track of things like that."

Either she's a commitment-phobe or one of those people married to their job. Or a bit of both. "And yet your hobby is"—I curl my fingers into air-quotes—"women." I nod as though I get it. It's fun to pretend sometimes. "Never just *one* woman."

"Nuh-uh. We were talking about you, Olivia." She

twirls the stem of her glass between her fingers. "I'm curious about your ex."

"Why?"

"Just to get an idea of the kind of woman you're into." She pulls the corners of her mouth upwards.

I could go through this entire conversation stringing together an endless array of 'why's' but my ex, who I'm supposed to be shedding some sort of light on, also assured me that's not how a conversation works. *Wait.* Why does Marie want to find out what kind of women I'm into? "She's…" How to best describe Sandrine? "Well, she liked attention a bit too much to live here alone with me."

Marie nods while doing a poor job of suppressing a grin.

"Our break-up was difficult. It's not that easy for me to talk about her."

"Okay. Sorry for pushing."

"She liked to push as well. She liked talking about our relationship all the time to see how we could make it better. In my opinion, that only made it worse."

"She hurt you."

"Big time." It's so long ago now that time has done its job of healing most of my emotional wounds. It left me with a lot of scar tissue, though.

"Fuck her, then," Marie says.

Although that sounds like music to my ears, I continue, "It wasn't all her. It never is. I played my part in the demise of our relationship. I can be pushy too, in my own way. We pushed each other to do things we didn't really want." I puff out a sigh. "It's not a story I can tell you in five minutes. Nor is it one I want to start the evening with. Too bleak. There's no happy ending."

"You look pretty happy to me." She shoots me a smile.

"I am happy. I love my life here." I've had about enough of this focus on me. "Tell me about your aversion to relationships. What's that all about?"

"All right. I'll play." Before she does, she refills our glasses. She leans back and crosses one leg over the other. "I was the cliché of the arrogant surgeon who had no time for anyone else's feelings. I always put myself first, often at the expense of others. I hurt many people in the process. It's not something I'm proud of, but it's also not something I can undo. I was that person. I'm still her, although I do believe that people can change. Perhaps I'm here to find out if that applies to me as well."

"Um." That's not really what I asked, but I guess she needed to get that off her chest.

"From what I've been told," she muses, "I'm very good in bed, but very bad at anything else relationship-related."

I nearly choke on my last sip of champagne. "I'm sorry, but…" I shake my head. "You're really quite something." I'm amused by her. Even a little bit touched by what she confided in me. Unless she's playing me. Putting on some elaborate act to get me into bed. I wouldn't put it past her. But I'll give her the benefit of the doubt. Besides, it takes a whole lot more than a semi-heartfelt confession to get me anywhere near anyone's bedroom, no matter how attractive they are.

I don't even know why I'm thinking about this. Probably because she just claimed to be very good between the sheets. Who says something like that about themselves? Where does she get the confidence? It must be the arrogance she just referred to. She doesn't have a boring bone in her body, I'll give her that. Although I'm quite the fan

of boredom. Its sameness suits my character. This kind of
loud bravado is what I'm usually allergic to.

"So I've been told," she says matter-of-factly.

"You've left a trail of broken-hearted lesbians all over
Brussels," I recap.

"Not just Brussels. Not by a long shot." She shoots me
a quick wink. Okay, she is playing me. Or balancing on
that knife-edge between being real and using it to her
advantage a bit too much. I'm still very much entertained,
however.

"And that's also why you're here. To find out why you
can't allow yourself to fall in love?"

"*Allow* myself?" She laughs. "I've never been in the
habit of denying myself anything."

"I don't know you, but from what you've told me, I
beg to differ."

"Really?" She sits up a bit straighter. "How do you
figure that?"

"You're what? Mid-forties? About the same age
as me?"

"I'm fifty-six."

"Oh." Say what now? She did mention her sister is a
plastic surgeon. Maybe she smoothed some of the wrinkles off Marie's face. "Anyway, it doesn't matter. My point
is that it's hard to believe that in all of your fifty-six years,
you've never fallen in love."

"I'm not sure I have." She pulls up one shoulder. "I
mean, the way love is gushed about, you'd think I'd know
if it had happened to me."

"That's what I meant when I said you haven't yet
allowed yourself to feel that way. Maybe you think it a
weakness to fall in love. Or you can't stand how vulnerable
it leaves you."

"Okay. Let's take a minute here." She tilts her head. "I've cooked you a feast. I didn't prepare for an impromptu therapy session."

"You're right." I'm intrigued by Marie and curious to find out more, but I've never been keen—much to Sandrine's dismay—to turn my emotions inside out for someone else either. "We don't have to go there."

"What's so great about love, anyway?" She distributes the remainder of the bottle of champagne between our glasses.

"You're asking me?" I exhale sharply. "I'm pretty much done with love. Or at least on a very long break. A holiday for my heart is what I've called it."

"Done with it?" She relaxes back into her chair. "Either way, you're ahead of me because it looks like I've never even started."

As I start talking again, I'm very aware this is the moment when my champagne buzz is optimal for conversation but dangerous for revealing too much about myself. Being aware of it doesn't really help me to shut up, though. So I say, "Done with it is maybe a bit too harsh. I'm only forty-four. I can't sit here and tell you I will never love again. But I can tell you that my life without love has not been worse than my time with Sandrine. It's just very different. When I was with her, I always felt like I couldn't fully be me. And maybe it's impossible. Maybe, when you're with someone, when you love them, you automatically compromise, because not to do so would make it unbearable." Definitely tipsy then.

"What did you compromise on?"

"Being me." Thank goodness for the tongue-loosening effects of champagne because this is hard to explain. "Being as close to myself and what I wanted as possible."

"But aren't you always you, by definition?"

I shake my head.

"And now? Talking to me?"

"It's a version of me." I arch up my eyebrows. "A pretty tipsy one, at that."

"You haven't touched my finger food."

"There's so much of it, it's like I'm waiting for the other guests to arrive before I tuck in."

"Are you saying my amuse-bouches are intimidating?"

"Not just your amuse-bouches," I hear myself say. Who's playing now?

CHAPTER 9
MARIE

D oes she know? Does she have any clue about how much I want to remove that champagne flute from her hand, lean in, and kiss her? But I haven't even flirted. Or have I? Either way, it's best if I remove myself from the situation for a little while. I need to plate my starter.

I excuse myself and head into the kitchen, which is open-plan, so I can still see her. Olivia gets up and wanders to the built-in bookshelf next to the fireplace. My gaze lands on her behind. It looks mighty good in those jeans—must be from all that running she does.

In many ways, it's a miracle she's here. My intuition is off kilter and it's hard to predict how she'd react if I tried to kiss her, but I can't risk chasing her away now I've finally been able to get a little closer to her. Although my inner, very petulant child is screaming to take what it can't have. The old me, the one I'm trying to subdue or at least mould into a better version of me, would drop the bowl I'm holding, swagger up to her, throw out some chatty line, and find a way to kiss her. It's what I do and there-fore, it's also who I am. Or who I was.

The old me is still there, screaming for attention and easy satisfaction, but I can keep her in check now. Or, just maybe, part of her left me the night before that fatal surgery. Earlier, when Olivia asked about my experience with falling in love, I lied. I do know what it feels like— and because of what happened, it's not a feeling I want to relive any time soon. I prefer to be in control. I need my mind sharp instead of fuzzy with a haze of romance. I need my hands dexterous instead of itching to be all over one particular woman.

"Need any help?" My gaze must have drifted from Olivia's behind because I didn't even notice her walking up to me.

"Absolutely not. Take a seat at the table. I'll be there in a few minutes."

"Yes, boss." She saunters to the dining table. "I'm sure you're aware of your bossy streak?"

"I am," I say as I position a piece of carrot on a plate just so. What I don't say is that a lot of the women I've been with appeared to enjoy that streak a lot. It's hard to gauge whether Olivia would. But no, again, I have to drag my mind away from that line of thinking. I focus on plating again. I want this dish to look exactly like the picture in the recipe book. Anything else won't do for me. After I've put on some microgreens using kitchen tweezers, I serve the starters.

"I've made for you scallop carpaccio," I solemnly declare, like I'm in a cooking competition.

"Damn," Olivia says. "That almost looks too good to eat."

"It does look rather pretty." My mother taught me the art of impressing myself at a very young age. My sister's even better at it than me, although I do a good job of it as well. I just did it again. "Enjoy."

"I'm sure I will. You weren't kidding when you said you were preparing a feast for me."

After I've speared a morsel of scallop on my fork, I find her gaze. "Some things, I don't kid about."

She chuckles. "If I'd known I was going to a Michelin-starred restaurant, I would have dressed up more."

I slant my head. I try to picture her in posher clothes. It's not hard. Olivia looks like she might brush up nicely. Her blonde hair is pulled back in a messy ponytail. The brown of her eyes could be accentuated with the right colour of blouse. She has great skin, although I mustn't forget she's more than ten years my junior. Earlier, when I revealed how old I was, I could tell the number surprised her. Must be the Botox my sister injects me with every few months.

"Are there any starred restaurants around these parts?" I'm not usually in the habit of asking questions I already know the answer to, but I'm curious to find out whether she's interested in fine dining. Something tells me she doesn't care one bit.

"The closest one is in Rennes, about an hour's drive from here," she says. "And there's Le Manoir in Saint-Brieuc, which was amazing when I went there, but it's been a few years now."

She surprises me again. I wonder what she was like before she retreated to the countryside—cultured and social, perhaps? I've also been wondering about her admission to taking a break from love and whether that includes taking a break from sex. For me, the two are not linked, but if there's one thing I've learned during my long stint of chasing after women, it's that most of them feel that the two are inextricably intertwined. If I have one goal for tonight, it's finding out Olivia's stance on the matter.

"Maybe we can go together some time?"

"Why would I go there if I can eat like this at yours?" She shoots me a smile.

"How about at your place?" I'm encouraged by that smile. "How would one eat there?"

"I have my weekly rota of dishes that I hardly ever deviate from."

"Seriously? You eat the same things every week?"

"Why not?"

"So many reasons," I say.

"I change my menu with the seasons. I wouldn't eat winter vegetables in summer."

"So, you're not one for experimenting?"

"I wouldn't say that."

"When was the last time you experimented with something?" I pour us some wine from a bottle I opened before Olivia arrived.

"You could say me being here is an experiment."

"Maybe it's out of the ordinary for you." It clearly is. "But that doesn't make it an experiment."

"Okay, well, maybe me living here is an experiment, then," she says.

"One that got a little out of hand, I presume." Earlier, she might have claimed to be intimidated by me, but that's not the impression I'm getting now. The more time I spend with her, the more I think she enjoys my company. Or maybe it's the excellent food and drinks I'm serving. Maybe a bit of both.

"It's hard to explain." She puts down her cutlery. "That was world class, by the way." She leans back in her chair. "Sandrine and I moved here because I wanted to. When she left, I was so heartbroken, I didn't have the energy to even think about moving away. As time passed, I found my groove here. Without her. Without anyone, really. Which has baffled me at times, because aren't we told that we need other people to be happy? That relationships with others are so important? It doesn't appear to be the case for me. I'm perfectly happy on my own."

Olivia likes to say something is hard to explain and then simply go on to explain it. It must be some sort of defence mechanism she picked up along the way—maybe when she was with Sandrine. "The human brain is fundamentally social and in need of connection," I say.

"So I've been told. Many times." She shrugs.

"You must have some connections. People you talk to in the village."

"The butcher and the baker. Sure. But I do most of my talking online. There are some people I correspond with via email. And there are the people I work with. Publishers and editors. That's about it."

"And no lovers?" Damn it. This is not the time to slip this into the conversation. I'm doing my utmost to be a good listener—it should be easy because I genuinely want to get to know Olivia. But change is hard. It takes time. I need to try again.

"Where would I meet those?" She shakes her head. "You do seem rather obsessed."

"Sorry." I'm not usually one to apologise in conversation. Sure, I like to speak before I think, but it has thus far always worked to my advantage. My bed is rarely empty— except for the past few weeks. But only because I wanted it to be. Why else am I staying here? It would have been easier, perhaps, if my closest neighbour had been an elderly male farmer, and not a fellow lesbian. But maybe Olivia is the temptation I need to resist. "Force of habit. I didn't mean to be insensitive." I need a break so we can restart the conversation. "Ready for the main course?"

"Sure." She gets up and clears the starter plates. "I'm curious to see what you've made." She doesn't sound too put off by my ways just yet.

CHAPTER 10
OLIVIA

After an exquisite main course of haddock baked en papillote with lemon and herbs, dessert is another astounding concoction of chocolate mousse on crumbly pastry. If Marie's as good a doctor as she is an amateur cook, I'd feel safe leaving my brain in her care.

"If you ever get tired of being a neurosurgeon, you can always open a restaurant." I'm more drunk than tipsy. Marie also has a very liberal pour when it comes to wine —she's very French that way.

"Who knows?" She looks up from her glass. "I'm glad you enjoyed it."

"Not just the food." Uh-oh! "You are unlike anyone I've ever met before."

"I'll take that as a compliment."

I chuckle—again. "Something tells me you've never suffered from a shortage of those in your life."

"Not really, but..." She leans over the table. "I know I come across as arrogant at times, but I've worked very hard for everything I am. You don't just wake up one day and think, oh, I might open someone's skull today. I sacrificed a different, perhaps more acceptable, kind of life for that." She rests her gaze on me again. "A bit like you, actually."

"With the big difference being that your life is considered high-achieving while mine would be thought of… like I'm running from something instead of towards it."

"You don't strike me as someone who cares a great deal about achieving highly." She plants her elbows on the table and rests her chin on her upturned palms. Her eyes really do have an eerie quality to them. The pale green of their irises and the heaviness of their lids create a dreamy effect. And those cheekbones look like they're made for the sole purpose of gently running a fingertip along them. I picture myself doing so, then shake myself from my reverie. I've had way too much wine. There goes my run tomorrow. The cats will be happy to avail of my lap all day while I sleep it off in the sofa.

"Sorry." I point at my wine glass. "A bit too much of that."

"You and me both." She nods her chin in the direction of the lounge. "Shall we sit more comfortably for the digestif?"

"You're going to liquor me up even more?"

"Only if you want to." Her smile is something else as well. Oh, damn it. It must be all Marie's talk of lovers and her sexual prowess. It seems to have awakened something inside me. When an attractive woman invites you to dinner, tells you, with zero qualms, that she's very good in bed, then proceeds to open bottle after bottle of wine, it's hard not to see her strategy shine through it all. Yet, she hasn't made a pass at me. There has been some mild flirty banter, but nothing to really build on.

"Why the hell not?" My last smidgen of good judgement went out the window hours ago.

"Cointreau?" she asks as she rises.

"Sure." I follow her to the lounge. I sit in the corner of the sofa where I started the evening. It feels like days ago that I arrived here. Time has done that funny thing where it warps, and I can't remember where it has disappeared to.

After she has handed me my drink, she sits next to me, her body turned towards me.

I must keep any remaining wits I have left about me so I don't accidentally invite her to dinner at my place. Entertaining dinner guests stresses me out like nothing else. I can't be all casually elegant about it like Marie has been all evening. Dinner parties at my house have, historically, always lead to burned steaks, overcooked potatoes, and limp salads. She also wouldn't fit in my house. Her grace would contrast too heavily with my rustic decor.

I take a sip and am encouraged by her direct, albeit slightly cloudy, gaze on me. "Can I ask you something?"

"Fire away." She leans against the backrest of the sofa, stretching her arm in my direction.

"You've made no secret of the fact that you've thoroughly enjoyed seducing, well, a vast number of women."

"Hm." It's like a low moan coming from her throat.

"Yet… you haven't come on to me in the slightest." Or has she? I panic. Did I miss it? My cheeks must be a fiery red by now. Why did I even ask that question? Bloody Cointreau. Sodding wine.

She tilts her head back slightly, exposing the pale frailty of her throat for an instant. "It's not that I don't find you attractive, Olivia, if that's what you're wondering."

73

My cheeks must have gone purple. I wish I could fan myself. From the very first time we met, when she showed up at my back door, I've felt a little out of my depth. "I'm being silly. I—I don't expect you to hit on me just because I'm the only lesbian in the village. It was a very stupid question to ask."

"I don't think it is." Her hand slides closer to my shoulder. "I've wanted to kiss you for a while now. Since you picked me up after my bender the other night, to be more specific."

I glance sideways at her hand. What those hands must have done. The lives they must have saved. The fire burning up my cheeks has descended to my core, melting the last of my defences. "Really?" I put my glass down and rest my arm on the back of the sofa as well, my fingertips mere inches away from hers.

All she does is nod.

I might as well continue now that I've gone down this path, and she's walking right beside me. "Do you want to kiss me now?" I ask.

"There's a lot of things I'd like to do to you." Something changes in her. Even though it's so visible, almost palpable, I can't quite fathom it. Her hand inches closer—any closer and it will be touching mine. I'm not sure how I will ultimately react to her touch. "But I'm not sure I should."

I'm the one who bridges the final, tiny distance between our fingers. I'm the one touching her and, with that, giving her permission. That's what it feels like. Despite her cockiness, she has always been respectful. She hasn't crossed any of my boundaries—not tonight. I have a feeling that's about to change.

"I'm sure," I say, which is the most flagrant lie I've

uttered in decades. I'm anything but sure. But I know I want something more from her than just her hand against mine.

She slides her fingers forwards so they interlace with mine. "In that case." She gets rid of her glass and shuffles closer. With her free hand she cups my jaw. "If you're *absolutely* sure." She doesn't wait for me to double-confirm, but leans in until her lips are a hair's breadth away from mine. I can feel the heat of her breath as she opens her mouth. She smells divine, like exotic flowers after a rainstorm. How did I get here? This was not the plan. The wine. The talk. This woman. I didn't even try to resist her. I came on to her. But I can't worry about any of that now—I have the rest of my life to analyse what happened here tonight. I haven't kissed another woman in a very long time. I haven't been in another woman's personal space in years. And it's as though, because this is the last thing I wanted, I want it even more.

I bridge the last of the distance between our mouths. I press myself against her. I taste the orange-flavoured Cointreau on her lips. Her tongue is not immediately forthcoming. What is she waiting for? Is she teasing me? The only way to let her know that I'm not into that is to tell her, but those words will never make it past the stubborn threshold of my lips. She seems like the type to make me beg for it even more if I were to do that, anyway. She seems like the dangerous, reckless type. The kind of woman who walks into a room, scans it for someone she might like, then just takes what she presumes is hers, just because it's what she wanted. Marie's entitlement has been clear from the beginning. Strangely enough, it hasn't put me off. On the contrary. Now I know that it didn't only intrigue me, it turned me on as well. I've barely kissed her and my engine is revving already, purring like a cat mid-pet.

She pulls back a fraction and regards me, as though she hasn't decided yet what exactly she's going to do to me. Because it's obvious that she's the one calling the shots. She's in control. She leads and I follow. That must be the change I spotted in her before. The aura that came over her that said, loud and clear, *I've got this. I'll make you cry out with utter joy soon enough.*

She narrows her eyes and a small smile plays on her lips. Maybe this is what she wanted all along. Maybe she was playing the long game. Maybe she wasn't even that drunk when Yvette called me to pick her up. Or maybe, we're just two women who really want this right now. Two women who don't want to think about consequences or tomorrow. Let alone the past.

"Kiss me," I plead.

She waits a beat, looks at me. "As I said." Her voice has dropped into a lower register. "I'll do much more than that." And then she does. Next thing I know, Marie's all over me, although she keeps her cool about it. She doesn't overpower or overwhelm me. She just pushes me gently into the sofa, undoes the buttons of my shirt, and locks an intense stare on me before she kisses me again.

This was the last thing I expected to happen, and I haven't dressed for it. I'm wearing an old sports bra and I have no idea what knickers are under my trousers, but they won't meet any modern-day sexiness standard.

She doesn't seem to care one bit about my faded bra. She runs a fingertip over my abdomen, all the way down, to the button of my jeans.

It sets my skin alight. I want her with long-lost abandon. Lust is one of the sensations I've denied myself for good reason. The last time I felt such desire, I paid the biggest possible price. But I won't let that happen again. Marie's just passing through. I don't know when she's leaving but knowing she inevitably will is enough. We can both take what we need from this. No emotions have to be part of this equation. Not that I don't like her. I'm drawn to her. Very much so as she hooks her finger underneath the waistband of my jeans and skates it along the sensitive skin of my lower belly.

It's a little bit of a tussle to get me out of my jeans but then I lie half-naked in front of her. I want to get that pretty-but-ridiculous top off her. I want to see her. I want to run my hands along her skin and see how she reacts, but I do none of those things.

Instead, I wait for her to come for me again. And she does. She presses me into the sofa with her bodyweight. It feels divine to have another woman's body against mine. After tonight, I might have to re-examine all the things I willingly go without. But let's see how it plays out first. Let's see if she's really as good as she claims to be. Although what does that even mean? She hasn't been shy to boast about the amount of experience she has in bed. No wonder she believes herself to be an expert. And in the end, it's not rocket science—nor neurosurgery.

Her lips trace a path along my neck, then hover over my ear. "Do you want to tell me what you like?" she whispers, her breath moist on my skin.

Hell no. I shake my head. I've always been an inadequate lesbian that way—according to Sandrine, at least.

"No problem." She latches onto my earlobe with her teeth for a fraction of a second. Her fingertips skate along the skin spilling out of my bra. "This needs to go." It's more a command than a request. I push myself up on my elbows and she gives me a hand removing my bra. I hope I'm not going to start worrying every morning about which bra to wear, thinking I might run into her and something like this could happen again. It's not the sort of dilemma I like to spend my mental bandwidth on. She's seen the worst of my lingerie now, although, despite the hostility of our first meeting, she hasn't come close to seeing the worst of me.

The look in her eyes changes again upon exposing my breasts. It's more ravenous, a touch less in control—a little more carnal. Her breath comes a bit faster, mimicking mine. My nipples reach high into the air, as though stretching towards her.

"You're beautiful," she says, apparently not minding the small curve of my belly. Those couple of kilos I can't seem to shed no matter how many kilometres I run. My wine kilos, as Sandrine used to call them, because I've always preferred three glasses of wine over two. Which is one of the reasons I find myself almost completely naked in the neighbour's holiday cottage tonight. That, and the current occupant, of course, whose enthralling gaze scans my body, following the movement of her hand. I'm not sure if I'm supposed to thank her for calling me beautiful, so I just emit a sort of groan in response to her compliment.

She kisses me again and I somehow manage to inter-rupt the endless stream of thoughts in my head, the chatter that's always there, and lose myself in the touch of her lips against mine, the gentle intrusion of her tongue into my mouth. Her fingertips are enchantingly close to the edge of my underwear. My heart pounds in my chest. I can't get enough of her kisses, of her soft lips. Her hand rides up again. She closes it around my breast. It feels like

the warmest embrace I've been the recipient of in years—
it probably is.

I could blame the copious amounts of alcohol, but
really, my body wants to catch up with all the absence of
touch I've put myself through. I claw at her top but it's too
complicated to get off her. I move my hand underneath it,
wanting to feel more of her. Her hands on me are not
enough. I need her skin against my fingers as well as her
tongue dancing with mine. Fuck, she's a good kisser. Of all
the unforeseen events that have already occurred, from me
showing up at her doorstep with an apology and a bottle
of cider, to me picking her up from the bar late at night, to
me being here, my eagerness to yield to her, for her to
ravage me, is the most astounding. There are instances,
when I come to my senses a fraction, that it doesn't feel
like it's me giving myself to her with such abandon. This is
the opposite of what I would do.

Marie's fingertip circles my nipple while her lips trace
a path to my neck and then downwards to where her
finger is revving me up even more. Did I ever want
Sandrine like this? It's impossible to remember, although I
can't forget her claims about my lack of passion in the
bedroom. Why isn't it like that now? I don't understand it.
Or is this the thrill that comes with having a one-night
stand? Something I've never previously understood. Why
hop into bed with someone you don't know? How would it
even be possible to share that kind of intimacy? But here I
am, living proof that strangers can be quite the turn-on.
Or maybe it's because, according to the dozen or so
unwritten rules I conduct my life by, I shouldn't be here.
I'm breaking most of my rules just by being here.

Oh, fuck. Her lips close around my nipple. I exhale
loudly, desperately. She flicks her tongue against my nipple

and sets every last one of my nerve endings ablaze. Her hand dips lower again and, this time, it doesn't stop at the edge of my knickers. A finger slides underneath the waistband and I swear I'm about to spontaneously combust. Maybe what makes her so effective at this is how she talks about herself and the self-fulfilling prophecy she creates by doing so. Or, let's be honest, she just knows, through many years of experience, how to expertly manage the vast amount of unspent lust that has built up inside me.

I can masturbate all I want—and I do—but it's an entirely different experience when another woman touches me there. Her fingertip is so close to my clit. I push myself towards her. But she doesn't let me come any closer. Instead, she retracts her finger. She narrows her eyes, then pulls my underwear down. She looks at me the way I've seen lions eye their prey on National Geographic, just before they go in for the kill. Am I her prey? She sure does look as if she's about to ravage me.

She kneels in front of the sofa and spreads my legs. I let my head fall back and enjoy the avalanche of sensations. Her hands on my thighs, followed by her lips. Her tongue teasing my clit. Her fingertips skating along my entrance. It all blurs into a crescendo of arousal, an abundance of lust set free. The touch of her tongue on me is deft, her fingers inside me feel like they should be doing only this for the rest of her life—and mine. The fire raging through my body is wild and untameable. It wants and demands more, and she gives it to me, until my poor, untrained-in-this muscles collapse, and the stars that you can see out there on bright nights are now also visible inside.

CHAPTER 11
MARIE

"No," I say. "Please."

Olivia looks at me with understandable confusion in her eyes.

"I can't." I've pleased plenty of women in my life and not asked for anything in return, but this is different. This isn't about not asking for something. It's about not being able to give something. Olivia's probably dying to get her hands on me—that's what the look in her eyes telegraphs at least. But I can't let her.

"Are you sure?"

"It's… not you. It's, um…" This is why I had to resist her in the first place. I hadn't expected her to come on to me like that—not Olivia. Although I hoped our moment of passion might remove some of my emotional barriers, it seems to have had the opposite effect.

She sits up, glances around, looking for something to cover herself with perhaps. I hand Olivia the shirt I took off her earlier.

"You don't have to explain." Her voice is soft. "I just… assumed."

"Will you stay, please?" I ask.

"Yes, of course." She reaches for my hand and grazes her lips against my knuckle.

"Thank you." I manoeuvre around in the sofa so we can sit more comfortably.

"I'll be right back." She grabs her discarded clothes and saunters into the downstairs loo.

I use the time alone to draw a few deep breaths. An image flashes in front of my eyes. A bright smile. Eyes sparkling with the only intention to seduce. Véronique. *Damn it.*

Olivia returns fully dressed. If I didn't know any better, if I hadn't just tasted all of her with my tongue, you'd think nothing had happened here tonight. That it was just two acquaintances having dinner.

I chuckle to lighten the atmosphere. To put myself at ease. "I was just thinking about going to bed, but you look like you're going out."

"I just felt a bit exposed. I can take all of this off again." She sits down close to me. "Are you okay?"

"Yeah, I... Before, when I told you that I'd never fallen in love, I wasn't telling the full truth." I glance at her sideways. "I was very much in the process of falling in love before I came here. I can see that now. But..." I hate being at a loss for words. Olivia presses her palm gently against the small of my back. For someone who doesn't appear very fond of people, she sure does seem to have a way with me.

"Take your time," she whispers. "I'm not going anywhere."

"Last November, a new nurse started working in the operating theatre. Véronique. I took an instant shine to her, but she made me work for it. She wasn't like any of the others. A mere flash of her smile was enough to make me melt into a puddle. I used to tell her that I was so grateful for having to wear face masks in the OR because a glimpse of her lips was enough to make me lose all focus on my task at hand, no matter how important." I lean into Olivia's touch a little. "We had a bit of a longer, multiple-nights thing, and I was considering letting it play out. To see what would happen. It was fun. *She* was fun. Until… the night before that dreadful surgery. Véronique and I stayed up way too late. Laughing. Fucking. Oversleeping." A shiver runs down my spine at the memory. "Things like that usually aren't a problem for me. I can easily get by on four hours of sleep per night, but… something must have caught up with me that morning. I wasn't focused. I was working on a very badly tuned autopilot. And then a person died on my operating table, because I had feelings for another woman I just had to indulge in."

"I'm sorry." Olivia's hand skates to my side. She pulls me close. After what we just did that kind of familiarity is possible now. "I understand you're having a difficult time processing all of that. Your job…"

"For years, I've been considered one of the best in my field. I get asked to consult on cases all over Europe. And then this happens. If it weren't so tragic, I'd be able to see the irony in it."

"What, um, happened with Véronique?"

My mouth goes dry, but I manage to push the words past. "Nothing. Literally, nothing happened ever again between her and me after that surgery. I couldn't bear to be near her and I made sure to have her removed from my OR. My leave of absence has worked wonders for putting distance between us as well." Even though what happened is still dreadful, a small sense of relief washes over me at having said these words out loud to another person—to Olivia.

"It's easy for me to say, but maybe you're being too hard on yourself. When it comes down to it, life will always be uncontrollable. The smallest thing can have the biggest impact. As trite as it sounds, mistakes happen all the time."

"It's different for surgeons. When we make a mistake, people can and do die."

"That might be so, but the result of a possible mistake by you doesn't make it so they don't happen. They're still an inherent part of life."

"I know, but... as I told you before." Maybe I shouldn't expect a mere mortal—someone not in the medical profession—to get this. "This one's different. This one has had such an inordinate impact on me. I can't disentangle it from my feelings for Véronique. Even though I am the most rational person you will meet, I'm somehow convinced that my feelings for her, that mind-blowing last night we had together, is the reason I fucked up." Olivia might not entirely get what this has done to me, but she has, somehow, managed to make me spill my guts to her.

"Is that why you weren't hitting on me?"

I'm not sure it's meant as a joke—I don't know Olivia that well—but I decide to take it as such. This evening has taken too much of a turn for the dramatic already.

"I wasn't hitting on you because you never gave me the impression you would welcome that. At all." I turn to look at her. "You're a tough nut to crack."

"Oh, sure." She chuckles.

She's right. Ten minutes ago, she was trembling at my touch on this very sofa. Not that that makes her easy by a long shot. "Besides, you came on to me."

"You poured me full of wine."

"That's the excuse you're going to use?"

Olivia nods, a sheepish grin on her face.

"Are you going to regret it in the morning?" Even though I can't yet bear the intimacy of her touching me the way I touched her, I want her again. I want to see her exactly the way she was earlier—ecstatic and fully surrendered.

"Let's not go there yet. It's not even midnight."

I exhale deeply, then lean closer to her. "Thank you for…" Giving yourself to me? I can't possibly say that. "Hitting on me. I think I kind of needed it."

"Believe me, it wasn't my plan when I came to dinner."

"I'm not only good in bed." Sometimes I think I overdo it with these remarks about myself, but too many women have gone nuts over them for me to stop. Confidence is still one of the biggest turn-ons for most. Olivia's no exception.

Olivia shakes her head, as though she doesn't really know what to do with me. I understand the sentiment. It's the very reason why I came here. To hide from my life instead of running towards it, as she put it earlier. But my confidence has been shaken. I wouldn't be here otherwise. It was just nice, for a little while, to pretend to be the person I once was.

"I can hardly deny that you have a way with your tongue." Olivia's cheeks pink up again. It's so adorable it touches me in that soft spot I've had trouble protecting the last few months.

"How about we go to bed and I show you what else it can do?" I really can't help myself.

"We'll see about that." She suppresses a yawn—hardly impolite this late in the evening. "I need some sleep."

So do I, although I haven't shared my bed with another woman since Véronique. I suspect sleep won't come easily and hope the Cointreau might help.

It's after three when I finally get up. Although I'm not used to taking bedfellows into account, I try to be quiet. I've waited for Olivia to fall into a deep sleep, although I can't be sure that she has. My neurological skills don't extend that far.

I tip-toe out of the room, throw on some clothes in the bathroom, and saunter downstairs. I could fill the dishwasher, but I don't want to make any more noise than I have to. I walk to the window and gaze outside. It's a clear night and the moon is almost full, casting a pale, hazy light over the garden and the meadows beyond. It's dead quiet. If it were summer, I'd go outside and sit in the darkness for a while, breathing in the night air until my brain calms down. But it's too cold so my only other option is to sit in the sofa where Olivia and I just had sex, or to sit in the chair opposite it and look at the same sofa.

I like Olivia and I most certainly enjoyed being with her, but I'm not sure I can have her in my house. It's too disconcerting. It unlocks too many memories I'm trying to forget. Why did I ask her to stay, anyway? As some sort of compensation for not allowing her to touch me? I walk to my unfinished glass of Cointreau. I consider drinking it, but the smell makes my stomach turn. I should have taken a sleeping pill like I do every night, but this being an out-of-the-ordinary night, I decided against it—I didn't want to show that kind of weakness in front of Olivia. I still could, but I'd be completely out of it when Olivia wakes up in the morning. Maybe that's a good solution, the two-birds-with-one-stone kind.

All of a sudden, I have no idea how I've kept Véronique's memory at bay for this long—her inviting smile. How she made me feel when she aimed it right at me. How I could never resist. And how, I see now, having Olivia touch me would have erased the memory of Véronique's fingerprints from my skin.

But I somehow did manage to banish her from my thoughts completely, as though doing so would magically solve all my problems. Nothing has been solved—I still let someone die on my operating table—and I can't seem to stop thinking about her anymore either. It would be easy to blame Olivia for that, but I only have myself to blame.

The creaking of the stairs startles me. I must have woken her. Maybe she's just using the bathroom and will go right back to sleep. I'm not sure what I would prefer. To talk to her or to be left in peace.

She's definitely coming downstairs. She's wearing that frumpy denim shirt she showed up in—although it does look kind of haphazardly sexy on her—and a pair of socks, that's it.

"Can't sleep?" she asks.

"Sorry to wake you."

"I'm not very good with strange beds." She walks into

the living room. "And my evening ritual was greatly altered tonight." She flashes a smile.

I just nod. I don't have energy left to flirt.

"Do you want me to make you some warm milk?"

Warm milk? I'm going to need something much stronger than that to stop the turmoil in my head. Can I ask her to leave now? I've asked other women I've slept with to leave in the middle of the night. Olivia basically lives next door. And she just alluded to preferring her own bed.

"Sure," I hear myself say, because I can't kick her out. It's different here, out in the countryside. Olivia's not someone replaceable to me, which, to my recent dismay, is how I've often regarded women in the past.

She goes into the kitchen and opens the fridge. I follow her and settle at the kitchen island. I watch her as she pours milk into mugs and puts one in the microwave. It takes her a few moments to figure out how it works. She's not wearing any underwear and her shirt isn't long enough to cover her behind completely. It really is very shapely. I wonder what it would look like if I made her bottom cheeks pink up the way her—I actively stop myself, because this is what I've always done to deal with the hard stuff. What happened a few hours ago is only more evidence stacked against me.

The microwave pings and Olivia plants a steaming mug in front of me. I can't believe she made me warm milk. It wasn't a lot of work, but it's the thought that counts.

"Thank you."

She shoots me a quick wink and puts the other mug in the microwave.

"Do you want to talk?" she asks, leaning her forearms on the surface of the kitchen island.

"I don't have much to say."

"Okay." She doesn't push. For Olivia, it's enough of an explanation. I appreciate that about her. It's so unlike the many women I've known who've wanted to pry deep into my psyche against my will—who wanted to find out why I am the way I am.

Olivia gets her mug out of the microwave, gives the milk a good stir, and then comes to sit next to me, pulling her shirt over her behind. We drink in silence for a while.

"Do you still want me to stay?" she asks, looking ahead. "It's okay if you don't. I understand."

"I was already planning what to cook you for breakfast." It's unlike me to beat about the bush like this.

"Let me rephrase my question." She turns fully towards me. "Would you be very upset if I went home? I know I won't be able to sleep for a few hours now that I'm awake. Unless... you, um, have other plans for passing the time."

I erupt into a chuckle. In her own convoluted way, she can be quite forward if she wants to be. "Why don't we save that for another time?" I put my mug down and plant my hands on her knees. "And no, I won't be upset if you leave."

Part of me expects her to invite me to brunch at her house, but she doesn't look like the type of person who would ever consider the notion of combining breakfast and lunch. The other part of me instinctively knows that I might have to wait a while before I'm invited into Olivia's home.

"Okay." She deposits her mug and covers my hands with hers. "Thank you so much for, uh, everything." The grin that follows is much more mischievous than bashful. I've seen her come. She can't hide from me anymore now.

"It was my absolute pleasure." I slant towards her. "I'm here whenever you want more of my cooking," I whisper.

She nods as though she fully understands what I really mean, then proceeds to kiss me tenderly on the lips.

CHAPTER 12
OLIVIA

Deneuve and Huppert have no clue what's happening when I come home in the middle of the night, and neither do I. My cats are easily reassured with some food in their bowls, but I don't have that option. My latest meal is what indirectly instigated this confusion in the first place.

I can't believe I slept with Marie. My mind simply can't fathom that it actually happened. It's like time sped up and my brain got tricked into believing I've known her for months instead of seeing her a few times since she arrived in Bonneau. The copious amounts of wine had a part to play as well.

Never in my life have I slept with someone I barely know. Never in my life have I wanted to, except with her. At first, I believed she'd played me expertly. That she had unlimited patience—not that she needed it—until I made the first move. But why would she even bother with all of that if she never had any intention of letting me touch her?

Now I realise it's all me. Although not really. It's my

reaction to her. To her confidence bordering on haughti-
ness—quite often teetering right over the edge between
the two. Maybe it's the combination of the two of us
together. Maybe I just really needed to succumb to
another woman's touch. I'm not immune to that, despite
how I've chosen to live my life. Maybe it's a sign that I'm
ready to open myself up to more people. But no, that's not
what it feels like.

I'm also happy to be home. I'm relieved to be here,
even though I'm pacing up and down my kitchen like a
madwoman. I have so many questions. What will she
expect from me now? What do I expect from her? Everything has changed. A headache is starting up at the base
of my skull. I drink a few glasses of water, erasing the taste
of the milk. Erasing the taste of Marie's kisses. What has
surprised me the most is how easily I yielded to her, as
though my pleasure was enhanced by her absolute belief
that she could give it to me. As though my own doubts
could be erased by her lack of them.

I go upstairs, followed by both cats, strip and hop into
the shower, hoping the warm water will help me relax.
Even though it's utterly insane to ask myself this question,
I wonder if I could fall for her. But she's not relationship
material. Everything about her screams danger, that I
should stay away. I should know. Yet, she keeps seeking
contact. Maybe she's as messed up as I am, but in a
different way. Aren't we all, I mumble to no one, my words
drowned out by the cascade of water running down my
face.

I wash the last of her scent from my skin. As I dry off,
I ponder her refusal to let me touch her and what she told
me about this nurse called Véronique. Marie's clearly
going through a difficult time in her life and she has

chosen to go through it away from her family and friends —that, too, sounds quite familiar. Some people process better alone, without any outside input. At the moment, even though she's had her hands, and tongue, all over me, she's nothing but an infinitely complex mystery to me. I'm not sure she's the kind of woman I want to scratch the surface of. I have an acute aversion to complications of any kind. More than anything, I like—I *need*—a simple, quiet life. Hence my chosen location.

Deneuve has this thing about helping me dry off my legs. After every shower, she's there, rubbing her fur against my skin. I praise her efforts despite it being ridiculous. If they had the capacity to understand, my cats would know more about me than any human on this planet.

I crawl into bed, surprised that I managed to fall asleep at all in Marie's bed earlier. Must have been the post-climax oxytocin in my blood. Deneuve settles at the foot of the bed. Huppert on the other pillow mere inches away from my head, close enough for me to hear her purr.

While the entire evening was pretty mind-blowing, and Marie lived up to the expectations she created for herself and then some, I can't see it happening again any time soon. This is the time to pull up the drawbridge, for me to protect myself.

Ideally, I wouldn't have let her come this close, but it's not the end of the world. It's manageable, and it will be even more so once she leaves. I make a mental note to ask her about her departure date. She hasn't mentioned it and from what she's told me, which isn't all that much, she's nowhere near finding the peace she's after. Although, perhaps for some people who are not me, these things can turn quickly. Either way, I have no intention of becoming some sort of surrogate therapist for her, nor her fuck buddy in Brittany. Besides, now that she's had me, she's probably done with me. Maybe I won't see her anymore at all. Maybe next time she drinks too much at Yvette's, she'll find another way to get home.

My endless thought loops about Marie must have helped me drift off because next thing I know, it's light and Deneuve is resting heavily on my full bladder—her way of telling me it's well past time for breakfast.

As soon as I stir, Huppert purrs joyfully into my ear— she's far less passive-aggressive than her sister.

My headache isn't as bad as I had expected. The wine Marie served was of excellent quality and I wouldn't be French if I hadn't learned the impact of inferior wine on hangovers from a young age.

As I jump out of bed, I consider that I never got to finish my pousse-café. Before I slip into my robe, I put a hand on my belly. Marie called me beautiful. When you've lived alone as long as I have, you stop thinking about yourself in that way because there's no one around to remind you. Not that I've ever believed myself to not be beautiful, nor the opposite. It's just not something I ever think about.

I hurry down to feed the cats. It's almost ten. If it hadn't been for the late-night feeding they received, they would have started rioting hours ago. Thank goodness it's Sunday. I stretch my arms above my head and look out the window. Damn it. It's different now. I can't actually see Marie's house from this vantage point but I'm too acutely aware of its presence and I can't seem to block it out.

I make coffee and open the Sunday paper on my iPad, but I can't focus. I try rocking in my rocking chair, but there's an agitation inside me that I can't shake. I'm probably going to have to talk to her, but what do I want to say? I have no idea because I don't know what I want, yet I feel the persistent need for a set of rules.

I move to my digital piano and put on my headphones so as to continue my practice in the art of non-performance. No one can hear me. I've never learned how to play but it doesn't matter. The goal is simply to play. To hear music. To listen for the next note. To tune into my intuition and trust that it will tell me where I should put my finger next. This usually has a calming effect, but not today. *Damn it, Marie.* I huff out some air and take off the headphones. Maybe I should go for a run, but my body is still recuperating from all the things that happened to it last night. A shiver runs up my spine at the memory. Is that my body's way of telling me it wouldn't mind being in that position, at the mercy of Marie, again soon?

"What do you think?" I ask Huppert, who apparently hasn't recovered from my unusual absence last night and is following me around making sure I'm not going anywhere. She perks up her ears, which she usually doesn't bother with when I address her because why would she? She must have heard something outside. My muscles stiffen. What time is it? Could it be Marie? And what on earth am I wearing?

Huppert glances at me as if to ask, who is disturbing our peace on a Sunday morning? Or perhaps that's just me projecting. The doorbell rings. It can really only be Marie. At least she's using the front door this time. I'm still in my robe when I open the door to her holding up a paper bag.

"Hungry?" she asks.

I know I'm supposed to say yes even though all I want to say is no. Although, I'm not entirely sure. She's no longer a stranger and I sort of feel like I owe her something. She cooked me a veritable feast last night and then…

"Olivia?" She stands there grinning. "Are you okay? Did I wake you?" She takes a step closer. "I waited as long as I could stand it. I even drove to the village to get croissants." She holds the bag up again.

"Come in." I usher her into the lounge, which looks very inadequate compared to her renovated cottage—kind of like how I look compared to her right now. "Make yourself comfortable. I'm just going to put something, uh, more on."

"You don't have to." Her grin has turned rather smug. "Nothing I haven't seen before."

"I will, anyway." I half expect her to reach out and loosen the sash of my robe. Or is that what I want her to do? I need more layers of clothing between us pronto. Clearly, my brain can't be trusted around her to keep me from doing something silly. Ending up in bed with her while inebriated is one thing, doing it again the next day when I'm stone-cold sober would be another thing entirely. It would mean a most dangerous decline in my defences.

I rush up the stairs. Deneuve is having her post-breakfast nap on the bed and glares at me briefly before closing her eyes again, unbothered by what's going on downstairs. I quickly throw on what I was wearing last night—that won't be anything she hasn't seen before either, then.

"Coffee?" I ask after I've slowly made my way down, trying to compose myself.

I should have known she wouldn't be the type to just patiently wait for me in a chair. She's standing by the sideboard next to the window.

"Is this the infamous Sandrine?" She holds up a frame with a picture of the two of us in better days.

I nod, trying to remember what I have and haven't told her about my ex.

"Didn't she break your heart?" Marie asks.

She sure fucking did. "Yes."

"Then why do you have her picture on display in your living room?"

"To, um…" I saunter over to her. "To remind myself of certain things."

She fixes her green gaze on me, then purses her lips for a split second and puts the picture down. Thank goodness. She gives me an ostentatious once-over. "For the record, I prefer you with a lot less clothes on."

I don't really know how to take that. She comes across as ultra-feisty today. As though she has something to prove. As though, she too, is on edge, but she expresses it in a different way.

"We should probably talk," I say.

"Sure." She narrows the distance between us.

I give it a few moments before I move away from her.

"Oh, you mean actual talking with words?" She cocks her head. She wasn't this obnoxious last night. If she had been, I wouldn't have slept with her. Or was I that far gone that I didn't notice? She juts out her bottom lip, then shrugs.

"Yes." I grab the bag of croissants and take it into the kitchen. The coffee should still be warm enough. Without waiting for her to reply to my earlier question, I pour us both a cup. By the time she makes it into the kitchen, I've set out two plates and napkins as well.

"Hey, I was just joking around. Are you okay?" She pulls back a chair and squints at me before she sits.

"I'm just… I haven't done this in a long time." I spend ninety-nine percent of my Sundays talking to no one.

"I'm a bit much. I know." She flashes me a smile.

I open the bag and distribute croissants. "I'm still kind of processing what happened last night."

"I get that." She tears off the corner of her pastry. "As long as you don't regret it." She looks as though she would need to perform an emergency lobotomy on anyone who would dare regret sleeping with her. "I'm no expert at dealing with that kind of sentiment."

I remember the mental note I made last night. "Do you have any idea yet of how long you'll be staying?"

"My initial leave of absence was for three months. If I want to extend it, I'll need to decide before the end of this month." She finally pops the morsel of croissant into her mouth. When she's done chewing, she says, "I'm seriously considering it. Part of me wants to go back and take up my life again but, if I'm being really honest with myself, which"—she lifts a finger—"is a bloody hard thing to do, by the way, then I know I'm not ready for that."

"So, you'd be staying in Bonneau longer?"

"If I decide to stay, yes, for another three months." She stares at her hands as though she can't believe they won't be performing any surgeries for that long. How does it work when you're a surgeon? Do you need to practice to keep your fingers nimble and your hands steady? "Until the end of June."

My brain starts whirring. It's only mid-February. If she's here until June, how will that affect me? I shouldn't get too close, I know that much. And I need to let her know that I'm the opposite of the clingy type.

"Whether I stay longer or not has got nothing to do with you, Olivia. I had a great time with you last night and

98

I'm up for that any time you want, but I'm not looking for anything serious. I hope that's clear."

Oh, snap. Looks like there's zero need for me to state my own intentions. "Oh, yes, very clear." I eat a piece of flaky croissant, its buttery flavour an instant comfort. At least we understand each other. Now, for the rules. "I'm not looking for anything romantic, either."

"Good."

I'm still slightly confused at what she's doing in my house today if she's not looking for anything serious. Is it courtesy? Is it boredom? "I appreciate you bringing breakfast, but I would appreciate it even more if you didn't make a habit out of coming round. If you could text before you want to stop by, that would be great."

"I was on my way back from the village earlier and I couldn't resist ringing your bell, what with the way we left things in the middle of the night."

"Okay." I guess I can understand that.

"I will respect your privacy, I promise." She holds up two fingers. "But I would like to spend more time with you. To be honest, if it weren't for you living here, I'm not sure I would even consider staying longer."

She must see the confusion on my face, because she continues.

"The reason for me staying longer is not that I want to pursue anything romantic with you, but the fact that you're here does make it easier for me to stay." She shakes her head. "Maybe I'm not making much sense, but perhaps we could be friends?"

"With benefits?" I add.

She chuckles. "Something like that, I guess, although, to be honest, I don't think I've ever had an actual friend with benefits before. In my view, it's pretty hard to

99

combine the two because if you're friends and sleeping together, what's the difference with being in a relationship?"

Fair point, and I'm hardly an expert either. "I don't know. But, um…" I take a sip of coffee. "I'm someone who needs routine. You showing up next door has meant I've had to make certain adjustments. Which is fine, but… I can't have my sense of being in control taken away like that all the time."

"Meaning?" She narrows her eyes.

"I live here for a reason." I can't give her much more today. Not after everything I've already given last night. And I need my energy to not fall into the greatest trap of all: feelings for another woman. Another glance at her is enough to know Marie would be easy to fall for. She has that easy magnetism about her that makes her irresistible. And I've already succumbed once. "It's hard to explain and I apologise for that." I take a quick breath. "But I'm going to need some rules in place."

"Rules?" She looks amused more than bemused.

"Like… that we only hook up once a month, for instance." I don't know where that rule has suddenly sprouted from. Probably from my dire need to have a rule, even a completely random one, while fighting randomness is the whole point of having rules. Oh, the tricks my brain plays on me.

"You want to quantify the number of times we sleep together?" Her brow furrows. "Why?"

"It was the wrong example. I—" If I keep this up, this conversation, nor any subsequent ones will be necessary. Marie will draw her obvious conclusions and avoid me for the remainder of her time here.

"How about I leave you be until you text me?" she

says matter-of-factly. "That way the ball's firmly in your court."

"Uh, well, yes." Did she read my mind? Or is she just placating me? The questions in my head are multiplying into an unmanageable spiral.

"All right. Just don't wait too long." She nibbles on the rest of her croissant. "And feel free to invite yourself to my place any time."

Deflation is quickly replacing the earlier elation inside me. Stunted, unsatisfying conversations like this are one of the core reasons why, most days, I prefer to not talk to anyone.

Huppert walks into the kitchen and meows as though something has greatly offended her.

"Hello, you." Marie leans down to pet my cat on the head. "When are you coming around to mine again?" She glances up at me. "Hopefully you won't make me wait like your mistress."

MARCH

CHAPTER 13

MARIE

"Can we go for a walk or something?" My sister gazes out of the window wistfully, at the heavy black cover hiding the pool.

"You've only been here two hours and you're already getting antsy."

"I'm more baffled than anything else, Marie. This is so unlike you. What are you still doing here?"

"Getting used to my own thoughts. Learning to love silence." I feel like I'm channelling Olivia, even though I haven't seen her in weeks. It has made me question more than my surgical skills.

Madeleine shakes her head. "Talk like that is what worries me the most." She walks away from the window and looks at me. "Who are you and what have you done to my sister?"

I've been in Bonneau more than two months and I've started to find some sort of peace, or at the very least comfort in the sameness of the days and the absence of stress. I've also started to realise that years of taking inadequate time off and never allowing my body to fully recharge have wreaked havoc on my sleep patterns. I'm finally beginning to sleep through the night without the aid of medication. Doctors are always the worst patients and I'm no exception.

"I'm taking a break from being me."

Madeleine shrugs and comes to sit next to me in the sofa. "But do you have to do it here? You have plenty of cash to go off to much sunnier shores."

"It has to be here."

"I don't know what it is about this place in winter. There's something so utterly bleak about it." She wraps her arms around herself. "That said, it seems to agree with you." She cocks her head and examines my face. "There's something almost tranquil about you." Her eyes darken and she puts a cold hand on mine. "You're not taking anything too invasive or addictive, are you?"

I chuckle at the things my family—a family of doctors, no less—worry about. "No. I'm totally off any meds."

"That's good, but, Marie, honestly, what do you do here all day?" My sister's reaction to arriving at the holiday house in Bonneau reminds me very much of my own two months ago. Dievarts can't sit around and do nothing all day. Even our mother, who's been officially retired for more than a decade, is always busy chairing some board or organising a charity event. *Sitting still equals dying* has been one of her favourite things to say for as long as I can remember.

I try to explain to my sister that it's not so much about what I do, which is the same every day, but what I don't do. The conversation stalls quickly because she can't quite grasp it and I understand her reaction completely—if the tables were turned, I'd react in exactly the same way. So we end up donning our heavy winter coats and venturing out.

"Take a deep breath," I say, risking my sister calling me a cliché. "It's different when you breathe deeply here. The air is much cleaner."

"Marie." She grabs me by the arm. "You are coming back, aren't you?"

"Of course." I huddle against her. It's good to feel another human's touch. "I'm glad you're here." Arm in arm, we walk in the direction of Olivia's house.

"Have you met the invisible neighbours?" Madeleine asks as we walk past.

"I have." My voice shoots up.

My sister stops to shoot me a look. "What does that mean?"

"It means that, yes, I have met the woman who lives in that house. Her name's Olivia. I've even had her over for dinner."

"And?"

"And... she's a lovely, if somewhat peculiar person. To say she's fond of her privacy would be an understatement."

"We shouldn't go knocking on her door, then?"

Heavens no. I've had to fight the impulse on a daily basis. We've texted back and forth a few times but, even though she claimed not to mean it when she said it, Olivia does seem to want to stick to the once-a-month rule. I can only conclude that seeing me, for her, equals wanting to do much more than talk. Why else is she keeping her distance like that? The real truth, of course, is that I don't know what to think, nor what to make of her. I shake my head.

"Why would we do that?" I say. "We have each other."

We continue our walk and talk about our mother and about Nicholas, Madeleine's husband, who is a plastic surgeon like her.

We don't encounter another living soul—at least not a human one—until we're on our way back home and a figure looms in the distance.

My heart jumps at the prospect of it being Olivia. The figure's too far away for me to be a hundred percent certain it's her, but who else can it possibly be?

"How exciting," Madeleine says, "another human!"

Said human approaches quickly and now it is unmistakably her. An image of her naked body flashes through my mind. As soon as my sister leaves, I will have to make some sort of move. I meant it when I said that having her live nearby made my decision to stay easier, although, since I've said it, the house around the corner might as well have been empty.

As we get closer to each other, our speed decreases naturally. Madeleine and I wait for Olivia to bridge the final few metres. She slows down a fraction, glances up briefly, says "*Bonjour*", and continues on her way.

What the hell?

"Olivia?" I shout after her. "It's me." What is it with this woman? What is she so afraid of?

She stops in her tracks, turns around and looks at me wide-eyed. Surely she recognised me and even if for some inexplicable reason she didn't, she could have worked out it was me.

"Hi, Marie." She shuffles her weight from one foot to the other.

"This is Madeleine, my sister," I offer. "She's visiting for the weekend."

"*Enchantée*," Madeleine shouts.

I walk a little closer to Olivia. Madeleine follows. When we reach Olivia, Madeleine offers her hand. Olivia shakes it quickly. Strangely, I don't know what to do with myself. I've slept with this woman, yet I feel trepidation about giving her a simple kiss hello on the cheek. Everything about her is screaming to get the hell away from her.

"I hope you enjoy your stay," Olivia says to Madeleine. "I need to go."

"Olivia." I ask Madeleine to give me a minute and rush after her. "Hey. Are you okay?" I grab her arm. "It's me." It sounds silly, but it feels like it needs to be said.

"I don't want to interrupt your time with your sister."

"Interrupt?" I find it hard to let go of her arm. "How can you even think you would ever interrupt anything?"

"You mustn't have seen her in a while. You should enjoy every minute with her."

"I wouldn't mind enjoying some more minutes with you." I put myself right into her personal space. Even though I don't know her all that well, I know her enough to reliably predict she won't like that. Just as I don't like being ignored.

"We can, um, get together after your sister has gone," she says.

"Can we?"

"Yeah. Sure." She steps back, her arm dropping from my grasp.

"Will you come to my place?" I need to lock down a date now. "Monday?"

"Okay. Text me the time."

"Any time," I shout after her as she starts walking away.

After I've rejoined Madeleine, she asks, "What was that all about?"

I huff out some air. "I can't make heads nor tails of that woman. She's so aloof, yet…"

"Oh goodness, Marie, no way." My sister squeezes my arm. "You slept with her, didn't you?"

"It's not a big deal."

"You're unbelievable."

I shrug in response.

"You solemnly claimed, with all the airs and graces us Dievarts are so blessed with, that one of the reasons for coming here was the lack of temptation it afforded."

"That was before I met Olivia."

"She can't have been very impressed with you; she barely acknowledged your existence just now." My sister appears to find this very amusing.

Sexual conquests are not something I boast about in a family context. I laugh it off, even though Olivia's odd behaviour does sting a little.

"Do you like her?" Madeleine bumps her shoulder gently into mine.

"She's the only person around."

"That's a non-answer if ever there was one."

"I do like her, but she's a challenge."

"What do you expect, Marie? Clearly, at one point in her life, she made the conscious decision to live alone, in the middle of nowhere. Then you turn up with all your unquenchable need for attention." Madeleine snickers.

I roll my eyes.

"I won't ask whether it's more than physical. There clearly wasn't much love in the air just now."

Love. What is she even talking about? "She's a friend."

"A rather distant friend."

"Yes." What else can I say? I might wish for things to

be different between Olivia and me, but I can only take what she offers.

"Do you know why she ended up here?"

"More or less." I'm not about to share Olivia's story with my sister.

"I know why *you* ended up here." She holds me closer again. "When are we going to talk about that?"

"We have all weekend," I say, as we walk back to the warmth of the house.

———

"Talk to me," Madeleine says, as if a bit of urging is all it takes for me to discuss the horrible events that brought me here. "Come on." She's more insistent than she usually is when it comes to things like this.

"A woman died on my table. There's really not that much else to say about it."

"You know as well as I do that sometimes patients die." Madeleine's tone is more compassionate than matter-of-fact. "It's what we learn to live with early on in our career."

"I know that very well."

"So? Why is it so hard for you to accept the death of this particular woman?"

"Hélène Cordier. That was her name," I say. "She had a husband, two children, and she was a teacher. She was a person, Madeleine, not just a patient, not just some brain tissue seen through the opening in the sterile drapes. An actual person. A mother and a wife, who died because I wasn't focused enough. If it weren't for me, Hélène Cordier would still be alive."

"Newsflash." Despite her earlier understanding tone,

Madeleine's not going to cut me any slack when it comes to this. She's a surgeon, too. People have died on her table as well. "*You* are a person, too. Not some operating robot. You're human, Marie. As much as you don't want to admit it to yourself, you make mistakes just like the rest of us. And yes, when you're a surgeon, the consequences of these mistakes are much harsher than when a plumber fits a pipe wrong, because our business is the human body. But the simple fact of the matter is that we are no more infallible than anyone else. You have to find a way to absorb this and forgive yourself. If that means sitting around in this house in the depths of winter for a while longer; if that's what it takes for you, fine. Take the time you need, but don't wallow. Snap out of it as quickly as you can."

"You sound just like *Maman*," I quip.

"I don't take that as an insult. *Maman* is the one who gave me a similar speech when I first qualified."

I raise my eyebrows. Our mother surely never gave me that speech. Maybe she didn't think I needed it. Madeleine's always been softer around the edges than me, hence the husband and daughter.

"*Maman*'s worried about you being out here on your own as well." Madeleine fixes her gaze on me.

"There's really no need to worry about me." I can't tell my sister about Véronique, who is another reason for me hiding out here in the middle of nowhere with only a grumpy neighbour I never see as a companion. "I'll call *Maman* later. I'll reassure her that there's nothing to worry about." I wouldn't even dream of mentioning Véronique to my mother.

CHAPTER 14
OLIVIA

"I didn't mean to be rude to you or your sister." My failed attempt at trying to ignore Marie the other day has been on my mind since it happened. I daresay it somewhat ruined my weekend, what with the avalanche of worry it set off inside me.

"Why were you?"

As attractive as I find Marie, I can't fully enjoy her company. She's too direct for that. She doesn't let me get away with things I'd prefer not to discuss. Even though they just are the way they are because I am how I am. I don't want to be explaining myself to her all the time— not to anyone anymore, for that matter. I no longer apologise for merely being me.

"It's hard to explain."

"You should get that tattooed on your forehead. It might make your life a lot easier."

Marie's not pulling any punches today. Then again, when does she? "I'm sorry. Will that do?"

"It's fine." She pours me a glass of wine and hands it to me. "I'm just glad to see you. It's been so long."

"It's been three weeks and one day."

"Out here, it feels like three months."

"I thought I made it clear that you shouldn't rely on me too much for distraction." I believed we were firmly on the same page about that after our last conversation.

"Crystal." She sits in the sofa with her back against the arm rest, her legs stretched in front of her, her toes resting against my thigh. Even when not talking, she's very forward.

When I glance sideways, I look straight into the cleavage her low-cut blouse offers. What she's after is quite obvious.

"Did you have a good time with your sister?" I avert my gaze and focus on my glass of wine instead. I make a mental note to not drink too much. I've reached the final chapters of the book I'm translating and I have a big, dramatic love scene to work on tomorrow morning.

"Yes, oh my goodness, it was great to have someone in the house with me, although I did have to adjust to it. You'd think it would have taken me longer than two months to get used to being alone all the time."

"Are you and your sister close?" I can't resist sneaking another glance at her inviting chest.

"Fairly." She grins at me. "As close as two work-obsessed siblings can be. We don't necessarily see a lot of each other, but we speak on the phone a few times a week."

"Did she have time in her busy schedule to produce any children?"

Marie snickers. "One daughter. Elodie's in med school. Doing the family proud." She presses her toes against my thigh. "Have I told you I'm happy to see you?"

"Not in so many words." I put a hand on one of her feet.

"I am very happy to see you, Olivia." Marie wiggles her toes. "I'm usually not averse to games, but out here, the waiting game you've made me play has been gruelling more than anything else."

"It's not a game."

"Then what is it?"

How many times do I need to repeat myself? "It's just how I am."

"You're giving me very little to work with."

"What do you mean?"

"I don't know... You're like one of those cupboards with dozens of little drawers. It feels good for a minute to unlock one until I realise there are so many more drawers that remain firmly shut and I'll have to look for a long time to find the key to open the next one."

I burst into a chuckle. "Which drawer would you like to open today?"

"This one." She slides her foot over my thigh and nudges the button of my jeans with her big toe.

"You're not even subtle about it."

"Why would I be?" She puts her glass down and, swift as the wind, straddles me and puts her arms around my shoulders. "I also feel I need to take what I can get when given the opportunity. For all I know, there's always a chance I'll never see you again." She gazes down at me with her intense green eyes. It stirs something in me that overrides the panic in my muscles, the impulse to throw her off me and run—and, as she just said, never see her again.

"I thought you wanted to talk," I manage to say.

"I do want that. Very much so, but I also want this."

She slants towards me and plants the lightest of kisses just next to the corner of my mouth. "I want this more than anything else," she whispers.

I've barely walked in the door. I've only managed a few sips from the glass of wine I'm still awkwardly holding in my hand. Last time we did this—when I came on to her and felt a lot more in control, whether I actually was or wasn't—we'd had a lot more to drink and my inhibitions were lowered. This is not the case today.

Marie kisses me squarely on the lips and it's easy enough to surrender for a little while. Stone-cold sober, she's still an amazing kisser, her touch soft and intentional at the same time. She's still gorgeous and suave and intriguing, but I'm also still me. The rigid part of me hasn't been softened by alcohol and I'm not sure I can give myself to her like this. I still hardly know her. Whereas a few weeks ago I could override my protective instincts, spurred on by years of being un-touched, it doesn't seem to be in the cards for me today.

When the kiss ends, in the split second of hesitation between it continuing or pausing, she pins her gaze on me.

"Are you okay?"

"I feel a bit…" The word I'm looking for escapes me. "It's a bit much." Not that her coming for me like this is unexpected. I, too, have thought about this, but I can't just launch into it a mere ten minutes after arriving.

Marie sucks her bottom lip between her teeth and looks at me as though that was the very last thing she expected to hear. She manoeuvres out of her straddling position and settles in the armchair to my left.

"Sorry. I assumed… again."

"It's not you. I just need a bit more time to warm up."

Marie shoots me a grin. "I got a little carried away, seeing you."

She makes it sound as though she finds me utterly irresistible, which I find highly unlikely. This must be more of a the-only-other-woman-in-the-vicinity scenario.

I take another sip of wine. "What have you been up to?" I ask.

"Nothing much."

"So, you've decided to stay longer?" She texted me this information a while ago, but we haven't had a chance to discuss it.

"Yeah." She draws up her legs and folds them underneath her, as though settling in for a while. "My sister thinks I'm crazy for taking so much time off, but…" She shakes her head. "I don't know. Maybe I am crazy and maybe staying here won't fix me or heal me in the way I had intended, but I feel like I've gotten a touch better at listening to my intuition. And my intuition might not have explicitly told me to stay here, but it has most certainly made clear to me that I don't want to go home yet." She paints on a small smile. "How about you?" A surprising enough question. "What have you been up to?"

"The usual."

"One poem a week." Her smile turns into a grin, the rather seductive kind. "How's the book going?"

"I'm working on the final chapters." I happily ignore her reference to my poetry. She sends a message on Instagram every time I post a poem, which I appreciate, but I only ever reply to with a curt thank-you.

"Lots of running?"

What's with all the questions? Is she trying to tell me something in some convoluted, roundabout way? She's usually much more focused on herself.

"Yeah." I shrug. "Every day."

She nods and gazes at me with an expression I don't know what to do with.

"Are you okay?" I ask.

"I'm trying to examine my actions around others more and I guess I just realised I did come on very strong earlier. I'm sorry about that. I should have known that would be too much too soon for you."

Should she have? I have no idea. I am amazed by her apology. It's entirely unexpected.

"It's fine, I mean, after how we left things last time…"

"No. I—" She reaches for her glass on my side of the coffee table, offering me a direct glance into her cleavage. "It's like I can be a different version of myself with you because you're so unlike anyone I know. The women I usually go out with are… they're more like me. Whereas you exude such calm. Your fierce quietness can be a bit unsettling but once you get used to it, it's pleasant to be around."

There's so much to unpack in what she just said. I take another sip of my drink to buy some much-needed processing time. "Thank you, I think." Does she really think I exude calm? Because, around her, it's the opposite of how I feel inside.

"Don't get me wrong. You're still very much an enigma to me, but there's something so unapologetic about you. I really admire that."

"You don't strike me as someone who's very apologetic about her ways."

"I'm not, or rather, I haven't been." She shakes her head again. "But I am now. Being here has given me the time and space to reprocess my life and all the things I've done. Despite what happened in the operating theatre that day, I know I'm a good surgeon, but I haven't always been an exemplary human being." She huffs out some air. "I've broken quite a few hearts in my life and caused a lot of unnecessary hurt. I've ruined relationships. I've been careless with other women's feelings. I've mainly been utterly selfish. All of those are more reasons for me to stick around here and take another long hard look at myself."

"I'm sure it can't have been that bad." She paints herself in such a surprisingly bad light, I can't picture it. Marie's definitely more than a touch arrogant, very in-your-face, and clearly used to getting what she wants, but I don't see her as how she just described herself to me—careless and ruthless.

"Oh, it was. And then some."

"I don't see it."

"Go to Brussels or Paris and you'll easily find a few dozen women in each city willing to call me a first-class bitch. They wouldn't be wrong."

I can't help but grin—and think that this might be a classic case of seeing yourself as much worse than you actually are. Something I happen to be an expert in. "What did you do to these women?" Maybe Marie needs a bit of a grounding exercise. A different perspective to show her that she can't be that much of a bitch.

She puffs up her cheeks and lets the air escape slowly. "Usually, I'm quite upfront about my intentions, which is fine, I think. But I've seduced too many women I shouldn't have. And I got off on it like nobody's business. That's the worst part of it, now that I'm taking the time to truly consider it. I've treated so many women with so little respect, without a care in the world for their lives and the ramifications of my actions on them."

"You're making it sound like you're some voodoo

priestess casting spells around the lesbian hot spots of Brussels. Like any of those women you've supposedly hurt lost every last ounce of their free will when faced with you."

"If I want something, it's usually a person I can't or shouldn't be with. That only makes them more attractive to me, and I can be extremely persuasive."

I can hardly argue with that. I know I drank too much that night, but I can usually keep my wits about me. I'm still not sure how I ended up naked with my legs spread before her in the very spot I'm sitting in—hence the voodoo priestess comment.

"Still. It takes two to tango," I say.

"Sure." Her eyes narrow. "That's why it's good for me to be here. I can reinvent myself. And you're here, of course."

Argh, it's not just her looks that make her so attractive, or her brazen ways. A woman who manages to look inside herself like that, tear herself apart a little bit even, is not something I've come across a lot in my life. A woman who doesn't blame others for all her problems—like Sandrine did with me.

CHAPTER 15

MARIE

"Maybe," I find myself stringing together a bunch of words I don't think I've ever said to anyone in this exact order, "we should just be friends."

Olivia furrows her brow, as though she's processing what I just said very slowly and deliberately.

"Oh," she says. "If that's what you want."

"For the first time in my life, I don't think it's so much about what *I* want." I was the one who jumped her. I've been the one pining to see her. She's barely been in touch. She never takes the initiative to see me. If I hadn't run into her with Madeleine the other day, I might not have seen her for another few weeks. I'm not stupid. I can put two and two together. "It's okay, Olivia. You're not direct the same way I am. You don't just come out and say things and that's fine. We don't have to sleep together. Maybe we're meant to be something else to each other."

A stiffness has settled into her features. She stares into her empty glass of wine.

"Do you want some more?" I reach for the bottle.

"No, I'm fine." She puts the glass away and pushes a stray strand of hair behind her ear. "I should get going."

"What? No." I scoot to the edge of my chair. "Please, don't go. I was trying to remove the tension between us." Wrong move, again, I suppose. "What is it that *you* want?" I wish she would just come out and say it.

"I don't know what I want."

Great help. This is the sort of behaviour I would either not tolerate or kiss away, but I can't remember ever being faced with this kind of attitude in another woman. Plenty of women have gone off me, called me obnoxious and much worse, but Olivia's wishy-washiness is something I don't know what to do with. Does she want me or not? Does she even like me? She's here, but it hardly feels like she's here of her own accord. If she wants to go, she should just go.

"I like you, Marie, and I'm attracted to you, but I... don't want to get attached to you," she says while rubbing her palms on her jeans. "I want you *and* I don't want you and it's driving me nuts."

"So... isn't just being friends a good solution to that?"

"It's confusing to hear you say that while earlier you all but jumped my bones."

"I wrongly assumed we were on the same wavelength about that. I'm just course-correcting now that I know that we aren't."

"I need to protect myself." She rises.

"What does that mean?" I stand as well.

"It means that I don't want to have feelings for you."

"Does that mean that you already do?"

"No," she says on a sigh. "Or yes, a little. I mean, I might, if we keep seeing each other."

Seeing each other? Oh. Is that why she's been avoiding

me? She's been under the spell of the old Marie Dievart charm already. I'm flattered but it doesn't get me anywhere.

She rests her gaze on me. "You're very self-aware," she says. "You're the kind of person who knows what effect she has on other people." Her lips stretch into something close enough to a grin. "Your hobby is"—she curls her fingers into air quotes—"women." A slight shake of the head. "I'm attracted to you, that much is clear, but... already, it feels much too complicated. Too much for me to handle."

"And everything always needs to be clear-cut for you."

Olivia nods. "I know it's not a very realistic expectation to have of life in general, but yes, that's how I prefer things to be."

"So..." I try again. I'm going to be here for more than three months, although I'm hardly sitting out a prison sentence. I can pack my bags and leave any time I want. Going back to Brussels doesn't mean I have to start work again. None of this has all that much to do with Olivia. So why am I so hell-bent on remaining something akin to friends, benefits or not? Before I came here, I would have cut someone like Olivia loose instantly. To be honest, I probably wouldn't have given her the time of day, her aloofness too much of a turn-off—not that I don't like a challenge, but I also like to win. She's so closed off, so guarded, so set on 'protecting herself' as she just put it, there's no way in. I should just let it go. "I'm giving you all the control you need." Even though I try to put some edge into my voice, it comes out like I'm the needy one. In a way, I understand her confusion. I'm not the same person I was before I came here—before I met her. Maybe the two are more related than I'd like to believe. "You call the shots."

"Just so you know…" She takes another step towards the hallway. "It's not you. I think you are… pretty amazing, in your own way. It's all me. I don't…" She waves her hand about a bit. "I don't do this. Not anymore. I was perfectly happy before you moved in. You're only here for a short time. While a big part of me wishes I was the kind of person who could have a casual friends-with-benefits fling with you, that's the opposite of who I am. It's just not me. I can't do it. I'm sorry, but I can't."

"Fair enough." What can I possibly say to that? Besides, I know very well it's not me. I walk her to the door. Even though I'm the one who suggested just being friends in the first place, a mild sting of rejection needles me. "I appreciate your honesty."

"That's what we're like around here." She grabs her coat from the rack.

"I'll try not to disturb your peace any more than I already have." As I let Olivia out, I'm not sure I'll see her again, despite her being my closest neighbour.

After Olivia has left, I take a long walk. It's mid-March and everything is still soaked in wintery bleakness. There's not a hint of spring in the air, yet I know it's coming, because, at the very least, nature can always be relied upon. I put Olivia out of my mind. It shouldn't be too hard—I've done it countless times in my life. Her ambivalence was starting to do my head in. It's something I can most certainly live without.

Instead, for the first time since I talked about her with

Olivia, I allow myself to think of Véronique. About what could have happened if everything had gone according to plan in the operating theatre the morning after. Would I have fallen in love with her? Or should I say further in love with her? It's impossible to tell, although simple deduction leads me to believe that I didn't only run away from my profession. I ran away from her as well. From the mere possibility of love.

My walking route leads me around Olivia's house. A faint glow of light comes through the windows and smoke rises from the chimney. I allow myself to feel that urge to ring her bell. The desire for her to open the door and usher me inside, into the warmth of her house, with open, welcoming arms. The desire for someone to say they're glad I came. They're happy to see me. They're over the moon to spend some unexpected time with me. With Olivia, it's an illusion. I'm no psychiatrist, but it's possible that I've been projecting some of my deepest, subconscious desires onto her—on the least likely person to respond to that. Although she hasn't been entirely unresponsive. I walk past her house, wondering what she's doing—what she does in there all the time, without any need for anyone else.

When I return to my house, I spot Huppert by the window. She walks over, her tail a question mark, and rubs herself against my shins as though she's my cat. I crouch down and pet her profusely. She starts purring instantly.

"Why can't your mummy be like this?" I stupidly ask the cat. "Why doesn't she turn up at my door for some of this?" I know it's silly, but at least having the cat show up has put a smile on my face. Maybe, when I go home, I should consider adopting a pet. It would need to be a cat.

A dog is too high-maintenance for someone with my schedule.

When I open the door, Huppert slips in, looks around and smells the air, before promptly settling in the sofa.

"Thank you," I say to her as I sit next to her, "for enjoying my company like that."

APRIL

CHAPTER 16
OLIVIA

Time passes, as it always does. Because I enjoyed translating the gay romance so much, I've decided to take on another romance. This time around, though, it's about two women falling in love. I've spent the better part of the past week getting absorbed in the story of Andrea and Imogen slowly realising they're in love with each other.

Not being the biggest believer in love, I usually stay well away from romance novels, especially ones involving two women. But this one has me so utterly engrossed, it makes me question my own beliefs at times, usually late at night. In the morning, it's easy enough to remember that I'm reading a piece of fiction that doesn't have much grounding in reality. For evidence of that, I just need to look in the mirror. Or at that picture of Sandrine I insist on keeping, its constant presence a reminder of why running as far away from love as possible has been the best thing I've done for myself.

Meanwhile, as the first shy but unmistakably green buds appear on the trees outside, life goes on. I compose my poems. I torture my treadmill. I play the piano solely for my own pleasure. I go about my business as though Marie has already left. I haven't seen her, haven't run into her, haven't received any phone calls to pick her up from the bar. She hasn't been in touch at all, which I hadn't expected.

Huppert disappears for longer stretches of time and I suspect she's going to Marie's, but it's not as if I can ask my cat where she's been when she comes home.

On an ordinary Tuesday evening, my phone rings. When I check the screen, my heart leaps all the way into my throat. Instead of picking up, I let it go to voicemail and I curse myself for letting my ex still have this effect on me.

I haven't heard Sandrine's voice in years. Surely, it won't undo me the way it used to. I listen to the message.

"Hey Liv," she says, her voice upbeat, "It's me. Sandrine." As if I wouldn't somehow already know that. "This is going to come totally out of the blue, but, um, I've been following your Insta and I love your poems. They're so beautiful but, then again, I always knew you were talented. Anyway, let me cut to the chase. I'm putting together an evening with a bunch of Insta poets in Paris in a few weeks' time and I think you should come." A pregnant pause. "Please, don't do your usual thing of already saying no before you've even reached the end of this message. I've emailed you all the details, but I wanted to call as well, even though I knew you wouldn't pick up." A small chuckle. "Please, please, please, think about it. You have quite the following and rightly so." Another pause. "I'm so glad that you finally started posting some of your stuff. Anyway, please don't dismiss this. I would really love it if you could come. It would also be a good chance for us to catch up. It's been so long. Thanks."

The dry click at the end of her message rings in my ears as though it's the loudest fire alarm. What does Sandrine want from me? Has she lost her mind asking me to this thing? She knows me better than most so she also knows that I would never go to a gathering of strangers. I'd rather close down my Instagram account and never post another poem again than expose myself in that way. Surely she isn't expecting me to read in front of these people? Cleverly, she didn't specify. But none of it matters. Maybe Sandrine thinks I have undergone some magical metamorphosis since she left and I somehow became more how she always wanted me to be, while the opposite is true. I've become more me and, being me, what she is proposing, is not something I do.

Out of curiosity, I do check my email. Her name sits boldly at the top of my inbox—a sight I haven't seen in years.

The subject reads: *PLEASE DON'T DELETE ME ;-)* in all caps.

What is Sandrine doing organising poetry nights in Paris, anyway? Last I heard, she lived in Rennes. But we haven't been in touch. I stopped following her social media accounts not long after we broke up, wanting as clean a break as possible—not that it stopped anything from hurting less. When someone you love no longer deems you suitable to be with, the pain tends to linger.

I open the email:

Hi Liv,
    Thanks for reading this far. ;-) Attached, you'll find an invita-

tion to the poetry night me and a few other like-minded souls are putting together. Don't worry, I'm not asking you to stand up and read for us. But just stop by, check out the vibe. You might like it. It might inspire you. You may meet some kindred spirits of your own. You're really talented and you know I'm not just saying that. I know that before we split, I wasn't very generous in the compliments department. I wish things could have been different between us. I wish I had been a bit kinder to you. It would be really great to see you, although I would understand if you don't want to see me. Nevertheless, you should still come by. I truly think you will enjoy it. It's a very low-key event. And when was the last time you were in Paris? ;-)

Sandrine

I check the attachment. The event is in less than two weeks. Even in the very unlikely event of me wanting to go, two weeks is hardly enough notice to arrange a trip to Paris. Who will feed the cats?

I close the email and try to put the whole thing out of my mind. The poetry night might be easy enough to not think about, although every time I open Instagram I will be reminded for a while, but Sandrine getting in touch will be much harder to forget. What does she really want from me? Why did I not know she was following me on Instagram? But that's the thing with social media, you never know who's reading along. I curse myself for giving in to my narcissistic tendencies and putting myself out there like that. Because of course I did it for the likes. For the lovely comments and messages people who connect with something I've written leave me.

I'm so worked up over all of this, I contemplate going

for another run, even though I already ran seven kilometres earlier.

Deneuve walks into the room, sits, and stares at me.

"You've been fed," I tell her. I walk into the kitchen and she follows me. "Look." I point at her empty food bowl. "You ate it all." Then it hits me that I haven't seen Huppert all day. I put food out for her as well, which has also disappeared, luring me into believing that she was here and ate it. Now, I suspect Deneuve gobbled it all up. "Where's your sister?" I say on a sigh, shaking my head. "Marie'd better not be feeding her." It's very unlike Huppert to miss a meal, but that was before she took a shine to our new neighbour. Then, maybe because I'm already so worked up because of Sandrine, it's like someone has hit a secret panic button in my brain. What if Huppert is not at Marie's? What if something has happened to her?

"Come here." I pick up Deneuve and hold her close as though her proximity can undo the fact that my other cat is not here. Deneuve can be a grumpy diva, but she can also be unexpectedly sweet. She purrs in my arms and it makes me worry for Huppert even more. I know I won't be able to relax until I know she's safe and sound. I also know where the first stop on my search for her needs to be.

CHAPTER 17
MARIE

Satisfying myself has become a part of my daily routine. I missed my window of opportunity with Olivia that time she ended up naked in my sofa, which seems like many months ago. But I wasn't ready then. Not to be touched by anyone else, anyway. I might not yet be ready for that now, either, although I wouldn't know. But I've always had a healthy sexual appetite and I believe that an orgasm a day keeps the doctor away—I'm a doctor, I should know.

I stretch out on my bed and sink into the mattress. I sleep much better these days and I hardly ever need to take anything to help me nod off. It just happens, the way it used to after a long day of surgeries. I slip my hand inside my underwear and let it rest there, not moving just yet. I have nothing but time and whereas that used to irk me, now, it feels like the only way it should be.

Which fantasy shall I conjure up today? Automatically, my mind drifts to Olivia. To how she surrendered to my touch that night. It was the last time I touched another woman and even though the actual memory is starting to fade, I still have plenty of it to hold onto. Because for all her distant behaviour and her efforts to keep me at bay, Olivia gave a piece of herself to me that day, and it makes me feel special somehow because I'm sure she's not in the habit of doing so. I also haven't been able to quiet the voice inside my head asking me what it would have been like if I hadn't stopped our actions short. With someone like Olivia, it's so enticing to wonder what she's like when she really lets go, when she gets out of her head and reveals her uncontrolled self—that part of her she's so keen on hiding.

My hand drifts lower. I close my eyes. It's no hardship to picture Olivia doing this to me. Her finger sliding down while she locks her dark gaze on me.

Was that the doorbell? What the hell? I can't imagine who it can possibly be. I'm not expecting any family or friends, unless someone wants to surprise me—but my family has never had any time for the frivolity of surprise visits. I quickly remove my hand from my knickers and get up. The bell rings again, making me think it might be an emergency rather than a surprise. I put on my trousers and hurry down the stairs, shouting to whoever it is on the other side of the door that I'm coming.

When I open the door and see it's Olivia standing in front of me, I erupt into a small bout of laughter, because it's as though what I was doing when she rang the bell conjured up her actual physical presence. Then my laughter turns to a frown because it's so unlike Olivia to show up unannounced.

"I'm sorry to bother you, but I'm looking for Huppert. Is she here?"

It's about the cat. *Of course.* For a split second, I'd hoped she'd come to see me, but I guess I shouldn't count on inviting her upstairs to re-enact what I was just imagining.

"Could be. Come in. We'll have a look." On any given day, I open and close the door for Huppert so many times, I sometimes forget whether she's inside or outside the house. "She seems to really like it here."

"I'm sorry. It's hard to keep her in all the time. She's not used to it."

Olivia and I walk into the living room where Huppert is lounging in the middle of my oriental rug as though she's lived in my house all her life.

"There you are." Olivia crouches down. "I was worried about you, you silly little thing." Her voice changes when she speaks to her cat. She sounds less uptight. "I know this place is super swanky, but you could spend some more time at home." Olivia picks up her cat and cradles her in her arms.

"Why were you so worried about her?"

"I don't know. I was suddenly in a panic." Olivia smiles sheepishly. "It's not really rational." She nuzzles Huppert's fur. "But it's not like her to miss dinner."

"She's been keeping me company." I take a step closer and scratch Huppert behind the ear.

"It's almost like we share custody," Olivia jokes.

"I promise to not lay any claims on your cat." I send her a warm smile—it feels like the least I can do considering what I was up to when she showed up. Thank goodness she didn't turn up five minutes later, when I'd have been much further advanced in my fantasy. "Would you like a drink?"

"Um, yes, sure." She puts down the cat, who rushes to the window. "I'll let her make her way home." Olivia opens the window, while I go in search of wine. Without asking what she prefers, I pour us both a glass of white.

"It's good to see you," I say, when I give her the glass. I let my hand linger a fraction of a second. What can I say? I'm still feeling a little frisky and I'm only human.

"Yeah." Olivia crashes into an armchair.

"I've been reading your translations." After I've sat down I nod at the pile of books she brought me. I've finished all but one. That's what happens when you have nothing but time on your hands. "How are the gays coming along?"

"I'm done with them. Sent off the manuscript last week. Happy gay endings all around."

It's hard to say whether Olivia is pleased to see me or not. Maybe it doesn't fit within the rules she lives by to show that she is—or isn't.

"On to something new?"

Olivia just nods. She's not in a talkative mood, then. She didn't come here for a chat, after all, only to look for her cat.

"How are you?" Finally, she looks me in the eye—like she was doing in my mind earlier. Of course, I want to play her a little, gauge whether I can pierce through that iron shield she has placed over her heart, test myself a little, but I've been here more than three months now, and that urge I used to not be able to resist, that lived like a wild animal inside of me, has subsided. I don't have anything to prove to myself in that area any longer. I can just sit here with Olivia and enjoy this conversation without sending out subtle hints about what we could be doing if we weren't chatting. I can even let her set the pace. If she wants more than this, it's up to her to let me know.

"Good." I pause. "Peaceful is probably a better word for it."

"I'm happy for you." Her gaze remains on me, surprising me a little. "You look quite calm. Less... frantic."

Frantic? What is she talking about? I'm a neurosurgeon. We don't go about our lives giving off frantic energy. "It's the surroundings. And all the walking I've been doing." I walk and walk and walk, until my head is empty and the endless churn of thoughts, of how I could have done things differently in my professional as well as my private life, just stops, and it's just my feet taking another step, and then another. "Maybe I'll have to start running soon, like you. Will you be running outside soon, now that spring is around the corner?"

Olivia looks at me as though I've just said the dirtiest word. "I never run outside." She shakes her head as though the mere thought of doing so is inconceivable.

"Why not?" This woman seems made up of nothing but 'nevers' and 'noes'. "It's gorgeous out there."

"It's just not something I do."

There we go again. Another one of her favourite phrases. I decide not to push. I'm just genuinely happy to see her, to be having a glass of wine with her. We decided to be just friends, after all.

CHAPTER 18
OLIVIA

I'm beginning to think I ended up at Marie's for other reasons than checking on Huppert. Maybe my brain played a vicious trick on me and made me panic so I would end up here, face-to-face with someone I actually quite like. Someone I can talk to. A living, breathing human close enough to confide in. Because this business with Sandrine is firmly at the forefront of my mind. I want to file it away so desperately, catalogue it as something belonging to my past, but it's nagging at me. It's doing so for a reason.

"Can I…" God, why is this so hard? I take another sip of wine. And another. "My ex called me earlier," I finally blurt out.

"The infamous Sandrine." Marie's eyebrows dart up.

What startles me most about this is that I didn't want to be alone with my thoughts. I didn't want to do what I always do, which is deal with whatever comes at me on my own. I don't know whether it's because Marie, despite her reasons for hiding out here, seems to have such a firm handle on life. She might be a bit of a mess in some areas, but not the same areas as me. For some reason, I want her take on this. And she has said she likes my poems.

"What did she want?" Marie asks.

I emit a nervous chuckle. "To invite me to some sort of meeting of Instagram poets in Paris in a few weeks."

"Wow. Is she a fan?"

I scoff. "Sandrine? A fan of something I do? I don't think so."

"Surely, she wouldn't have invited you if she didn't like your work?"

"No. That's true." I can't argue with simple logic. "But she knows that—"

Marie holds up her hand, stopping me. "That's not something that you do." Her smile is warm enough to convey she's not viciously mocking me.

"Well, yes. She knows that better than anyone."

Marie points a finger at herself. "I've become pretty well acquainted with how you *don't* do things as well."

Even though it doesn't come natural to me, I know I have to have a sense of humour about this. Those are the rules. "Don't take yourself so seriously all the time," Sandrine used to say. "Have some fun once in a while. Let go."

"I haven't heard from her in such a long time. She said she'd like to see me."

"Why wouldn't she?" Another kind smile from Marie. "There's plenty about you to like, you know."

If it were anyone else saying that—if it were Sandrine saying it, post break-up—I'd immediately dismiss it as just talk, something that people say, but it's different with Marie. I've given her plenty of reasons not to like me— and I'm sure there are plenty of things she doesn't like about me—yet here we are. Here I sit. "I'm not used to talking about, um, things like this anymore."

Marie just looks at me. She doesn't push, which I had kind of expected her to do. Maybe time has done its thing with her, mellowed her, shaved off some of that edge she likes to show off. She still looks too posh for these parts. And hot. Damn it, she looks good. I'm trying to remember why I rebuffed her advances the last time I was here. In this moment, sitting across from her looking all delicious and composed, I can only plead temporary insanity. But of course I know that, as always, it was just fear. Panic. The slightest hint of losing control over something. Same as it always is.

Because we're talking—and perhaps also because she didn't jump my bones the minute I walked in—the vibe is different. There are no expectations. Just two people having a conversation.

"So… correct me if I'm wrong," she says, "but it sounds to me as though part of you would like to go to Paris, while the other part of you is too afraid."

"No. I really don't want to go." She's right, though. She hit the nail right on the head. Even though I'm not telling the truth, it doesn't really feel like a lie either. 'I just don't want to' is the excuse I've used all my life. It's as simple as it is effective—and it used to drive Sandrine absolutely crazy.

"Then why are you here?" Marie looks like she's ready to give me some tough love. "If it's a done deal and you've made your decision, why are you telling me?"

"It's not about the poetry night. It's about Sandrine."

"What about her?"

"She and I… we didn't part amicably. I drove her away, or at least that's what she would tell you if asked.

143

Maybe I did. I mean, I know I kind of did, but... It's complicated."

"What if someone other than your ex had invited you to this event?"

"In that case, I wouldn't be here talking to you about it."

Marie cocks her head, narrows her eyes, then reaches for her phone. She taps the screen a few times, then starts reading the last poem I posted.

"*In these wilds I ramble. Does it not make you stir? To pause here naked with me. Underneath this sky of birds.*" After she's done, she fixes her gaze on me. "Despite my many faults, I can safely say I possess an above-average intelligence and I have impeccable taste in many things."

I will never understand how someone can talk that way about themselves, but, admittedly, it does drive me a little crazy when Marie does it.

She holds up her phone to me. "This is a beautiful poem. Seriously, I wouldn't be able to keep a straight face and say that to you if I didn't mean it. And it's not the only one. You have a gift. Why wouldn't you share that? Why wouldn't you be proud of that?"

"I'm already sharing it."

"Aren't you curious to meet the poets behind the Instagram accounts you follow?"

"No." At least that's the absolute truth.

Marie chuckles. "Oh, fuck, Olivia."

"What?"

"Okay." Her eyes sparkle as she looks at me. "How about this…" She keeps her gaze firmly on mine as she puts her empty glass away. "But before I say anything else, you're not allowed to reply with your usual rebuff."

"Who says I'm not allowed?" My hackles go all the

way up. I live by no one else's rules but my own, no matter how silly and rigid they may appear to any other human being.

"My house, my rules," she says, as though where I am makes any difference.

"It's not something I can promise."

"Just don't immediately say no, please."

"You are pretty hard to say no to."

"Oh, really?" She huffs out some air. "I hadn't noticed."

By now, I'm more curious than trepidatious about what she wants to ask me. "Fine," I say. "I will wait at least ten minutes before I say no."

She erupts into another chuckle. "Okay… how about we go to Paris together? I haven't been there in ages. We can treat ourselves. Stay in a nice hotel. Go out for some fancy meals. And just casually check out the event. You could even pretend to your ex I'm your new girlfriend."

All of this sounds so utterly ridiculous, I can't help but burst into laughter. "I'm not saying anything." I pretend to lock my lips with an imaginary key that I throw behind me.

"You have to say something," Marie says, "just not 'no'."

"Pretend you're my girlfriend." I would never say this out loud, but I wouldn't have issue with that. For a split second, I allow myself the fantasy of walking through the streets of Paris with someone like Marie by my side— because this is my imagination, we could even be holding hands. The thought is highly pleasant, but I know that's because a thought is all it is.

"Just to get under your ex's skin a bit."

It's so very much like Marie to assume that her mere

presence would get under Sandrine's skin. For her, there doesn't seem to be any other way to think about herself. I can't help but admire the capacity she has for unconditional self-love.

I ostentatiously check my watch. "Have ten minutes passed yet?"

"Actually, I'm changing the rules. You need to sleep on it. You can't say no until tomorrow." She sits there with a triumphant smirk on her face, as though changing the rules like that is even an option.

But whether I decline her offer now, in ten minutes, tomorrow, or even next week, doesn't matter. I know she knows it's a no from me. I'm not going to Paris with Marie. The deep well of anticipatory stress is already making my hands go clammy. But what I will do is play along, just for tonight, because, as it turns out, I don't feel like going home at all.

"When you say go to Paris together and book a nice hotel, does that imply separate rooms or not?"

"Whatever you want." She gives a throaty chuckle. "But if you're explicitly asking for my preference, I would suggest sharing a room."

CHAPTER 19

MARIE

W hat did Olivia expect I was going to say? My friskiness hasn't subsided one bit since she has arrived, on the contrary. I've let her set the pace. I've listened to her with more patience than I would give anyone else who behaves like she does. Truth be told, pre-Brittany Marie would surely have been interested in Olivia, and might even have tried something, but she would also have given up on her a long time ago.

Time is all I have now, time to spend on Olivia and her odd ways and challenging personality. It's time I enjoy because, even though I think she tries, she can't shut me out completely. I can tell. Look at her now. She's flirting again, despite herself. She can't help herself when it comes to me and that thought is so pleasing, so alluring, that I have to respond. Nothing's stopping me. I don't get attached so easily and I know exactly where I stand with Olivia. And it's not always up to me to take every last one of her many possible feelings into consideration.

"The only time we shared a bed," Olivia says, "I found you wandering around the house in the middle of the night. You won't be able to do that if we stay in a room together."

"That was ages ago." I push myself out of the sofa to get more wine. "A lot has changed for me since then." I make sure to give her a lingering sultry look before I head to the fridge.

When I turn around, Olivia's in the kitchen, standing right behind me.

"That thirsty, are you?" I sink my teeth into my bottom lip. Fuck, I want her. Maybe I just want someone. But it doesn't matter. She's here—and she's making a move.

"Yeah." Her voice is throaty and a little ragged. She takes the bottle of wine from my hands and puts it away. "I—" She bridges the distance between us. "Is this okay?" She cups my cheeks in her palms.

"It's okay with me if it's okay with you," I whisper.

"I—I didn't come here for this." I figure she's saying it more to herself than to me. That she needs something to take the final step towards me. She leans in, brings her lips to my ear, and whispers, "You're so fucking hot."

I resist the urge to say "I know", because I now realise how utterly obnoxious that sounds, even though it has proven a turn-on for many women in my past. But Olivia is not like the women I used to sleep with. She's different in so many ways and her lips are warm against the skin of my neck, her breath hot and promising, and I already know, this time, I won't be asking her to stop. Already, I want her inside of me, but I'll need to find some patience within myself. Olivia seems to have the uncanny ability to tap into reserves of it I never even knew I possessed. Her lips hover along my chin, to my cheeks, and then, finally, brush against my lips.

We kiss and any remaining tension I was carrying inside my muscles dissipates. My time in Bonneau has calmed me, has stilled something in me, but, despite my daily acts of self-love, it hasn't quenched the renewed need for this particular activity. I am, after all, the person who, mere weeks ago, boldly proclaimed that 'women' were my hobby. I cringe a little at the memory, but not for long, because Olivia's tongue is insistent in my mouth. I'm not the only one who wants or even needs this.

"I've missed you," she whispers, when we break for air.

I realise I've missed her, too. Not just the attention of any other human, but *her*. She might be taciturn and too difficult to reach most of the time, but it hasn't stopped me wanting her, not only for what we're doing now, but also for her company, which has come to represent something for my time here.

Even though I barely see her, she's my neighbour and she's an integral part of my stay in Bonneau. She stands for a ray of hope during my exile here. She's the personification of the rugged but beautiful landscape of Brittany in winter. She's the weather with its sudden storm clouds and now, as spring approaches, with its increasingly long patches of sunshine and breaks in the rain and slowly rising temperatures. She's the person I met when I came here and, like her surroundings, she's not pliable or easy, but she's here and, at times, more than willing. That's all I need from her and that's all she's willing to give. Her heart's not open for business; neither is mine. In that, too, we're a good match.

"Come." I grab her hand and take her upstairs. Once we get there, I assume my natural role, and push her against the bedroom door. She pulls me close again, her hands in my hair, her lips hot on mine. *Oh, fuck it.* For once, I don't want to take on the part I always gravitate to. I don't want to be in charge—besides, Olivia's such a sucker for control, she'll happily take the reins.

Instead of pressing myself harder against her, I drag her onto the bed with me. I let her lie on top of me, let her push a knee between my legs. I let her undress me and I let myself enjoy the lustful look in her eyes. She wants me all right. It's clear as the stars out here at night. And maybe it's only to someone like her that I can give myself like this—the way she gave herself to me the first time. Someone who doesn't want anything from me. Someone so dead set on being on her own with the freedom that gives her to be this person I rarely allow myself to be. Because for me, the thrill is almost always in the chase, the conquest, the moans of pleasure coaxed from another woman's throat. If I do let them touch me the way Olivia is touching me now, I always try to retain a semblance of control. I always try to guide them, as if my body works in different ways than other women's, just to let them know that I'm still with them, that I'm still in charge, that they shouldn't expect anything close to surrender.

Just like I let Véronique have her way with me all night, I let Olivia discover me at her own pace and devour me over and over again. I allow Olivia to do whatever she wants. I don't tell her what to do or what I like or, heaven forbid, what I expect. Not only because I know that I don't need to—I've never really needed to—but because I feel safe with her, here, in the middle of nowhere, where we have zero obligations in the morning. No medical proce-dures need to be performed. Nothing intimate needs to be discussed. She'll just go home. I might or might not see her—it took a while, but I'm used to that now. There are no expectations. With her, I don't need to put on the front

I present to the world. I can let go of my bravado and show her part of my hidden side. I can just be a woman in the throes of lust instead of the female Lothario surgeon and all that entails. I can embody the version of me I am out here in the sticks. The calmer, quieter, thoughtful person who doesn't operate to the relentless beat of the city, who was crumbling under the pressure of a too demanding job.

With Olivia, I can let all of that go and, as I've been doing, very slowly since I arrived here, I can come a little closer to the real me who, perhaps, isn't as bad as I thought she was.

I can't stop kissing Olivia. I can't get enough of the softness of her lips, the nearness of her warm body, the sensation of her fingertips roaming across my skin. The old me is still hiding in here somewhere, so when I can't take it anymore, I do say, "Fuck me," but only because I want her so much, not because I want to exert any control over the situation.

Olivia smirks down at me and I look into her dark eyes, trying to read something in them, trying to learn more about her, but there's something so utterly unknowable about her, even now, when her hand glides along the apex of my thighs, and she's about to do what I just begged her to do.

Her fingers brush against my lips, light as a feather. Months of abstinence, of not practicing my favourite hobby, have left me desperate for her. When her fingers slide inside me, I surrender everything. I give myself to her in ways I rarely do. I shed another layer of the person I was before I fled to Brittany, before I met her. The person Olivia might have caught glimpses of, but might never really know. With her, I can be someone else. I can be the real me. With every stroke of her fingers, I let go more. I leave behind what happened that day on the operating table and become the person who can handle it, who can move past it, who no longer has to associate this very act with something going so terribly wrong. I can focus again on the lives I've saved instead of the ones I've lost. I know it's not Olivia specifically making this change happen inside of me—it's me—but she's here with me for this moment, and for that alone I'm grateful. Because even when I didn't see her for weeks on end, I knew she was always there. Maybe she was more than a non-returned phone call away, but I always had Huppert to remind me that her mistress was always there, in the house around the corner.

My eyes have fallen shut as I enjoy Olivia's thrusts inside me and when I briefly open them, she's gazing at me, her face a mask of concentration. I pull her to me and I kiss her as her fingers delve deep inside me. I'm the last person on this planet to believe that having sex with someone can fundamentally change you, but, as her tongue swirls in my mouth and her fingers coax pleasure from me, I'm convinced of one thing: I'm almost ready to go home.

CHAPTER 20
OLIVIA

I wake in Marie's bed. It's still dark outside, but not the pitch black of the dead of night. I look around for a clock, but can't find one. Marie's not a woman on a schedule. She doesn't need to be woken up in the morning. She has an arm slung over my belly and I have to stop myself from reaching for her hand, for intertwining my fingers with hers, because I know what this is. I know what a few orgasms can do to me. For a little while, they make me feel as though I'm a different person. Someone normal, without a million hang-ups and rules she has to live by.

"It's time," Sandrine used to say, before taking me by the hand and leading me to our bedroom in the middle of the day. "To take that edge off." I didn't always protest, because I knew she was right.

Instead of taking Marie's hand in mine, I scoot to the edge of the bed and roll on my side, watching her. She's too good-looking for me, anyway. The kind of good-looking that doesn't fit in around here. She's city-good-looking. I bet when she struts around the streets of Brussels, heads turn. When I venture beyond Bonneau, I immediately feel like a fish out of water because I no longer fit anywhere else. I feel out of sorts because I'm too far from home, too out of control and out of my comfort zone.

Because morning hasn't fully come yet, I allow myself a brief bout of imagining what it would be like to go to Paris with her. To walk through Paris with her. Even though I slept on it, although sleep might be too big a word for what we did most of the night, I still think the idea ridiculous.

I'd go to Paris with Marie, though—oh, there's a surprising thought if ever there was one. Would I, really? I only have to look at her to know the answer to that, but it's not the real answer, because I'm still under the intoxicating influence of whatever hormones got released into my bloodstream after the night we just had. I can't take myself seriously. What I should really do is go home and feed my cats. Maybe Huppert is sitting by the window downstairs. Maybe she even brought Deneuve, who mustn't have a clue of what's happening to her mistress. Truth be told, her mistress doesn't have much of a clue either.

But it's hard to drag myself away from Marie—and the cats will be fine. It was such a treat to have her give herself up to me like that. I had expected her to be bossier because that's the air she tends to exude. But she wasn't. She was soft and gentle and hot and present and... Oh, damn. *Oh, no.* I do need to get out of here. I know I can't be trusted right now. Past experience has taught me that this feeling will dissipate, hopefully as soon as dawn fully breaks, but still. I'm not sure I can trust myself entirely. Marie has a way of breaking through my meticulously constructed armour.

Just as I obviously used my cats as an excuse to come over here yesterday—I can see it so clearly now, although I didn't at the time—I will use them as a non-offensive excuse to flee her bed before she wakes up. Because I no longer feel safe. My defences don't work the way they should around her. She's too many things I secretly long for. I'm no match for her, although, for those few delicious hours before we fell asleep, it sure felt as though we were beautifully matched. As much as I want her, I don't want to put myself through any of that again. In the end, it's a matter of self-respect. Time to hide behind the distance again.

I get out of bed without waking her, but I need to gather my clothes from the hardwood floor and some of the boards creak despite me trying to be light-footed. She shifts under the sheet, but doesn't seem to wake up. I'm missing a sock and I can't find my bra, but I'll go home without them. A bunch of clothes stuffed under my arm, I make my way down the stairs, feeling like someone who is some place she really shouldn't be, fleeing like a thief in the night, as though what we did was somehow wrong. I throw on my clothes and hurry home. Both cats are waiting for me by the door, looking as though what I did was very wrong and deserving of the most disapproving glances. Huppert will forgive me swiftly. Deneuve will need some more time. I feed them and sink into a chair in the kitchen, my naked feet cold against the floor, reminding me of what I just did.

I send Marie a text message to let her know I had to feed the cats and didn't want to wake her, so she knows it wasn't her that I skulked away from, even though it is. Because I still feel it now, in the safety of my own home. I can still smell her. When I close my eyes, I can still see her.

I feel her lips on mine and in every other spot she kissed me. What I really want to do, now that my cats are fed and happy, is go back to her house and crawl into bed with her. I even allow myself a short debate over it.

But my reasoning, that she was a safe person to do this with, doesn't hold up any longer. She might still be leaving, but it doesn't seem to make much difference anymore. The fact that she will at some point in the near future leave Bonneau now feels more like a trigger than a safety net. I've watched one person I cared too much about load her belongings into the boot of a car and drive off to never come back. I'm not doing that again. I'd rather not see Marie again if I can protect myself from a dreadful moment like that. At least I can count on my infallible logic to make the right choice.

My phone beeps. A message from Marie.

COME BACK NOW

A second message comes in immediately.

NOW!

So much for her not being bossy. I can't help but smile, but the reason why I'm smiling is the same reason why I can't go back.

Huppert jumps into my lap. She has forgiven me already.

"Why do you always go over there?" I ask my cat. "Why can't you stay away?"

She responds by pushing her nose against my hand, demanding to be petted.

"You're just like her." I scratch Huppert under the

chin and she breaks into a loud purr. "What am I going to do?" I let my head fall back and as soon as I close my eyes for a fraction of a second, Marie's all over the back of my eyelids. Her seductive smile. Her beguiling green eyes. The way she seems to see right through me. Her breathy voice when she asked me to fuck her.

"I'm sorry," I say to Huppert as I lift her off my lap, or maybe I'm saying it to myself, because I know what I'm about to do to myself.

On my way back to Marie's house, I break into a jog —it reminds me that I told her I don't run outside. There are so many things I don't do—that I shouldn't be doing. Like this. My head knows I shouldn't be hurrying back to Marie's bed, yet here I am, making my way to her house as the sun peeks over the horizon.

"Thank fucking goodness," Marie says when I enter her bedroom. "I thought you'd done a runner." She lifts the sheet for me.

Fully clothed, I hop back into bed with her, thinking that a runner is exactly what I did. And then I ran straight back.

"I've been thinking." I press myself against her warm body. "Maybe we should go to Paris. There's a woman in Bonneau who moonlights as a pet sitter. I'll ask her to come take care of the cats."

"I knew an excellent night's sleep was all you needed." She kisses my forehead and I lose my mind a little more.

MAY

CHAPTER 21

MARIE

For the past two weeks, Olivia has no longer been the stranger she once was. To my utter surprise and delight, I've seen her almost every day. I'm even allowed to turn up at her doorstep without texting beforehand these days. Sometimes, when I look at her, I feel like I'm looking at a different person.

"When were you last in Paris?" I shoot her a quick glance across the car.

"Years ago, with Sandrine. There was a place we used to go to every year for our anniversary."

Sandrine remains a touchy subject. Even though she and Olivia split up years ago, I get the impression Olivia hasn't fully recovered yet. I'm so curious to meet the elusive Sandrine, and even more to witness how she and Olivia will interact. However, we might be on our way to Paris, but Olivia made it very clear that she couldn't guarantee us actually going to the poetry night her ex is throwing.

I'm just happy to be out of Bonneau for a few days. To

be driving towards the buzz of a city. I feel like I need the practice. It will be my life again soon enough.

"When were *you* last in Paris?" Olivia asks.

"Also years ago. I—" What to tell her? When I first arrived in Paris I was at the peak of my most appalling behaviour. I burst in and played my usual games. "It was fun while it lasted."

"Did you leave a trail of broken hearts?" I can hear the smile in her voice. "I still don't see it, you know. The person you described to me. The person you claim you once were."

"That's because you met me under very different circumstances." It's hard to ignore that Olivia has fallen for me. Why else is she flouting all her own rules all of a sudden? Why else has the woman with all the noes transformed into someone saying yes to many things—although far from everything.

"Does that mean you're going to transform into a different person once we cross the Paris city limits?"

"I don't know." I take my eyes off the road for a moment to look at her. "I've been hibernating in Bonneau for so long. It's hard to predict what will happen when I'm let off my leash."

"At the very least I can vouch for the agility of your fingers," Olivia says so matter-of-factly it makes me chuckle. "They are in perfect working order."

I laugh along with her. The prospect of performing surgery hasn't filled me with dread for a while. It's early May and my sabbatical ends at the end of June. I figure I'll be raring to go by the first of July. I've missed the adrenalin of being a surgeon most of all. That rush of knowing that only a select number of people in the world can make a patient's brain better.

"I'll be sure to tell my boss upon my return."

"I'm glad you decided to stay longer." Olivia puts a hand on my knee.

"So am I." I send her a quick smile.

"Huppert's practically been beside herself since you arrived."

"Cats know things humans can't always see."

"Some cats. Deneuve hasn't quite taken to you yet."

"Some cats are just too difficult." I put my hand on Olivia's for an instant.

"I know I'm difficult," she says, as though I was just referring to her instead of her ever-aloof cat.

"Everyone's difficult in their own way."

"I don't know whether that's true, but it doesn't really matter."

"In the end, you really didn't prove to be that difficult." I give her hand a squeeze before returning it to the wheel.

Olivia chuckles. "I was powerless against the woman whose hobby is 'women'."

"I wish I'd never told you that. I have a feeling you're going to hold that against me forever. Fine." I turn my head to her and give her an eye roll.

"Forever?" she says. "I don't know about forever." She looks away from me out of the window. The trees lining the motorway are only a few days away from bursting into full life. When she looks at me again, she has a grin on her face. "I think you made a mistake in booking only one hotel room. How will you be able to practice your hobby?"

"Hey, this trip is for you." I do hope she's joking, but Olivia's hard to read sometimes.

"I'm not into threesomes, nor any of that kinky stuff you tried on me the other day."

A few nights ago, in the throes of passion, I turned Olivia over and asked—very politely, which is not always how I've done it in the past—if I could spank her behind. She looked at me as though I had just asked if I could sacrifice one of her cats to the devil.

I decide to laugh it off. "Don't I know it."

Despite our previous banter, Olivia goes quiet again—although, I have also learned, this is hardly unusual for her. Whereas I can usually appreciate her silence and I've certainly learned to respect it, in the confines of the car, it's hard to deal with.

"Are you okay?" If her hand was still on my knee, I'd give it a reassuring squeeze, but she removed it earlier.

"I am. I, um…" She doesn't look at me when she speaks. "I feel like there's so much to say and I don't know how to say it."

"Maybe you should read a poem about it tonight." I'm not like Olivia. I don't mull a thought over in my head a dozen times before I express it.

"Please, don't push me. I don't respond to that well."

"I was hardly pushing you." Okay, I was pushing her a little, but only because she needs to be pushed from time to time. If she hated me doing it so much, we wouldn't be in this car together right now.

"I'm nervous." She turns to me, her lips drawn into a pout.

"You don't have to say or do anything you don't want to."

"That includes threesomes?" She arches up her eyebrows and her face looks funny.

"You're the one who brought up threesomes. I never

even alluded to them. Sounds to me like a threesome is on *your* mind." I shoot her a quick look. "Is that one of the many things you can't say to me?"

She looks at me as though I've just lost the very last one of my marbles. "Don't tell me you've never had a threesome."

"I've never had a threesome."

"So it's one woman at a time?"

I shake my head, unable to hide my glee. "I had a foursome once."

"Oh, for crying out loud."

I erupt into laughter. "It's not true, Olivia. I'm just messing with you."

"You enjoy doing that a bit too much to my liking."

"But it's so much fun."

"Aren't you going to miss having a laugh at my expense once you've gone back to Brussels?" She brings her hand to the back of my neck, her fingertips in my hair.

"Very much so." I push my head against her fingers a fraction, just so she knows that I feel something for her too. It's not something I feel the need to express in words, let alone discuss in detail, but I'm willing to take her feelings into account. "You could come visit me." I try to find her gaze again, but she looks away.

"Ask me again after you've seen me in action in Paris. Cities and I don't go together very well."

"Brussels is hardly Paris."

"Even Le Havre was too much for me."

"I'll come back to Bonneau in August." As I say it, I realise that's not a promise I'll necessarily be able to keep. With anyone else, that wouldn't bother me, but everything about me and Olivia is based on being honest with each other—I've been more honest with her than I've ever been with anyone else in my life. "I mean, I'll try." Even though I want to make some changes to my life, my profession doesn't allow for many concessions. Neurosurgery is not a part-time position.

"It's okay. Part of me knows you won't. I've always known. That's why I kept my distance for so long, but, argh…" Her fingertips press against my scalp a little harder. "Even though you are arrogant and way too full of yourself, I've had to…" She huffs out some air in exasperation.

When I think about my life back home, Olivia stands out like a square peg. Nothing about her would fit into my life in Brussels. But it begs the question whether I would want her to fit into my life in the first place.

"We don't have to think about that yet. We have time." To my surprise, something coils in my stomach. Olivia has hinted how hard it will be for her to say goodbye to me, despite her best intentions to protect herself from that, but I never thought I would have such a difficult time with it too—and who knows what will happen in the time we have left together? But from the start, I've seen her as someone who can only be a part of my time in Brittany, nothing more.

"Do you think that maybe after this trip we should go back to how things were before?"

"Before what?"

"Before we—"

"—started sleeping together every night?" I can't help but scoff. "Do you want to go back to once a month?"

Olivia seems to be able to laugh at her own silly rule for once. "No, but maybe we should keep our distance."

"Why? There will be plenty of distance between us once I'm back in Brussels."

"To prepare for when that happens."

This is so typical of Olivia. She needs to prepare for every single possible scenario, while it's impossible to do so. "No." I make sure I sound firm. "Absolutely not. We are going to enjoy the hell out of every minute we have together. That goes for this weekend as well."

"In the beginning you hid it quite well, but now your bossy streak is coming through more and more."

"Don't pretend you don't get off on it a little."

"Sure, if you keep it outside the bedroom," she says laconically. For someone so worried about every little thing, Olivia's always so much herself, and she seems incapable of too much compromise—of changing something about herself simply to please me.

CHAPTER 22
OLIVIA

The swanky hotel room Marie has booked is tiny because that's how things are in Paris. It reminds me why I never want to live in an overcrowded city again.

While I seem to have crossed over into the zone where proximity to her is no longer an issue for me—I crave it more than I like to admit—I wonder how being this close to her will affect me over the course of the weekend, because there's nowhere else to go. If I need to be alone, I will have no choice but to ask her to leave the room. Truth be told, I could do with a few hours on my own after the drive, but I remind myself to be a good sport. She didn't drag me here against my will. We're only here because I brought it up. We're here for me, as she said in the car. The least I can do is be my most gregarious self, which is hard at the best of times, and much harder in stressful situations like this.

"Do you want to go out for a glass of wine?" Marie asks. "I could murder one right about now."

When I look at her standing there, all suave and effortlessly Parisian, I want to say yes to everything she suggests

—within my own limits, of course—because that's how it is with her now.

"Sure." I send her a smile, but keep myself from closing the distance between us.

"Let me quickly change into something a bit classier." She opens the large suitcase I can't believe she brought. We're here for two nights. How many clothes can you possibly need other than a few changes of underwear?

I brought my most fancy blouse just in case I want to face Sandrine tomorrow, but that's it.

Then again, it's no hardship to lounge on the bed while Marie changes from one silk blouse into another. Lately, I've found myself quite captivated by her elegance and her obvious worldliness—by all the things I'm not, nor have any desire to be.

She disappears into the bathroom for a few minutes and I think about the oddness of being here because I would never have come if it weren't for Marie. It's yet unclear whether I'll be able to thank her for persuading me in the end.

When she exits the bathroom looking all glitzy, her hair just so and her make-up touched up, I'm beginning to think that I wouldn't mind one bit pretending to Sandrine that Marie is my girlfriend—although she is no such thing. And I would be lying to my ex-partner.

"You're looking at me as if a glass of wine is the last thing on your mind right now." Marie leans against the closed bathroom door, her gaze firmly locked on mine.

It's in my nature to want to stay inside, to hide myself from the possible peril of the outside world. But now that I'm here with Marie, whose confidence is the most beautiful thing she wears, even more than her blouse which is fit for any fashion magazine, I want to step out with her. I want to bask in the aura of how she carries herself. And I need a glass of wine to be able to articulate the thought I just had, about us pretending. Ideally, we wouldn't have to, but we both know what this is.

Paris is not Bonneau and all we have to do is turn a few corners to find the perfect terrace and order a delicious glass of wine—it's not even that overpriced.

The noise coming from the nearby street is deafening to my ears; the roar of the motorbikes pierces my ear drums like a pointy needle, but I can endure it when I'm sitting next to Marie, who seems to be greatly enjoying her first hit of city atmosphere in months. She has leaned backwards in her chair, totally relaxed, one leg slung over the other, her eyes almost closed.

"Enjoying the lovely smell of car fumes," I joke.

"It's all part of it," she just says, her voice as calm as her demeanour.

We sit in silence for a while, sipping from our wine. My nerves need to get used to this onslaught of unrelenting input and, at one point, I stop myself from reaching for Marie's hand. We might be in Paris, but our affair has only been conducted behind closed doors, hidden away in the Breton countryside. It's a while before she returns to Brussels, which is a bit of a double-edged sword because it leaves plenty of time for my feelings for her to deepen and I don't know how to deal with that. I've already bypassed my instincts so many times when it comes to her.

And I'm no fool, nor am I in the habit of deliberately fooling myself. As the days have passed, ever since I allowed myself to rush back to her bed that morning, I've become a little crazier about her. Because she's kind and delicious and patient and overflowing with charisma and she can tell me all she wants about the myriad of women whose hearts she's broken, whose feelings she's cruelly played with, but that's not the person I see when I look at her.

Granted, I'm probably rather blind to her personality flaws, what with my growing infatuation, but I still can't see it. Because all I see when I look at Marie is her grace, her style, those long strong fingers she can work magic with, the intelligent sparkle in her eye and, also, to my dismay, how utterly incompatible we are. Now that we're here, it's obvious that a city like this is where she belongs. We've only been sitting here ten minutes and already I've seen women and men alike glance at her. That's the kind of presence she has. You have to look.

And me, I'm just part of the penance she prescribed herself.

I finish my wine and gather my courage. "About tonight," I say. "I think I'd like to go."

"Good." She sends me the kind of lopsided smile that always make me melt a little. "Let's do it."

"And, um, maybe we can also do that other thing you suggested."

"What thing?" Great. She doesn't remember. Of course, she doesn't.

"You said that you would pretend to be my new girl-friend." It sounds so silly. What are we? Fifteen years old? "Sorry. Forget I said that. It's, um, really stupid."

"I'd hardly be pretending," she says in a way that makes me swallow hard. "This." She's the one who takes my hand in hers. "It's not nothing. We have a thing going, you and I. It may only be temporary, but that doesn't mean it's not…"

Something to rub into my ex's face. I can't help but be

a little caustic about this. I also can't wait to hear what she'll say next, but words seem to fail her. I get it. What we have is temporary and hard to define.

"It is what it is, for now." She cocks her head. "I'm no expert when it comes to any of this." She looks at our joined hands. "I'm not in the habit of sticking around, but I didn't have much choice with you."

"You could have left Bonneau any time."

"True, but… things only started getting a bit more intense two weeks ago and it's been… highly pleasant, so why would I take off now?"

"Huppert would be heartbroken if you just upped and left." Marie never calls me out on my jokey first line of defence. Towards the end, it was all Sandrine did. Then again, Sandrine was my partner. Marie is… whatever she is.

"I may have to adopt her."

"She's not up for adoption," I'm quick to say, wondering, like so many times in my life, what we're really talking about.

"If I took her with me to Brussels, you'd have to come and visit."

"Oh yes, I'd visit Huppert, of course, not you."

"Hey." She pulls my hand a little closer. "I'll be all over you tonight. Trust me, I've annoyed many exes in my day. Sometimes, they weren't even exes." I can't tell if her chuckle is mirthful or embarrassed. Maybe the reason why things have been so *intense* and *pleasant* between us, once I finally surrendered to that option, is because the woman Marie claims she was before she came to Bonneau is of no interest to me. It's like I know that she's a neurosurgeon, but to me she's something entirely different. She might as well be a carpenter or an accountant. In my neck of the woods, it doesn't matter.

"I'm touched," I reply. It may sound like banter, but there's a ring of truth to it as well.

Marie wasn't kidding when she promised she'd be all over me. Because our affair has been limited to our houses in Bonneau, public displays of affection have not been something to worry about, but now we're in this tiny café, with tables pushed so close together it feels like all of us are sitting together, it takes a bit of getting used to.

But the strangest thing about tonight isn't Marie's hand being glued to one of my body parts at all times, it's that I haven't seen Sandrine.

"Is she even here?" Marie asks.

"I don't know." I glance around. There's not much ground for my gaze to cover. Most French Instagram poets might very well be like me and prefer to hide behind their screen name.

"Are you a poet?" A man with one of those ridiculous buns on the top of his head, asks Marie.

"I'm not, but she is." Marie points at me. I should have laid out the rules to her before we came here, but I was too nervous to come up with any—and too grateful to her for coming with me to subject her to any of that.

"What's your Instagram handle?" he asks.

As I talk to @un_gram_de_poeme, Marie strokes my back, and while it has a calming effect on me, it's utterly strange to sit here like this, talking about something I never talk about, with Marie by my side, waiting for Sandrine to make an appearance. I'm so caught up in the spirals in my head that it takes a few minutes for me to realise that the guy I'm talking to, whose real name is Cedric, is actually an Insta poet I follow and admire.

"Are you reading?" Cedric asks.

I shake my head. "Just here to listen and, um, absorb the vibe."

"Fair enough."

After our conversation has ended, Marie pushes her chair closer to mine and whispers in my ear, "It's really hot to listen to you talk about your poetry."

If she keeps this up, I'm going to have to ask her to be a little less all over me. Then the door opens and as if everyone in the bar instinctively knows that someone important has just arrived, we all look in the same direction.

Sandrine walks in, hands held high, in a gesture still so familiar to me. "*Desolée*," she says. "Sorry, I'm late. There are no excuses."

"Is that her?" Marie asks.

For some reason, I can only nod.

In response, Marie wolf-whistles in my ear. Wonderful. That's all I need. My pretend-girlfriend having the hots for my ex.

"Let's get this show on the road," Sandrine says, just before she clocks me. Her eyebrows arch up and she starts to say something, but someone from our cluster of tables addresses her and the moment passes.

"She looks so different in real life," Marie says, no longer whispering.

Does she? To me, Sandrine looks the same but she must have changed. We are both different people now. Older, hopefully a little wiser, and more in command of who we are and what we want.

"Let's talk later," Sandrine mouths to me before busying herself with getting this night of poetry off to a late start.

I'm glad for Marie's hand on my neck when Sandrine turns the spotlight to herself and introduces herself as the editor of an upcoming poetry collection with an esteemed publishing house. I never even knew she was that interested in poetry. Then again, she could say the same of me. I only started taking my poetry more seriously after she left, probably to fill the hole inside me that her departure created.

She's still as gorgeous as ever, and it's as though time has done its thing and erased all the insults she threw at me, all my inadequacies she suddenly couldn't live with anymore and had to voice over and over again. All I can see is the person I once loved—and who inspired many of my poems.

After she has announced the first poet, she pulls up a chair and comes to sit next to Marie. She gives us both a once-over, her gaze halting at Marie's hand on me, and I have to stop myself from engaging in a public display of affection. I'm glad that I do, because even though we might not be pretending entirely, it would still feel wrong.

It's strange to sit here. It's also impossible for me to absorb any of the poems being read out loud. There's too much going on. I'm too far out of my comfort zone and my nervous system is on constant high alert. And I haven't even had a conversation with Sandrine yet.

CHAPTER 23
MARIE

I've known for a while that I'm ready to take up my old life again, that I'm ready for the delights of city life once more, but being here tonight cements my decision.

In previous times, I'd likely have ditched Olivia in favour of pursuing her hot ex, Sandrine. The picture I saw of her at Olivia's really didn't do her justice. Or maybe she's changed a lot in the years since they broke up. But it's only a fleeting, amusing thought to me now. I'm here with Olivia. We're here as an actual couple. I can't even flirt with Sandrine—not even for the hell of it. Oh, how times have changed.

I can sense Olivia's unease and as soon as Sandrine announces a break, Olivia hurries off to the toilets.

"*Bonsoir.*" Sandrine has sidled up to me. "I'm Sandrine. Olivia's ex-partner. I take it you have a great deal to do with why she's here tonight." Sandrine flashes me a big smile.

"Marie Dievart."

"Olivia's new squeeze?" She eyes me suspiciously.

"That's right."

177

"I'm glad she's, um, with someone." She chuckles. "This is a bit weird, actually. Olivia and I haven't exactly been in touch."

"I know." I nod slowly, gauging the woman who broke Olivia's heart to such an extent, she had to take a holiday from all things romance-related for years.

"How long have you two been seeing each other?"

"We met on the first of January, if you can believe it."

"I'm sorry, but your accent… are you from Belgium?" Sandrine asks.

"Yes. Brussels. My family owns the house around the corner from Olivia's."

"Oh. I see."

"The one that sits mostly empty, as you may remember."

From the corner of my eye, I see Olivia approach. This is going to be interesting. Will they kiss? Hug, even?

Olivia stands beside our table awkwardly.

Sandrine rises. "*Mon dieu*," she says. "It's so good to see you." She's the one who opens her arms—I guess it's not very hard to be more gregarious than Olivia. Olivia gives a slight shake of the head, then steps into her ex's embrace. Hm. Was that a pang of jealousy? No. I shake it off. It can't be. I've never been the jealous type. I've never had the need to be.

"I have so many questions," Sandrine says after they break apart. "But I'm mostly so glad you came, Liv. I do have an ulterior motive." She puts her hand on Olivia's upper arm. "I want one of your poems for my collection, but we'll talk later."

Olivia does that Olivia thing where she doesn't say anything with words and her body language is all over the place, making her impossible to read.

"Will you be in Paris for the weekend?" Sandrine asks. Olivia just nods.

"Let's have lunch tomorrow?"

Olivia glances at me.

"Go for it," I say, as though she needs my permission.

"Okay. That would be good." Olivia has finally found her voice again.

"I'm sorry, but I have half a dozen people to talk to." A short queue has formed next to where Olivia and Sandrine are talking.

"Of course. Let's talk later."

"You're one hundred percent certain you don't want to read tonight?" Sandrine likes to push, then.

"I am."

"Had to ask." She gives Olivia's upper arm one last squeeze, then turns and is swallowed up by everyone who wants a piece of her.

Olivia crashes down on her chair. "More wine will be required."

I like a glass of wine as much as the French, but it has become very clear to me over the past few months, and the past few weeks especially, that Olivia uses wine as her favourite coping mechanism. I'm not one to come between a woman and what gives her comfort, so I look out for a waiter.

"I know this is not the time or place, but meeting your ex has made me very curious about what exactly went down between the two of you. You seemed quite chummy just now." I put a possessive hand on Olivia's knee.

"Chummy?" Olivia scoffs. "That was not chummy, that was just… I don't know, nostalgia maybe. We were together for a long time. But it's been so long now. It's strange to see her after all this time. She's…" She doesn't finish her sentence, but turns fully to me instead. "I have zero intention of wasting the little time we have left together discussing my ex and why we split. It's no longer important." To my utter surprise but great delight, she leans in and kisses me on the lips.

When the last poet of the night has been announced, Olivia whispers in my ear, "Let's get out of here before it ends."

"Are you sure?"

"I don't want to talk to Sandrine again tonight."

"Okay." It's a bit of a kerfuffle to make our way between the tight squeeze of chairs and tables, but we manage, and then we're outside in the fresh air, and I'm kind of glad to have Olivia all to myself again.

"Let's walk." Olivia takes my hand. I guess we're still pretending.

"How do you feel?" Another new string of words in my vocabulary.

"I feel like having lunch with you tomorrow instead of with my ex." She throws me a quick glance, then looks away.

"Don't you want her to publish your poem?"

"I honestly don't care about that." Her shoulders slump. "It's not even about Sandrine. I'd have the same reaction if it was someone else suggesting it. I'm already three steps ahead and wondering what I'll have to do in return."

"You mean reading your poetry in front of a group of people?" I tug her towards me.

"Yes, and none of them would be you."

"What are you talking about? I'd come and see you read wherever, whenever."

She gives me a wry smile. "That's nice of you to say, but it's not relevant. I'm not interested in any of that. I didn't come for the poetry, although it was lovely. I came because the circumstances allowed me to, because you could be here with me, and I was curious about Sandrine. My curiosity has been satisfied. I can move on now."

"Do you mean you want to end the long holiday your heart has been on?" A light drizzle starts to fall but having spent the past few months amidst the cold winds of Brittany, it doesn't faze us.

"Maybe." Olivia holds on to my arm a little tighter. "My heart isn't as closed off as it used to be. Seeing Sandrine made that clear to me as well."

"Seeing *Sandrine*?" And here I was thinking it was all down to me.

"It's not just one thing. Obviously, it's mainly because of you. But, apparently, Sandrine doesn't hate my guts any longer. She was so nice to me, like all the bad stuff that happened between us wasn't even that bad."

"Maybe it wasn't. Maybe your memory is playing tricks on you."

"Oh, no. It was bad, but... maybe I don't have to be so afraid anymore."

Is she trying to tell me something? "Afraid of falling in love?" I ask.

Olivia stops in her tracks and gives me a lopsided grin. "I remember you telling me you're not one for falling in love and that's fine. I'm sure you have your reasons, just as I have mine, but... something has changed in me." She drops my hand. "Don't worry. I'm not talking about you. You've always been very upfront, which I have always appreciated. I know not to have any expectations about this." She takes a step away from me. "I know it's not what you're after."

"But, Liv…" If Sandrine can call her that, then so can I. "If you're not talking about me, then who are you talking about?"

"I don't know." She looks away again. "Someone I haven't met yet."

"Okay." I reach for her hand again, acutely aware that our days together are numbered. "But until then…" I start looking around for a taxi. "You're all mine."

Olivia's been broody all the way back to the hotel. In the back of the taxi, she kept gazing out of the window instead of looking at me. I leave her be because she's probably going through something; she's processing seeing her ex again. We have all night in a tiny room together. She's going to have to talk to me—or do something else with me—at some point.

"Come here," I say, once we're in our room, holding out my hand.

She looks at my hand as though it's a knife I'm holding out to her. "Look, I know what you want, and… Part of me wants it too, especially because we're in Paris and we had a nice time and the mood is romantic, but I can't do that with you right now. I can't get there. I—I'm too preoccupied."

Not one to easily throw in the towel, I keep my hand extended. "You can sit with me, can't you?"

"Yes." A hint of a smirk appears on her face. She reaches for my hand and takes it in hers. She looks at it now as though she's in great awe of this particular body part of mine. "Today has been a lot for me. As you know, I don't get out much."

In response, I pull her to me. The only place for her to sit is on the bed, anyway. "I had noticed."

"I need some down time. I'm sorry."

"You don't have to apologise for what you need."

"Do you think we can just lie in bed together... without any expectations?" She bumps her leg against my knee.

"We can do whatever you want." The tenderness I feel for Olivia surprises me. I might be a doctor, but this need to take care of someone in my private time is pretty alien to me—I do enough of that at work.

"Thank you." She looks into my eyes, and I see some of the things she can't say. Some of the things I might also feel, but I know I can squash. I know how to keep my feelings in check. It's what I've done all my life.

We strip to our knickers and slip into bed. I lie on my back and Olivia nestles in the crook of my shoulder. For all the orgasms I've doled out in my time, this is one of the more intimate moments of my adult life. I hold Olivia close to me. And while it's true that we could have found ourselves in this exact position in one of our houses in Brittany, it feels like this could only have happened here, in Paris, after she did something she was afraid of doing.

"Do you want to talk?" I ask, after a while.

"Not really. Do you?" She pushes her nose against my neck and whereas with anyone else I might not have noticed the subtlety in that gesture—I might have pounced on it and bent things my way—with Olivia, I know it's not sensual. It's intimate and, perhaps, I can't help but think, she's already starting to say goodbye to me.

CHAPTER 24

OLIVIA

"I know I'm difficult," I say, before taking another sip of wine. I feel refreshed and only a touch mortified. When I woke up, Marie's side of the bed was empty but for a note on her pillow saying she'd gone for a long walk and that I should take my time. "If I wasn't, I'd be having lunch with Sandrine instead of you."

"In that case, I'm glad you're such a challenge," Marie says.

"I just don't want to get into the whole poetry thing." While I had some time to myself this morning, my finger hovered over the delete button of my Instagram account several times, but I haven't pressed it yet. "Nor do I want to rehash the past with her. I just don't want to go there."

"She probably would have given you the third degree about your hot new girlfriend." While Marie was surprisingly tender and understanding with me last night, she's back to full-on confidence today.

"I wouldn't have minded singing your praises." Except that Marie's not my girlfriend, of course. "I'm sorry I got a bit maudlin last night."

"You're telling the woman who decided to take six months off work to go sulk in Brittany?"

"Yet you've always come across as very chipper."

"Even that time you had to pick me up from Yvette's way past your bedtime?"

I smile at the memory. I distinctly remember not being very happy about that. It also seems like it happened a lifetime ago, even though it's only been a few months. A few months of trying to keep my distance, because I knew what this would do to me. I might have failed at keeping my feelings for Marie from blossoming—and I think she knows this—but seeing Sandrine has taught me that it doesn't have to be the end of the world. Compared to my relationship with Sandrine, my affair with Marie is just a blip in the grand scheme of things.

"I might have made it sound as though Sandrine was the culprit in our romance gone wrong, but I know that's a one-sided view."

Marie nods.

"This"—I tap my chest—"Is not always a walk in the park to be with, especially when it's just the two of you in the middle of nowhere."

"I only met her briefly, but she seems way too pushy for you."

"I need to be pushed sometimes."

"Maybe," Marie says, because she's never been one to mince her words.

"You pushed me to come to Paris this weekend."

"It hardly felt like pushing to me."

"Maybe you just have a way with me."

Marie slants her head. "You have a way with me too."

I'd very much like to know what she means by that exactly, but I'm the opposite of the pushy type. I let the moment pass because the sun is out and we're sharing a wonderful meal in this beautiful city.

"How many hearts did you break in Paris?" The words sound silly as they come from my mouth, but she's the one who's brought up her sketchy romantic past a few times.

"I don't really keep score of things like that, but..." She whistles through her teeth. "I seduced a woman who was spoken for and then slept with her partner's best friend." She looks away from me briefly. "Let's just say I owe a few women a huge apology for how I treated them."

"Yet you've always been nothing but kind to me."

"That's because... it's different with you. There's a certain pureness to you. There's something about how you are that grounds me and... Well, let's not forget the reason why I fled my life in Brussels in the first place. I was very shaken when I first arrived."

Again, she could have fooled me, what with how she turned up at my doorstep seemingly unable to take no for an answer.

"It's funny," she continues, "but it seems like you ever so slowly lowering your guard with me has happened in parallel with me becoming myself again. Now, here we are in Paris, back in civilisation, and it kind of feels like the end of a long road." She takes a deep breath. "I've missed the city so much more than I realised. I've missed just walking out of my apartment and going for a coffee or a meal. I've missed having people, bustling life, around me at all times. And for someone who never takes the time for it, I've missed going to the cinema and the theatre and the opera so bloody much."

"You're a city dweller. It's a strange affliction."

"I hate to break it to you, but living in the countryside

on your own is considered much more of a strange affliction."

I just shrug. Already, I can't wait to go home. To breathe in the fresh air. To see the trees that are at their very best this time of year, full of returning vigour and life. To have the first thing I hear in the morning and the last thing before I fall asleep be a bird's melody instead of the incessant hum of cars. To have space and my cats around me and the stillness of my garden. To be at ease instead of always vigilant.

"Don't be too surprised if you find you miss it. Breton winters are harsh, but there's so much beauty in the sheer tranquillity of it."

Marie smiles at me as if she has just realised something, but again, I don't push. If she needs me to know, she'll tell me. She's not the kind to keep a lot to herself—not the kind to keep quiet if she can be talking instead. Just like I'm sure she will miss Bonneau when she's back in Brussels, I will miss her boldness, her inquisitive green gaze, her hands all over me, her sleepy face in the morning, and the way she has taken to talking to Huppert as though she's human. There will be a lot to miss and her passage through my life will have a lasting impact. She has made me a little less afraid, a little more open to the possible beauty of connection, and I'll be the first to admit I can always do with more of both.

The Monday after we've returned from Paris, I know it's futile to work on the translation I'm doing. My brain is otherwise engaged, busy with sorting through everything that happened over the weekend, which was so much more than what I go through on any given day at home. The smells. The sounds. All the sights. The pompous opera I let Marie take me to because I felt I had to do something for her. The proximity of other people with all their energy and movements and antics. The drive out of Paris which I had expected to be smooth because it was Sunday afternoon, but was hectic instead. Being with Marie almost twenty-four-seven. Seeing Sandrine again.

The weather's lovely, and I sit outside in my rocking chair with Huppert glued to my lap. The poor thing's not used to me being away for more than a few hours at a time and she's planted herself firmly on my lap to make sure I don't do that again anytime soon. I'm happy enough to have her so close. I'm happy to have her at home with me instead of at Marie's. Huppert will be out of sorts when Marie leaves as well. She'll have to go back to only having one home and one pair of hands to pet her. But I push the thought of Marie leaving from my mind as soon as it comes up. She was always going to leave and there's nothing I can do about it. And she was right when she said that going back to only seeing each other occasionally until she does leave is nonsense. It won't help to protect my heart. And maybe my heart is ready for the tiny dose of pain that's coming. Maybe it will make me stronger and, in the end, help me to let someone else in again—as I alluded to on that walk in Paris.

Huppert's ears perk up. Footsteps approach. It can only be Marie. Even though I told her I needed some time on my own, I mostly don't mind that she's come over. My subconscious is equally aware of our limited time together. I'll recover from all the excess input into my nervous system later, after she has gone.

"Hey." Her voice is soothing now instead of jarring.

Instantly, Huppert jumps out of my lap to rub herself against Marie's shins. Marie ruffles her hands through my cat's fur before kissing me hello.

Her smile quickly recedes as she pulls up a chair and sits down next to me. "We need to talk," she says, sounding ominous.

"We do?" My heartbeat triples in pace, but I curse myself for wanting her to say what I've been dying to hear —if I'm being really honest with myself. That she feels the same way about me as I feel about her, even though it wouldn't change anything. But still, it would give the month and a few days we have left together a different tinge.

"Yes," she says on a sigh. "I just got off the phone with my boss at the hospital. They want me to go back a month early."

My heart feels like it's being squeezed into a pulp by an icy hand.

"I'll spare you the details, but, um, I've said yes." She rubs her palms on her jeans. "I'm ready to go home, to take up my life again."

"W—when will you be leaving?"

"The day after tomorrow."

Another cold hard punch to the gut. I don't do well with emotions that need to be absorbed and processed very quickly, especially when I believed I had time to adjust. "No," is all I can say, unwanted tears welling behind my eyes.

"I'm sorry, Liv, but maybe it's for the best."

I swallow hard. I look at Huppert. I wish she'd jump in my lap. I need all the comfort I can get. "Yeah. Maybe." Oh, fuck. Of course I don't want her to go. And of course, I didn't want to explicitly admit that to myself. I don't want her to go the day after tomorrow and I don't want her to go at the end of June.

"Look." She leans towards me and puts her hands on my knees. "You told me you're ready for, um, someone new."

I did say that. Just as I said that that someone wasn't her, although it is her. It can only be her.

"The day after tomorrow," I mumble. "That's…"

"I'm starting work again on the first and I need a day to get my bearings back home."

"Okay." My voice chokes.

She digs her fingertips into the flesh around my knees. "Here's a thought out of left field." She tries a smile. "You could come with me. Just for a few days. See where I live. Spend some time with me in Brussels. You can work anywhere."

I'm flattered that she asks—that she's thought of this. That she acknowledges how hard this is. But as appealing as the idea is, there's no point in dragging any of this out. It has to end at some point. "I'm not sure."

"Think about it." She presses down on my legs. "Promise me."

"I promise I'll consider it, but you're kind of springing all of this on me and…" I cover her hands with mine. "I don't want you to go." My voice cracks.

"I'm sorry, but I can't keep hiding out here forever. Spending time in Paris made me see I'm ready for my life again. This…" She pauses. "This has been wonderful, but we always knew it would end. I was never going to stay here. It was always temporary."

"I know. I just thought we had more time." The first tear trickles down my cheek. I've never been very good at crying in front of another person, but today, I don't care.

"When I said that I was ready for someone new... when I said that person wasn't you..." The words die as my throat swells so I don't say that person could only ever have been her and how, with all her brain surgeon intellect, could she not see that?

Marie kneels beside me and wraps her arms around me. "I know," she whispers. "It's hard for me too."

It might be hard for her too, but it's not the same. She's going back to her old life, while I'm staying here, left with the void she has created by coming here, forcing her way into my heart, and then leaving.

Tears stream down my cheeks, into Marie's hair, which she had cut into a fancy do in Paris. Maybe that should have been a sign that she was getting ready to go. Once again, I was so preoccupied with all the thoughts in my head, I forgot to inquire about hers. I know I can't take this out on her. Not only because it's not fair, but even more so because there is no time.

"How many hours do we have left together?"

Marie looks up at me, wiping a tear from her chin— it's impossible to tell if it sprouted from her eyes or mine. "About fifty, I think."

"Fifty hours." Fuck. "Can't you stay a little longer?" It's the shock of her early departure that has me in such tatters. I was unable to prepare for this, to pull up the drawbridge to my heart that I lowered to let her in.

"No, but you *can* come with me."

What good would that do? I want to ask. It would only postpone the inevitable.

CHAPTER 25

MARIE

N one of this was meant to happen. Olivia and I weren't meant to grow this attached. I don't even know how it happened. At first, she was just my cranky neighbour. Then, she was a life raft in the storm that I let my life become. She represented some human warmth in the cold Breton winter. But I pushed and pushed, because that's what I do. And now here I sit, crouched beside her, simultaneously so certain and utterly uncertain of what I have to do. It's doubts like these that I tried to escape when I came here. It's doubts like these that I believed I had overcome. I had.

In Paris, I felt it. I knew what I wanted. I could reach my deepest intuition again and I knew I was ready. I *am* ready. The prospect of being in the operating theatre again, of doing what I do best, is intoxicating. This type of sentimental scene has never been my forte, yet here I am. Attached to a woman I can't seem to let go of.

I know Olivia's not going to come to Brussels with me, but I had to ask. It would be far less complicated if she didn't accompany me home. I could have a much cleaner break, although this is still going to be messy, because feelings I never even knew I had are involved.

Olivia takes a deep breath. I push myself away from her, become myself a bit more again.

"I wasn't going to tell you this," she says, her voice constrained but much more level than when it broke earlier. "But... now that you're on the cusp of leaving, I feel like if I don't tell you now, you will never know, and I think you should."

I try to steel myself for what she's about to say, because I know what it is. She doesn't have to say it, but I know she needs to, for herself. Because she's not always good at articulating how she feels, but she will go through the effort of communicating. I give her a small nod of encouragement.

"You must have heard this so many times in your life while being unable to reciprocate." She chuckles nervously. "But I am so stupidly, so foolishly in love with you." She leans back in the rocking chair and fishes a handkerchief out of her pocket. She quickly blows her nose, and it breaks my heart a little to see her like this. To have her say this to me.

She's right. I've had plenty of women confess their love to me, but with Olivia, the impact is far greater. I can't just shake this off and hope it all goes away by saying a few dismissive words. I don't want to dismiss her. I feel for her; maybe not the same as she feels for me, but still. Her heart might be a tightly sealed fortress, mine is more like an underdeveloped muscle, like a recalcitrant adolescent refusing to ever grow up. But with her, I'm never cruel, and I love that about her. I love how she has brought out my softer, more caring side. I love how this distant, fully independent woman suddenly seems to need me like her life depends on it.

I can't say it back. I simply can't. Even if it were true, I still wouldn't say it. But I have to say something, no matter how inadequate.

"I have feelings for you too, Liv. I really do, but…"

"It doesn't matter." Her limbs stiffen. "I just wanted you to know."

"I do know." I've known for a while. She wouldn't have rushed back to me that morning after she fled my bed if she didn't have feelings for me—she's not the type. She can try to hide all she wants, but Olivia is made up of nothing but deep emotion. She feels it all so much that she had to move to the middle of nowhere in order to deal with it all. I can see that now. Her skin is so thin, she has no choice but to keep her distance from everything and everyone. Perhaps I should have respected that, but I didn't know she was like this when I arrived here. I didn't know she was only pretending to be this stern, hardened country woman who didn't want to have anything to do with me. But she did open up to me and whereas before I would have easily shrugged off the responsibility she saddled me with, I can no longer do that. Just like Olivia, something in me has changed.

"You mean so much to me. You really do." I make sure to look her squarely in the eye. "I appreciate what we've had so much. It's taken me by surprise as much as it has you. Truly. This… thing we have. That's not really something that I do." I throw in a small smile because I'm using one of her own favourite expressions. "You've made my stay here so much more delightful and interesting and I'm so glad to know you, to have witnessed this other side of you." I might be pushing it again, but just as she needed me to hear what she just said, I need her to hear this. "You don't have to be alone for the rest of your life. Most of the time, you might feel as though you're better off alone, but I'm not sure that you are. You are kind and smart and funny. You're one hell of a poet as well. You have so much to offer, Liv. Don't hide yourself away like this forever."

"What about you?" I should have known she would use her powerful skills of deflection. "You've been alone all your life as well."

She's right. I have, but in a very different way than her. "I don't know." I'm always looking for something but not for anything serious. Maybe it's time I changed that. Earlier, on the phone with the head of neurosurgery, after I'd said yes to going back early, the first thing I thought about was seeing Véronique again. She might not work in the operating theatre anymore. Maybe she's at a different hospital altogether. Either way, she must have moved on from me. So have I, I realised then—and now. "I'll be focusing on work for a while." I push myself up and stand next to Olivia in her rocking chair, suddenly feeling awkward.

"Thank you for saying those things about me." She stands as well, facing me, but leaving some distance between us. "You're not so bad yourself."

I no longer automatically think "I know" when someone says that to me, especially when that someone is Olivia. I'm also not feeling particularly special at the moment, what with me being the cause of Olivia's tears.

"You're going to make someone very happy some day." As I say it, I know how utterly trite and ridiculous it sounds, so I make sure to follow up with a chuckle.

"Look at us." She smiles as well, although it's a tight

smile. "When did the cold-hearted surgeon and the dyed-in-the-wool loner become so sentimental?"

"Excuse me? Who are you calling cold-hearted?" She might mean it in jest, but it stings a little all the same.

"I take it back. I know you're anything but cold-hearted." She tugs me towards her by the hem of my blouse. "What are we going to do for the remaining fifty hours together?"

"What do you want to do?" If it were anyone else, I'd be kissing them already, but I know by now that's not how it works with Olivia.

"Give me an hour or so to process this, then I'll come over and I won't leave your side until you get into your car."

I have a hundred phone calls to make. I have to pack up my stuff. I have to find a way to quickly adjust to life away from this cocoon I made for myself with Olivia. But I know myself. The transition might be rough for a minute, but it will be quick, and I will have acclimatised to real life soon enough.

"I'll be waiting for you," I say, and kiss her tenderly on the lips.

CHAPTER 26

OLIVIA

I t was always going to come to this, I think as I knock on Marie's door. It's open and I find her talking on the phone in the kitchen. It looks like a small tornado has passed through her house. There's an open suitcase on the living room floor and an assortment of clothes hanging from the dining room chairs. The disarray in the room reflects how I feel inside.

I sit on the sofa and look at her—at this spark of energy that coursed through my life. Already, she seems a little different, a little more city than country. She gesticulates wildly and her voice has gone up a pitch. It strikes me that I might not even like the person she is in her real life. Because this is the effect being surrounded by nature has on most people. It softens their hardest edges. It makes you feel like so many things that mattered before, no longer do—until you have to go back. God, I can't imagine. I can't imagine ever leaving this place, this safe haven tucked away from too much noise, too many people, too much life. The heartbeat of this place is much slower, far less frenetic.

I predict that Marie will not adjust so easily to the life she consciously fled—a life that, at least for a while, she didn't want anymore. She's been in Bonneau for five months. The stillness must have gotten under skin. The need for it must have grown inside of her as time progressed. Or maybe she's just totally different from me. Look at Sandrine. The quietness, especially in winter, drove her nuts, drove her back into the arms of the city. I forgot to ask if she lives in Paris now. I'm working on an email to her, explaining why I bailed on lunch, and why I don't want my poetry published, but how it was really good to see her. But that's for later. For after Marie has left. I'll have oceans of time, then.

Time never used to be an issue for me. I've always been able to fill it, using only myself as a resource. I'll need to adapt to that again. To not seeing Marie's face first thing in the morning. At least Deneuve will be happy to no longer have to share me with another human.

"Sorry about that." Marie walks over.

And so it begins. Society will swallow her up again in no time. She'll surrender herself to a life in which there is not enough time for reflection, and, in her case, not enough time for love.

"I'm all yours now." She straddles my lap and wraps her arms around me. "How are you feeling?"

Sore. Tender. A touch embarrassed for confessing my true feelings to her. Sad. Deflated. Robbed of a month's worth of her heavenly kisses, her warm embrace, her easy self-assuredness. Instead of telling her how I feel, I show her. I pull her close and kiss her as though there's no tomorrow. It's a strange sensation to kiss a woman who will be leaving me. Someone who means so much to me, but will be gone from my life in two short days. It's incongruous and it makes it hard for me to lose myself in the kiss, even though soon I won't be able to kiss her anymore and I want to make the most of the time we have left.

"Was this about sex?" I ask, rather bluntly I realise, after the fact.

"Maybe a little, but not really." Perhaps one of the things I've appreciated about Marie from the get-go is how she always gives me a straight answer. She's not coy about anything.

I can feel my heart close down already, and I'm not sure I can open myself up enough again to do more than kiss her. Can I again surrender to someone who will so easily walk away from me, even though it was always part of the deal? But now that it's so close, now that I know that it's going to hurt, I need to shore up my defences as quickly as possible—as if that will make it hurt any less.

"What are you really asking me?" Marie stares down at me.

"I don't know. I feel like we *have* to do this now. That we need to squeeze out a few more orgasms in the time allotted to us."

"Jesus." She moves to sit next to me.

I'm guessing this is the side of me she's not going to miss—if she misses me at all. The side that always needs some sort of illusion of being in control.

"I'm sorry. I have no idea how to deal with this." I don't want her to go. It's as simple and as complicated as that.

"I can leave tomorrow if this is too hard for you."

I examine her face to see if she's joking, but I can't tell.

"Please, don't." I heel off my shoes and lie on my back with my head in her lap, looking up at her.

She runs her fingers through my hair, her eyes a little moist in the corners when she looks at me.

"I can find a tenant for the house," she says, a hint of a smile on her lips. "Someone you will like."

"I won't like her." I mean to sound every bit as petulant as I do.

"That's a given. Not at first, anyway." Her face goes serious. "Promise me you'll be okay."

"Why? Are you going to be that worried about me?"

"Yeah, I might very well be."

"Nah, you'll forget all about me as soon as your life picks up its regular pace again. It'll be like you never even knew me."

"I'll never forget about you, Liv. Don't say that."

"I'll just blend in with all the other women you've been with."

"Stop it. Okay?" She sounds as though she means it.

"Okay." I'm behaving like a child because I don't know how else to behave. I don't know what to do with myself. "Sorry."

She traces a fingertip over the lines on my forehead. "I *am* going to miss you."

"Me too." Where's the time that I wanted her to go? That I wanted this house to be as empty as every other winter? That I wanted to be left to my own devices and not have anything to do with her?

"I want you." Her voice has dropped into a lower register. "At least one last time. It doesn't have to be now. Whenever you're ready—and if you feel the same, of course."

I want her so much it has crossed over into wanting to push her away, because surrendering to her one last time will hurt too much. But that's the irrational part of me acting up. I want to make a few final memories with her as well. I want the two nights we have left to be as special as they can be. As special as the two of us are together—because there's nothing ordinary about our temporary union. In any other place but here, I wouldn't be lying with my head in her lap, thinking about whether to sleep with her again or not. This place brought us together and is about to tear us apart. "I do." I meet her gaze.

"Thank goodness," she whispers, and skates her finger down my temple, across my cheek, to my lips. Her touch is light as a feather. Oh, how I will miss those fingers and all they represent. Not just the pleasure they have coaxed from me, but because they make her who she is. Her hands save lives. It's a notion so foreign to me, it makes me feel special just to have them dance across my skin, for the privilege of it. For the privilege of having met her and got to know her.

I open my lips to her finger, suck the tip into my mouth, and let my tongue sweep against it. It makes me see the utter foolishness of my earlier ways, because why would I possibly try to resist her now? Why would I deny myself this heavenly sensation of being with her? Of allowing her in and having her divine hands all over me. I need to take what I can get, not in the cynical way I expressed earlier, but in the beautiful way I can be with her. I've already told her I'm in love with her. I've already been at my most vulnerable. I have nothing left to lose.

Marie leans down as I reach up. Our lips meet in the middle. Our tongues dance. I close my eyes and give myself up to her, to how she makes me feel when she does this, which is unlike any other sensation I've experienced for years—until she moved into this house. I give up the need for control, the need to think ahead, to plan for whatever disaster might or might not occur. She's leaving. I already know that. The worst is already happening. But we still have today, and tomorrow.

"Let's go upstairs," she says when we break from our kiss.

I follow her to the bedroom, getting a good look at her shapely behind as we go up. I've always been very aware that a woman like Marie wouldn't look at me twice in a city like Paris or Brussels. That climbing the stairs with her now is an anomaly in my life. Of the five months she's been here, we've only spent a few weeks together. Surely, whatever this is between us, this infatuation I have developed for her, will dissolve into the greater scheme of my life. It will decrease to a tiny blip on the long timeline of my life. I will go back to how I used to be, before her.

Summer's coming, the most glorious season in this part of the country. The sky will be blue and the evenings long and inviting. I'll sit outside with my cats, reminiscing about that elegant city woman who descended upon us on the first of January and I will say to no one in particular, "It was fun and special and now it's over and I'm fine with that." I'm glad it happened, that I finally let it happen, that I gave myself that little present of being with another woman like that, and the fact that it was always finite in time was part of that gift. Otherwise, if by some twist of fate Marie had ended up staying, it would surely have ended the same way it did with Sandrine. I can't see how else it could possibly have gone. Because we are so different and we want other things from life. She wants constant excitement, the adrenalin of surgery, to be admired for what she does. I just want to be left alone in my quiet, perfectly pleasant life. So no, I actually don't want her to stay, despite my feelings for her, which, truth be told, are partly based on how she looks. So glamorous. So effortlessly stylish all the time. Her peculiar green gaze on me when she slips a finger inside will stick with me for a while, but, in time, I will forget, and the colour green will remind me once again of the leaves on the trees and the meadows outside instead of her eyes.

I don't love you, I try to imprint in my brain as she takes my clothes off, her strong fingers working the buttons of my shirt as though it's their primary job, as though her fingers are not destined for far greater things. But tonight, all of her is only for me. *I don't love you*, I think, as I try to meet her gaze. It's impossible when I try to rationalise myself into not having feelings for her. I can't look her in the eye with that thought running through my brain because I feel so much for her. I'm about to show her, again, exactly how much.

CHAPTER 27

Olivia's all over me. She's much more assertive than she's been before. Her lips trace along my neck, her hands are in my hair. Even though we've done this many more times than I've done it with anyone else, she still feels like a stranger to me. The taciturn woman next door. The cat lady who never answers her phone.

She pushes me down onto the bed and then suddenly stills. Her body is pressed against me but her hands have stopped roaming across my body and so have her lips. Maybe she needs me to take over. Not a problem. I start coaxing her onto her back, but she resists.

"Let's just lie here for a bit," she whispers.

I turn my head to face her and smile, nodding. I understand. Already, I have a million thoughts running through my head about things that need sorting out now that I'm going back to real life, because that's how my stint here has felt. Like stepping out of my life and taking a break from it. But Olivia is a real person as well, a human being with oh-so-many feelings. And she has taught me so much more than she will ever know, than she will get credit for. She has taught me what it's like to live with the brakes on. To not rush through life as though you'll miss it if you dare to blink. Because of her, I know that there's another way to be—there are many other ways to be.

She runs her fingertips over my belly and although light, her touch rushes through my entire body. I sense her intention behind it even more now that she's explicitly told me that she's in love with me. I turn on my side and stroke her the way she's stroking me. I need to feel her skin against my fingers. I need to see her eyes light up when I circle her nipple. Familiarity has never really been my thing but it's a surprisingly pleasing sensation to know how Olivia will react when I take her nipple between my lips. When I slip my fingers between her legs she'll make a low sound in the back of her throat, a gravelly groan of desire, of letting go, and my own body will respond in kind. It will keep up with hers, because when have I ever not wanted to keep up with someone else?

When I came here, of course. When I decided to stay longer. My stay here has been good for me in many ways, although some days just being here, surrounded by all this nothingness and lack of excitement nearly drove me crazy. But it's the actual staying, the not running away when I wanted to most, that has had the greatest effect on me. Not that I sat with my demons every day until they slowly, as time passed, disappeared, to make way for confidence again. I've also learned that it doesn't work that way. I will always carry with me the memory of the woman who died on my table that day, but it doesn't have to crush me anymore. It doesn't have to define me any longer.

All along, even when she didn't want to see me, Olivia was in the house around the corner. Knowing that she was there always made me feel less alone, made me feel that wherever I go, wherever life takes me, there will always be someone. To be honest, even though it hasn't always felt that way, and I'm used to being treated with more adoration, it has been good for me that Olivia is, as she said so herself, the opposite of the clingy type. She's the opposite of needy. She made me work for it. She made me take myself—and my so-called charms—less for granted.

But through it all, since she picked me up from Yvette's that night, I knew she would be there if I really needed her. She's here right now and I need her now, too. Just like she needs me. In this unusual union we've formed, we are equals. I might not be able to express it the way she has, but I have deep feelings for her too. Nothing I've done with her has been trivial or in any way replaceable. But it always had to end.

I cup her breast in my hand and marvel at how her lips form an O-shape, but no sound comes out just yet. I look into her eyes and know I will miss her inquisitive gaze as well as her contemplative one—the look she gets when she goes completely silent, when she's had enough of talking. But that's not the look I'm getting from her today. Her gaze blazes desire and need. And I'm right there with her. I didn't come all the way to Brittany for this, but I'm so glad I found it. I'm so happy to have found Olivia as my quiet companion on this road I've been on.

Her hand mirrors mine and I moan when her hand closes around my breast. I moan even louder when she leans in and sucks my nipple into her mouth.

While it's also true that, at first, I wanted her mainly because she was there, that stopped being the case a long time ago. Now, I want her because she's so unmistakably, so irreversibly her. I meant what I said when I told her she'd make another woman very happy one day, even though, in a way, it was a dreadful thing to say. Because part of me was sad that I couldn't be that other, more suitable, woman. But right now, I am still that woman. I'm the woman I can't be for her in the future. It adds another dimension to our lovemaking; it adds intensity and a touch of melancholy.

After she has feasted on both my nipples, her lips find mine again and I lose myself in a kiss I don't ever want to end. Precious time passes as we kiss and kiss and my body melts into her more. I go wet like a river for her, again, and I need to feel her. I bring my hand to the apex of her thighs and am met with her desire for me. While our tongues keep dancing, I circle her clit and revel in how she stiffens against me. She groans, and her lust reverberates through my own body. I catch her hot breath, her throaty sounds, and open my legs to her.

Instead of mirroring my motion, she slides her fingers all the way inside me, and I'm the one who's out of breath now. I'm the one who can't keep my desire in check, the heat that rushes through my veins, that's been living under my skin for weeks now. I've been unable to get enough of her, of this, because every single time she slipped her fingers inside me she left me shaking and breathless and utterly satisfied. Maybe it's because I've become much more relaxed here, and more attuned to my body. My orgasm-a-day routine started it—although since Olivia really got involved, I've had many more than one a day. Or just maybe, it's Olivia making me feel this way. Or the two of us together. I don't know what it is, but as soon as her fingers slide inside me, I lose my mind a little.

I try to keep my eyes open, to not lose myself in the slipstream of my desire just yet, and look into hers. How she manages to appear so composed is a mystery to me—

maybe because my finger has halted its motion on her clit. I want to touch her but I simply can't. I'm too consumed by the exhilaration her fingers are causing me.

She drives high inside me, as if she wants to possess me, as if she won't stop until she's had all of me, but she's still in control. She's still in charge. And maybe that's what it is. When I first came here, this was unthinkable. Another woman's hands all over me after the last time I let that happen.

But here, with Olivia, nothing bad can happen. There's great safety in hiding away—Olivia should know. And sometimes, all we need is to feel extremely safe for a while, for our nervous system to restore itself. I feel restored. I'm ready. Nothing has made that clearer to me than Olivia pushing her fingers inside me like this. If I'm ready for this, if I can accept the pleasure she's willing to give me again and again, if my body is so eager for it, and my mind doesn't have any more objections to my absolute surrender to another person, then I can do anything. I've never looked at it like that before, but here I am, with Olivia inside me, giving myself up to her more with every single thrust.

And Olivia knows how to thrust. Being a doctor, I want to examine our actions in great anatomical detail and get to the bottom of why her doing this makes me feel like I'm the greatest woman alive, like I can face that mad world outside again, but I suspect no scanner or scientific study would yield any results, because this is not a matter of anatomy.

This is a matter of two women coming together in the kind of circumstances that neither of us could ever have predicted. Because of my arrogance, I never saw myself ending up in a place like this, with Olivia as my only neighbour and closest human connection. I know she tried to fight it. It was written all over her face from the very beginning. But Olivia's need for control didn't win out in the end either. Because here we are.

Her breath is coming faster as well. Did she say something? I'm sure her lips just moved. I don't want her to ever stop what she's doing but I want to hear what she has to say even more. I try to still a little, try not to meet her thrusts halfway so much. I look at her and I listen.

"Come for me," she says, and it's so unexpected because it's the very last thing I ever thought Olivia would say to me—would ask of me.

"Come for me," Olivia repeats, her voice a breathy whisper. She looks deep into my eyes, and it connects us on a more profound level.

She surrendered to me, but I surrendered to her as well. I feel it now more than ever. The shudder that starts at my core and runs through me is caused by her, by what she's doing to me but also by what she means to me. What she stands for. By who she is—a gorgeous, strong woman I don't want to leave behind. I couldn't close my eyes now even if I wanted to. I'm beguiled by her gaze on me. By the shallow lines bracketing her lips, by the pillowy curve of her upper lip, by her eyes that can tell me, without the words she never really wants to speak anyway, how much I mean to her. Because this is how Olivia communicates best, and I hear her loud and clear. I feel it all as her fingers do their thing inside me, as the heat sparks off my skin and the fireworks ignite in my flesh. As I do as she has just asked of me. As I come for her—and only her.

CHAPTER 28
OLIVIA

W e're sitting in Marie's garden. Deneuve has made the short trek from my house as well, as though she sensed I need her with me tonight. Or maybe she has grown fond of Marie in her own way.

It's a gorgeous evening full of promise of a beautiful summer to come. We're surrounded by all shades of green and the purple of the wisteria. The air is just the right temperature and the birds sing loudly and freely and I have one last thing to tell Marie, although I'm sure she's already guessed.

"I can't go with you tomorrow," I say.

"I figured as much." Marie has her bare feet in my lap. I can't stop myself from stroking every patch of skin I can get my hands on. Ever since she broke the news of her early departure, about thirty hours ago, it's like my feelings for her have cruelly deepened. Like only now, on the cusp of her literally driving away, I can well and truly see her for who she is. Because she's been different too. More affectionate. More all over me. More as though her leaving pains her too.

She lets her head fall back. "That feels good," she says, as my fingers rub her ankle. "Your fingers are like magic."

"Says the surgeon."

"Exactly. I should know. I know quality fingers when I encounter them."

The conversation is silly and the opposite of deep but that's the only way it can be right now. We have to keep it light until she leaves.

"Will you come visit me?" she asks, after a while.

"Ask me again in a few weeks."

"I'm asking you now." She sits up a bit straighter.

"Maybe."

"Please, just say yes. Just this once."

"Okay." Oh, fuck. The beginning of a tear pricks behind my eyes. It's not as if I haven't thought about it. I could even take the train. I'd be in Brussels in a few hours. Maybe it's about time I broadened my horizons and visited a new city. Marie may want me to make some sort of hollow promise to her now so she can feel better about herself, but I'm not convinced she'll still want me to visit her after a few weeks have passed. I'm also not convinced I should. How else am I going to forget about her?

Huppert jumps into her lap, as though she knows Marie will be leaving soon.

"I'm going to miss you too," Marie says in the voice she reserves for the cats. "I've never had shared custody of a pet before."

"Aren't you going to miss this?" I spread my arms wide to gesture at the splendour of the landscape around us, that was so rugged and barren when she first arrived.

"Yes, very much." She lifts her gaze from my cat to me. "Just so you know, I'm going to miss you most of all." She purses her lips. "Look, I want to say something to you,

Liv, because it's our last night together and… well, you know."

"Go ahead." When I look at Marie with her hand on my cat like that, the very picture of serenity, and of how a summer night out here should look, she can say whatever she wants.

"I know Sandrine hurt you and that it has taken you a long time to put all of that behind you, but… the reason I'm asking you to come to Brussels is because if you always stay at home, if you always try to control what's going to happen next, you're missing out on a lot."

"I guess."

Her words are pretty much a carbon copy of something Sandrine said to me before she left me. "There's so much life to live out there and, yes, it can be scary and it's definitely unpredictable, but you just never know what's going to happen. You can't give up on all that possibility, Liv." She takes a sip of wine. "Somehow, it would make me feel better if I knew you'd just… put yourself out there a bit more."

I nod. In a way, she's right, because me sitting here with her, albeit with my heart in my throat, is the direct result of me living life instead of trying to make it do what I want—which is usually nothing much.

"The same goes for your poetry. Keep putting it out there. And when an opportunity presents itself, as it did with Sandrine wanting to publish your poem, don't immediately say no. Call me. Let me talk you into saying yes."

"Call you?" I can't imagine myself doing that, because what would that make us? Some type of friends, but unlike the friends we tried to be a few months ago, with benefits.

"Yes. And while you're at it, pick up the phone when I

call you. I don't have time for long emails and texting back and forth. I'm going to be calling you, okay? So, just pick up."

"I'm confused… what are you insinuating with all of this?"

"I'm not insinuating anything. I just don't want you to lock yourself away anymore. Obviously, you can do what-ever you want, but… I think it's such a waste."

Of all the things I expected tonight—a couple more orgasms, maybe a few tears—I wasn't ready to get an earful on how I've chosen to live my life. "At this point, what you think is quite irrelevant."

"The hell it is. We're friends. Whether you like it or not, I care about you. I worry about your well-being."

Friends, uh? Once again, I'm way ahead of her. "You don't have to worry about me. No one has to worry about me."

"You worry enough about everything, yourself included, that's true."

"It's just what I'm like." Even though she's annoying me, I can't bring myself to remove her feet from my lap. Despite her being a royal pain in my ass at times, I still want her to stay.

"I expect a brand-new poem on your Instagram every week, okay? You've been slacking." She says it with enough jest in her tone I know to take it as a joke.

I wisely decide not to tell her I've been thinking about closing down my account altogether.

She nudges me in the thigh with her big toe. "I know very well I can't expect anything from you. I have zero claims to make, but…" She falls silent and looks into the distance. "Maybe this is harder for me than I thought it was going to be." She looks at me briefly but, very much unlike her, her gaze skitters away. "It feels like whatever we have between us, has only just started." Another nudge with her toe. "If only you hadn't been so bloody difficult in the beginning. We could have had a lot more time together."

"You still would have left." I sound much more laid-back than I feel.

"Fair enough." She pauses. "You're right, I still would have left."

"Besides, you were going to stay until the end of June."

She just nods, still looking away. "I know," she says, after a few seconds have passed. "Maybe I feel like I need to protect myself too."

That's a new one. "Protect yourself from what?"

"From…" She makes a vague gesture that makes Huppert mew in protest. "This. Whatever this is. You and me. How it makes me feel."

"So, you're running away." *Again.*

"Maybe, but not really. Come on. I'm going back. It's a big step. I'm nervous."

"Of course, you are." I curl my fingers around her slender ankle. "I promise you that I'll come to Brussels at least once." Now that I've said it to her like this, I will have to keep my promise. "If you promise to make time for me when I'm there."

She brings her hand to her chest. "I'm not only promising you that, I also promise you'll have the time of your life."

"Big words."

Marie shrugs. "I've always been a touch cocky." It's when she's like this that I find her most irresistible. I'm guessing I'm not the only one.

"Just don't introduce me to your many lovers."

A hearty laugh bubbles up from the back of her throat. "You have my word." Her face suddenly goes all solemn. "I, on the other hand, hope to be introduced to the new love of your life sooner rather than later."

"Don't say that. Not yet." I swallow hard. "My head's still too full of all things you."

"I'm sorry." She walks her toe up my thigh. Huppert has had enough of all her sudden movements and jumps out of Marie's lap. Her toe reaches the crotch of my shorts. "I see a tree over there with your name on it. Let me make it up to you with some alfresco loving."

"Not in front of the cats," I joke. "They'll never recover." When I say that, I'm not entirely sure if I'm referring to the cats or my own fragile heart.

CHAPTER 29

MARIE

I've barely rounded the corner when I need to pull over on the side of the road because I'm crying too hard to drive—because I'm driving away from Olivia.

I find my gaze in the rear-view mirror. "Pull yourself together, for heaven's sake." I bang my hand on the steering wheel. Damn it. This was not supposed to be this hard. A surprisingly large part of me wants to turn around and head back to Olivia's house, leap out of the car dramatically and run into her waiting, open arms. This is ridiculous.

"You are Marie Dievart," I say to my reflection, as though that means anything at all. Out here, it didn't mean a single thing, which was exactly what I needed to put myself together again.

I put the car back in gear and drive through my tears. I can't go back to Bonneau. I need to go home. I need to put distance between Olivia and me, and hope it's enough. Because that strange, unbendable woman has gotten under my skin much more than I'd like to admit. I need to focus on other things now. I can no longer afford to have my spirit scooped up in an idyllic countryside love affair.

My foot is heavy on the accelerator and I'm probably breaking the speed limit but I don't care. Suddenly, I can't get out of here fast enough. This transition from the version of myself I was in Bonneau and the one I intend to be back in Brussels can't happen fast enough, but it's a long drive and it's just me in the car—me and my thoughts.

I was different out here. There was no one to impress, no one to fool, except Olivia, who wasn't easily fooled, although I did get through to her in another way—oh yes, I did. But her having feelings for me doesn't change anything. This is still my life. I might have taken a break from it for a while—like she claimed to have taken a holiday for her heart when we first met—but I have to go back. I don't have the kind of job that allows me to hide myself away in the middle of nowhere, nor would I want that. Rationally, I should be able to get past all of this very quickly. It's normal that it's difficult at the moment. Because I'm not only driving away from Olivia. I'm driving away from an entirely different kind of life, free of stress, free of obligation, with every day wide open for me to do with it as I pleased.

A lot of those days I actively chose to do nothing at all. I honestly didn't think I had it in me, but there you go. Sometimes you need to take a break from your life to see what else you're capable of. I was able to live a much simpler life for a while. It was great to take the pressure off for those months. To just *be*. To sit in the garden and giggle at Huppert's silly antics and cook a leisurely dinner and not have to be *on* all the time. But that's over now. The day after tomorrow, I go back to what it is I do—healing people. I won't be scrubbing in on the first day back, unless there's an emergency, but I will be soon. I glance at my hands on the steering wheel and it's as though I somehow know for certain they won't betray me any longer. They will be steady when I next hold a scalpel. They will be ready. I will feel like myself again.

I take a few deep breaths. There is a lot to look forward to as well, aside from work. Time with my family. Catching up with friends. Walking into my apartment. Breakfast in the sun on the Flagey Square, surrounded by a myriad of different people. Cinema. Opera. The Museum of Fine Arts. A smile forms on my lips at the prospect. I didn't run from my life because it was so horrible. I ran because of something very specific that happened and that I needed to digest. I've taken plenty of time.

Then there's the other thing—what I told Olivia was my hobby. The thrill of the chase. How a woman I'm pursuing lets me know she's up for it with a particular hint of a smile. Knowing that it's done. That I'm in. Strangely, the prospect of that doesn't fill me with the same glee as it used to. But I will only know how I truly feel about it the first time I go out, probably after a long day of surgery when I'm too mentally stimulated to go home. Or maybe there will be new staff at the hospital to get to know better. No. I shake off the thought. I don't want a repeat of what happened with Véronique.

When I stop to fill up the car and get something to eat, I see a sign for Brittany and I wonder what Olivia's doing right now. Is she thinking of me? The prospect that she might spreads a small wave of warmth throughout my flesh. Then I'm back on my way and the drive is long but there's something cathartic about it, like I need the hours it takes to get from one place to the other to get closer to the me I was before I left—the best parts of me, not the broken ones. As I approach Brussels, and traffic gets a whole lot denser, I'm cocky enough to conclude that I've left the broken pieces of myself in the wide open fields of Bonneau, to be picked up and scattered about by the fierce Breton wind.

Unlocking the door to my penthouse apartment overlooking the Ixelles Ponds is a vastly different experience to arriving in cold, unwelcome Bonneau five months ago. Even though I haven't been here for a long time, instantly, I'm hit with the vibe of home. My cleaner has taken care of my plants—as she always does—and stocked the fridge and made sure everything is spic and span. I walk to the floor-to-ceiling windows and bask in the light that streams in. In the pond across the street a mother duck and her ducklings float by and the moment couldn't be more perfect.

I congratulate myself on another good decision made, although it wasn't an easy one at the time. But going away for a while has reinvigorated me. I wish I was going back to work tomorrow, that's how great I suddenly feel. How right with the world. How self-assured about who I am and what I'm meant to do.

The biggest difference with who I was before my sabbatical is that I don't immediately make plans to go out. The drive back was long and tiring and I kick off my shoes, open a bottle of wine, and sit with myself for a bit. I can do that now. My brain no longer plays tricks on me when I unwind. I vow there and then to take time for myself like this on a daily basis, to carry a tiny bit of the essence of my time in Bonneau with me every day and just let the world go by for half an hour or so. Then I grab my phone and instead of texting Olivia that I've arrived safe and sound—now that I've crossed the border into another country, I feel like keeping my distance is the only right thing to do—I order something for dinner, just because I can.

JUNE

CHAPTER 30

OLIVIA

This summer is not going as planned. It's already halfway through June and I'm still gloomy like it's the middle of winter. When I work on my current translation, the words don't come. It doesn't help that the book's about two women falling in love. Branching out into lesbian romance was a grave error in judgment on my part. When I play the piano, the notes don't come to me the way they used to and I find myself trying to play pop songs just to occupy myself, but a lot of the easy joy I experienced when I used to sit and just play, just go with the flow, just listen for the next note, has escaped me as well.

To my surprise, the biggest joy I find is in running outside first thing in the morning. I always go by the Dievart house and I always look for a glimmer of life, a sign that someone might be there. But the house is empty and Marie's still gone.

Most nights I'm in front of my laptop, trying to decide when to book a train ticket to Brussels before the usual doubts set in. Marie has barely been in touch. We've exchanged only a few text messages. I wonder why she hasn't called, like she said she would. If she had, I would have picked up after the first ring. I haven't gone as far as to call her. I know what I am—what I *was*—to her. A momentary distraction. A bit of fun while she took a break from her life. With every day that passes, I try to live with that a little more and I can perhaps accept it a little more as well.

There won't be any grand romantic gestures, not from me—I'm not the type—and most certainly not from her. It's over and, in a way, that's fine. It's how it was always going to be, but the interim period between her leaving and me returning fully to my former self is frustrating because I miss her so damn much.

The other thing that has been working for me is writing new poems. Whenever I sit, they just flow out of me as though my pen has a direct connection to the pain inside me. But these are not the kind of poems I want to post to my Instagram account. This is the kind of poetry, if you even want to call it that, that I should only ever keep to myself, because the sentiments are foolish and the sentences too dramatic. But writing them does help. So I just write and put them in a folder I may never open again. I keep it all to myself, the way I'm used to, safe in the knowledge that doing so will, hopefully some day soon, help me forget about the previous five months.

Meanwhile, I'm engaged in the kind of email corre-spondence with Sandrine that can only be described as vigorous. Every day, we send long messages back and forth, and a lot of it is rehashing the past, which doesn't bother me as much as I thought it would. A big part of her emails is trying to convince me to let her publish this one poem of mine, "The Rain", she apparently can't let go of. She needs to print it in her precious collection. I'm about to say yes because she has made it very clear that having one poem in one collection isn't going to upend my life in any way. Signing a contract for one single poem to be published doesn't come with any obligations nor expectations and can I just be happy and proud about it already? She has a point, of course. That was always the thing with Sandrine, whenever we fought about how I was and how I behaved, she always had a point, which made it extra hard for me to bear.

I've just pressed send on my email saying yes to Sandrine when my phone chimes with a message. If I believed in that sort of nonsense, I would claim it was the universe giving something back to me for putting myself out there, because it's a message from Marie.

I'm impatiently waiting for your next Insta poem. Huppert is very cute, but just pictures of her aren't cutting it. ;-)

It's true that Huppert has been overly featured on my Instagram account, what with me not having written anything I want to share with the virtual world. Then I read the message again, trying to unearth a deeper meaning behind it. I'm well aware I wasted a lot of the time she was here not getting to know her. Once I let her in, there was barely time to scratch the surface of what she was really like, so it's hard to tell if she means anything else with what she's written. Maybe she just wants another poem. Maybe I should be glad she still follows my Instagram—that she hasn't become so busy as to forego all social media. I reply.

I've not written anything fit for publication.

I quickly follow up with:

How are you?

I can see the three dots indicating that she's typing, but it takes a while for her reply to come through. I take my phone outside and sit in my rocking chair overlooking the garden.

So busy my head feels like it might explode most days. It's been a tougher adjustment than anticipated, but it's good to be back. You? P.S. You're not getting off the hook re. a new poem that easily!

I just agreed to have that poem published by Sandrine.

It's not pride I feel when I send that last message, it's more a satisfied notion of having pleased Marie, because she urged me to go for it. But what am I still doing trying to please her? I stop myself from asking if she's picked up her old *hobby* again—I don't want to know the answer. I stare at the three dots again for a while. The longer it takes for her response to come through, the more furiously my heart starts racing. Maybe her fingers are tired from being a surgeon all day.

Since you're in a yes kind of mood, shall we pick a date for you to come to Brussels?

I don't think my heart can go any faster. My fingers are too excited to type anything coherent back so I do something that's wholly out of character for me, yet, right now, feels like the only right thing to do. I call Marie and my heart leaps all the way into my throat when she answers.

"Hey." I don't remember her voice being this sultry.

"Hi. I—" That's the thing with phone calls. You need to know what to say because silences without body language are unbearable. "Yes, I would like to set that date." I hop out of my chair and go inside so I can look at the train schedule on my computer.

"Wow." Marie chuckles. "Such enthusiasm. I wasn't really sure what to expect from you."

I've missed you so much, I want to scream into my phone. I'll book the ticket for this weekend. But I don't say that out loud, of course.

"I'm looking at the train schedule." I sit in front of my laptop, the French railways website open on my screen. "When are you free?"

"I've been very bad at taking weekends off. You coming here would be a perfect excuse. Let me have a look." I enjoy the simple sound of her breathing as she checks her calendar. "How about the second weekend of July?"

My heart sinks. That's more than three weeks from now. But beggars can't be choosers. Bloody hell. I'm going to need to give myself a stern talking-to. One minute on the phone with her and I feel like a lovesick teenager already. Maybe I need those three weeks to gather myself.

"Liv?"

"Em, yes. Just checking the available tickets." I search for the dates. "Would that be from Friday to Sunday?"

"Unless you want to stay longer." Is that a hint of hope in her voice? Surely not. I'm just projecting. "We have woods here too, you know, if you need some nature to tide you over."

"I can't leave the cats for too long," I say sheepishly. They'll be well taken care of by the woman who looked after them when we were in Paris, but they'll miss me. *Get a grip. The cats will be fine because they're cats. This is your chance to spend some time with Marie.* "Although I guess I can tack on an extra day."

"Do it, Liv. Why the hell not?"

Why the hell not, indeed. This thought is also very unlike me, but all my protective, controlling instincts are overridden by my desire to spend time with her.

"Okay. Just a minute." I select the new dates on the website. "You're absolutely sure?"

"Positive. Over the moon you're so willing. This is Olivia Chevalier I'm talking to, right? Notorious recluse and avoider of people?"

"Very funny." I make my purchase. "There. It's done."

"That's really great. I look forward to it already."

"Will, um, we be in touch before then?"

"Yes," Marie says on a sigh. "I'm sorry I haven't called you, but it's just been so crazy. Going back to work was a real shock to my system after having been out of rotation for so long. I'm still adjusting, to be honest. I need much more sleep than before, for instance, and I haven't been out nearly as much just because I'm so exhausted all the time."

"It's only normal. Your body was running on a very different kind of clock out here."

"Yeah." The kind of sigh she utters isn't one I associate with her.

"But you're coping? You're not overdoing it?"

"I'm most certainly overdoing it because there's no other way to do this job. It's more an issue of getting used to the insane pace of it again. And taking enough time to recover in between. I've had to make changes."

"You're not in your twenties anymore," I hear myself say, sounding like my mother. "I'm sorry. I shouldn't have said that."

"It's good to hear your voice, no matter what you say," Marie replies.

"You too."

"Write me a bloody poem already."

I've written you so many, but you will never know. "I'll see what I can do."

"Give the cats a hug from me."

"Huppert still goes over to your house sometimes, hoping that you'll be back."

"My sister and her family are going to the house in a few weeks. Maybe she'll take a shine to them."

Fat chance of that, I think, once again projecting my own feelings onto my cat.

We chit-chat for a bit longer and it's lovely, and maybe even a touch more romantic than I thought possible, and when we ring off, I'm left with a return ticket to Brussels and three weeks of not knowing what to do with myself.

CHAPTER 31
MARIE

"Remember that woman you met when you visited me in Bonneau?" I say to my sister.

"The one who talked our ear off?" Madeleine smirks.

"Olivia." I've seen my sister a few times since I got back, but this is the first time I'm addressing the topic of Olivia.

"What about her?"

"I've invited her to stay with me for a long weekend."

Madeleine quirks up her perfectly sculpted eyebrows, but she doesn't say anything. Why would she? She doesn't know what Olivia means to me. To her, Liv is this weird woman she saw walking around our neighbourhood in Bonneau. How easily Olivia could have just been that to me as well.

"I grew kind of fond of her while I was out there."

Madeleine slants her head. "Meaning that you continued to sleep with her?"

I nod, although I can't go into detail about that. I can't tell my sister how Olivia made me feel alive again, like I could do anything, but also how, when she looked me in the eye when she slipped her fingers inside me, she could make the entire outside world disappear, because she let me into the tiny universe she'd created for herself and, for a while, that was enough for me as well.

"Wait." Madeleine narrows her eyes. "Is there more going on here?"

"I don't think so, but I don't really know."

Madeleine huffs out some air. "In that case, how is it a good idea for her to come here? Shouldn't you be focusing on other things?"

Work. My career. My high-end life in my luxury apartment with the best view. I've tried keeping the promise I made to myself when I just got back from Bonneau to take a few minutes to myself every day—half an hour is simply too long—and just sit and remember what I was like in Brittany. The last time I sat in my chair overlooking the pond, I couldn't take it anymore and I ended up texting Olivia.

"I'm fifty-six years old," I say matter-of-factly.

"Yet you don't look a day over forty-five, thanks to my unrivalled Botox-injecting skills."

I ignore my sister, whereas before, her making a remark like that would have been cause for an age-inappropriate bout of giggles—no matter how much Botox has been injected into our skin. "I've, um, met a lot of women in my life." *A lot.* "But with Olivia, everything was different. I know it was because of the circumstances and our surroundings as much as anything else, but it wasn't only that." Most days, I wish it was. That I could just forget about my time in Bonneau, but it has proven impossible, no matter how buried in work I am. No matter how much I enjoy being a surgeon again, no matter how satisfyingly exhausted I am when I fall into bed at night, there's a part of me that wishes she was in bed with me, every single night.

"You've only been back a few weeks."

What's with Madeleine, anyway? It's like she's totally against the mere notion of Olivia, even though she barely met her. "I know she didn't make a very good first impression on you." Making a good first impression isn't part of Olivia's skill set, although it's become harder for me to remember the grumpy woman I met that day when I knocked on her back door. "But she is a kind, smart, talented woman."

"That may be so, Marie, but…" Madeleine narrows her eyes further. "What am I missing here? Are you trying to tell me something?" She slants towards me as though that would give her a better understanding of me. "Are you in love with this woman?"

In love? "God, no. As I said, I'm very fond of her. She may appear unlikeable at first blush, but she's the exact opposite." An inadvertent smile tugs at my lips. "But no, I really wouldn't say I was in love with her. I'm a Dievart, I don't fall in love that easily."

"That has nothing to do with being a Dievart." Madeleine hooks her finger into her wedding ring, which she wears on a chain around her neck because it's easier with all the scrubbing in for surgery that she does. "Several times over the years, I've believed you to be incapable of falling in love. Believe me, I've racked my brain over this. By all means, you are a catch, yet you've always been single. And so… promiscuous." Madeleine makes a tsk-ing sound as though this is now suddenly frowned upon by her, whereas this is not something we usually talk about. She goes about her life; I go about mine. She's married with a child; I'm single. That's how it's been for the past few decades. "I figured it had something to do with you working in such a male-dominated field and wanting to be one of the boys, but the brain and its workings are far from my speciality, so I don't really know why you are the way you are."

"Neither do I." I could take offence at what my sister's said, but I choose not to because my stay in Bonneau has allowed me to go deeply inward and every time I allowed my thoughts to drift to all the women I've hurt, it wasn't pretty. I've been rude and heartless and, most of all, utterly selfish. "I've just always accepted that's the way I am. I never really questioned myself. Never really looked back, only forward. There was always another woman waiting for me on that road ahead." I shrug, as though this is the most self-evident claim in the world. "I never really had to try very hard, you know." Except with Olivia. She made me work for it and she made me wait for it. She came to me eventually, but only on her own terms.

Madeleine chuckles. "So I've heard."

"I'm not sure I want to be that person anymore. In fact, I'm not sure I *can* be that person any longer."

"Because of this woman?"

I shake my head. "No, because of the much-needed introspection I did in Brittany. I stayed there two months longer than planned because if I had come back in April, I believe I would have just reverted to my old patterns. I already knew that's not what I wanted, but I needed more time to let that thought consolidate." What a two months they were. Especially the last three weeks, when Olivia, finally, let me in, and a version of myself was revealed that I never knew existed—a version I also grew quite fond of. "But, yes," I correct myself. "Also because of her."

"So, her coming here is what? Something exploratory? Would she move here for you?"

The thought of Olivia moving to Brussels is so preposterous that I burst into laughter. "No, nothing like that. We parted as friends. I'm not going to get sucked into some sort of long-distance thing. I don't have the time nor the energy for that."

"Yet, you invited her here. Why?"

"Because I want to see her. I want to spend some more time with her."

"Before you say your final goodbye?" Madeleine has always been very good at playing devil's advocate.

"I don't know."

"What about her? How does she feel about you?"

I will never forget Olivia admitting that she was in love with me—'stupidly and foolishly' were her exact words.

"Well, you know me," I joke. "I'm easy to love."

"The hell you are." Madeleine sends me a cheeky smile.

"She was much keener to come than I thought she would be."

"Let me put it this way, then." Madeleine leans back in her chair and pins her gaze on me. "Are you going to properly introduce her to the family when she's here?"

Again, a prospect so ridiculous, it elicits nothing more than a snigger. "No, she would hate that, and I want her to have a good time."

"Sounds like you're giving me no choice but to go and say hello to her when I'm in Bonneau in July."

"Sounds to me like you have plenty of other choices."

"We'll see," Madeleine says and gives me another look I can't decipher—maybe she's noticed something in my expression when I talk about Olivia that isn't there when I look in the mirror. Or, knowing my sister, she's probably evaluating when I should visit her for my next round of Botox.

After Madeleine has left, I scan the bar like I used to do, for possible prey. I always believed my biggest talent, outside of work, lay in being able to find someone to deploy my charms on in the most unlikely of places. This bar has a clientele of all ages with a pretty even mix of males and females. It takes a finely tuned gaydar to pick up any signals in a place like this, but I've learned from decades of experience that there's always one who will return my look with a lingering stare.

People are curious by nature, and they want to know why someone like me would look them in the eye like that. Sometimes, they might just inquire whether they know me from somewhere. It has even happened that I've met them before in a professional capacity—I meet a lot of people in my job of whom I can't possibly remember all the faces. Most of the time, they're more than happy to play my game, if only for a little while. Just to see how it fits them. How they'll react to a woman like me hitting on them. And, oh, the thrill of adjusting my strategy as I go along, according to the type of woman I've set my sights on. Of playing this game that I've played for so long, it's like second nature. It's what I do—as opposed to all the things Olivia so easily claims she doesn't do. *Damn it.* Olivia's the last person I should be thinking about when I'm out and about—when I'm on the prowl.

There's a woman with a group of friends who reminds me of Véronique. I'm momentarily tempted but decide pretty quickly I don't want to go there. Ah. There we are. A woman alone at a table is already giving me the eye—I didn't even have to try. Late thirties, probably. Short black hair. Big brown eyes. Why not? I wait to see if she's joined by friends any time soon, but she sits there, on her own, perfectly pleased with herself, occasionally sending a glance in my direction. Sometimes, it's just too easy. Sometimes—and I know how this sounds—I just have to show up and bat my lashes a few times.

With a confident smile on my lips, I walk over to her table, ready to buy her a drink and see where it goes. She's smiling back. All I have to do is pull back the chair to make my intentions known. Instead, I find myself walking right past her table, and out of the bar. As though my legs wanted different things for me tonight and they had to take charge, dismiss my foolish notions. All I was after was some innocent flirting, some chit-chat back and forth. I blame discussing Olivia with my sister. I can try to push her from my mind all I want, but that doesn't mean her memory's not still inside me.

I start walking home. I'm not unhappy with how my evening ended—on the contrary. I slip my phone out of my pocket and call Olivia in faraway Bonneau.

JULY

CHAPTER 32
OLIVIA

When I arrive at the station in Brussels, I need to get my bearings. I had hoped Marie would pick me up, as was the plan all along, but she texted that it would be a great help to her if I could make my way to her place on my own. Friday late-afternoon traffic in Brussels is insane and her last operation took longer than expected. Just take an Uber, she said in her text, as though that's all I ever do in Bonneau—as though that even exists there.

I need to find a quiet corner to take a few deep breaths as I'm reminded why I'm not a city person. Simply too much of everything. I really should ask Marie how anyone's brain is able to process so much noise and information all at the same time. I head outside and spot a taxi rank. The line is long but that will give me time to adjust to this madness. At least the weather's sunny and, once I make it in and out of a taxi, Marie will be waiting for me. It's been seven weeks since I've seen her. It feels more like seven months—if it hadn't, I doubt I'd be here, putting myself through this.

A normal Friday evening in summer consists of me sitting outside in my rocking chair, listening to the gentle rustle of the wind in the leaves, with at least one of my cats in my lap. Maybe a glass of cold wine nearby. Working on a poem, perhaps. The mere thought of it right now sounds like utter bliss, like what I should be doing instead of subjecting myself to this relentless rush of overstimulation.

Once I'm in the taxi, I just mumble the address to the driver so as not to have to make conversation. I look outside and I'm astounded by how busy it is—at first sight, it's definitely on par with Paris. Traffic remains constant, but the streets become broader, and the houses grander as I approach Marie's place. It's clear she lives in the upscale part of the city, just as I had expected.

The taxi stops in front of a five-floor apartment block across the street from a large pond. My heart races as I pay the driver and get out. I'm drawn to the water, to the sense of respite it offers from the frenzy of the city, but I want to get inside that building even more. Although I'm not quite sure why, just as I'm not quite sure what I'm doing here—although I also know I'm fooling myself.

I'm still in love with her. I haven't been able to shake Marie's presence, despite her having left seven weeks ago. I still think of her all the time. I dream of her heavy-lidded green eyes, her high cheek bones, her slim surgeon's fingers. Deep down, I know that's the only reason I'm here, but because Marie doesn't exactly feel the same way, I need to at least pretend, also to myself, that I'm here just as a friend.

I've hardly rung the bell before I'm buzzed in. I take the lift to the top floor, fearing I might not make it there alive because my heart keeps pounding against my chest.

But then the lift dings and the doors slide open and there she is. Her smile is as wide as her arms. I hurry out of the lift and step into her embrace.

"There you are," she says, and curls her arms around me, pressing her body against mine in a way that makes me wonder if this is how friends usually greet each other —something I don't have much experience with either. "I'm so sorry I couldn't pick you up from the station." She seems reluctant to let go of me—I feel the same way about her. She smells different here, but her body pressed against mine feels the same—like it should stay in place for a long time, until my most acute need for physical contact has been met. "Come inside." She finally lets go and pulls me inside an apartment that is so bright, I blink my eyes a few times to adjust to the light.

"Bloody hell," I stammer. I'm instantly drawn to the floor-to-ceiling windows overlooking the pond I saw earlier.

"You're not the first person to like the sight of those ducks more than the sight of me." Marie has sidled up beside me.

"It's a little… overwhelming. That's all." I give Marie my full attention. "It's gorgeous." Those last words I speak looking her straight in the eye—something Marie will most certainly not misinterpret.

"Thanks." She slants her head. "It's so good to see you." She reaches for my hand and takes it in hers. "How was your trip?"

We make some small talk about my train journey and her work schedule and all the while she's holding on to my hand as though she has no intention of letting go of it any time soon—and I don't know what to think.

"I've planned wisely," she says after we've sat by the

window with a gin and tonic. "I haven't over-scheduled. Tonight, we'll have dinner here, so you can relax after your journey. You can take a shower while I prepare you a small feast. Get acquainted with the place. Do a bit of unpacking."

I could kiss her just for saying that. Even though I haven't been to a restaurant since we were in Paris together, I can't bear the thought of having a meal surrounded by a bunch of strangers—and Marie's a wonderful cook.

"I've missed your cooking."

"On to the summer rotation of weekly dishes for you?" It doesn't sound as though she's mocking me. It sounds more like she's stating a fact about me that she has come to accept. "Tomorrow, we can sleep in…" She stretches her neck. "I look forward to that a lot myself."

I look forward to finding out the sleeping arrangements. The single backpack I brought is still standing by the door.

"Then we can go for a gander through my neighbourhood. Maybe have brunch on the square if the weather's nice. There's a market much like the one in Bonneau. Let's see how the mood takes us."

"How about a tour of this place first?" I look her in the eye—I simply can't look away. "I can't imagine seeing anything swankier than this all weekend."

"You'd be very much correct." She takes a sip, then gets up and takes me to the open kitchen. It's all glistening marble and fancy appliances—everything of an even higher spec than the house in Brittany. Then she leads me into the hallway and shows me her bedroom, which is vast and boasts the same floor-to-ceiling windows as the living room, catching all the light. Because her apartment's on the top floor and there aren't any taller buildings around, it's as though we're towering over our surroundings.

"The guest room's at the end of the hallway," she says and then I just need to know because not knowing is no longer an option and I'm not someone who can play things cool.

"Is that where I'll be sleeping?"

Marie sinks her teeth into her bottom lip briefly. "I don't know, Liv." She reaches for my hand again. "I have this urge to touch you. I'm not sure I can bear the thought of you sleeping in the other room."

Still as forward as ever, then.

"But I don't want to presume anything. I—" She pulls me closer. "We're not together. I don't know what we are. But we aren't just friends, are we?"

She's asking me? I need to shower. I need to process. I need to find some sort of control in this unfamiliar situation, yet all I really want to do is walk her into that room and push her onto the bed. But we haven't even kissed.

Last time we saw each other in the flesh, I confessed my feelings to her and she wasn't exactly forthright about them being mutual, and if there's one thing I know about her for sure, it's that she wouldn't deliberately hide her feelings for me. On the other hand, the other thing we did when we were together, is exactly what I want to do now.

"The last thing we are is just friends," I say.

"I've been so busy," Marie says. "It's been rather convenient in a way, because I hardly had the time to think about you, but now that you're here…" She walks back into her bedroom, taking me with her. "The way I feel is not something I can ignore any longer."

"W—what do you feel?" My heart hasn't had a break

from its restless, reckless hammering since I got out of that taxi.

"I want you so much." Her voice has lowered into a throaty whisper. "I want you right now."

It's a start, I guess, and certainly a feeling that's entirely mutual. Maybe it's just physical for her—from what she's told me about her history with women, it's plausible. For me, it's much more than physical. It always has been, even when I didn't know it yet, although I should have because 'just physical' doesn't exist in my world. But I'm here and I'm not going to ruin this moment by demanding more of her than she can give. Even if this is all I will ever get—her eyes full of lust and her voice ragged with desire—I will gladly take it. I'll deal with whatever pain comes next later.

"You have me," I whisper back, because some things are too much to say in full voice.

She looks into my eyes and my knees buckle. At first, I didn't even dare dream of a moment like this, because I know dreams are not always harmless—I know how they can spiral into unbridled fantasies and take over your thoughts; how they can border on illusions. But as time progressed, of course I fantasised about Marie looking at me the way she does now, as though there's only one other person who exists in her universe: me.

We stand facing each other for a silent moment, our lips close enough to drive me crazy, the anticipation of our first reunion kiss hanging heavy in the air. We just stare at each other and I know what I see. A woman with whom it was impossible not to fall in love from the beginning—the woman I'm in love with. What does she see when she looks at me? It's impossible to know and now is not the time to ask, but I vow, there and then, as I lose myself in her gaze a little more by the second, to find out the answer before I go home. I need to know. Feelings like these are not ones I subject myself to easily—not that I always have a choice. But I let her in, knowing full well—fearing it, at times—that I am in love with her, and all that entails. She doesn't owe me anything and she's always been honest and direct, yet she will need to tell me.

"I should take a shower," I say. I need to wash the journey off me, but my feet are nailed to the ground. My body won't go anywhere she isn't. This is why I didn't want to come to Brussels. This is why I so fiercely kept my distance those first few months. So I could remain the person I am, someone who can operate independently from everyone else instead of pining for another human the way that I've been doing—the way I did so ridiculously, so weakly, after Sandrine left me.

The promise I made after I put myself together again, after I made myself strong again, to never let that happen again, went out of the window the moment Marie Dievart turned up. There's no defence against infatuation multiplied with hot sex and the kind of attention Marie bestowed on me in Brittany, and now here. All the walls I've hidden behind for years started crumbling when I first looked into her eyes.

"We can shower later," she says, before closing the distance between our lips. She waits another beat before pressing her lips to mine, but when she does, when her mouth touches mine, I'm reminded once again that, when it comes to her, I'm a lost cause. And I'm willing to be, just to share these brief moments with her, to have this long weekend with her. To have her kiss me like this.

Her hands slide to the back of my head, pulling me closer as our tongues meet. I let it all fall off me. The weeks of anticipation. The built-up stress from the journey. All the things I don't know and might never know about her and what we are together, or what we are not. All the things I can't control when I give myself up to another person. I let it all go so I can open myself up to her all the way, so I can feel it all. The impossible smoothness of her skin. The strong grasp of her fingers. How she groans in the back of her throat like she's already overcome with lust.

My hands drift underneath her blouse, wanting to feel more of her. She lifts up her arms and I hoist her blouse all the way over her head. Her bra is black and very much in the way. I need to see her breasts. I've missed the feel of them in my hands. I've missed putting my head against them first thing in the morning. I've missed her arms around me.

Marie starts unbuttoning my shirt and I give her a hand by pulling it over my head. We dispose of most of our clothes in a frenzy of tugs and groans until I'm only wearing my knickers. Instead of falling onto the bed, Marie walks me to the door, closes it behind us, and pushes me against it. She can do whatever she wants to me tonight. I'm all hers. No conditions. No reservations.

Her thumb stroking my neck, she leans towards me and takes my nipple in her mouth. She might as well just have swept her tongue over my clit, that's how my body reacts. To her. To this. To us together. She flicks her tongue against my nipple and slides her other hand between my legs, cupping me softly over my underwear. All I want right now is concentrated in my aching clit. I want her so badly, I reach for the hand she's been stroking my neck with and suck her fingers into my mouth. I'm of half a mind to press her other hand harder between my legs, but I use my last smidgen of restraint to let her control me a little. I know she gets off on it. She gets off on many things, I have learned, not all of which I've always agreed to, but this is easy to accept.

She skates a fingertip over the panel of my knickers and I lose my mind with every millimetre her finger moves.

"Please." This is unbearable. If I'm going to be consumed with desire like this, it can't go on for too long. I may never find myself again in the mess she might leave me in. And by god, do I need some sort of release. After all the lonely nights without her, with nothing but her memory keeping me company. To finally feel her against me is much more than a dream come true. For a moment, she can erase all the conflicts in my mind. She can dissolve all the tension I carry with me day in and day out. It's not just an orgasm I crave, it's so much more than that.

It's a short reprieve from the rigidity of being myself. It's the sensation of fusing a part of myself with her. Because I know that I always want too much in situations like this without being able to give enough in return— that's what I've been told, at least—except in moments when this is happening. When my personality doesn't matter. When it's two bodies meeting and I can get over myself enough to experience climax after climax. I might be terrible at everything else a relationship requires, but at least I have this.

Marie drags her lips along my neck but instead of kissing me again, she looks at me. Her fingertips are in my mouth. My heart is in my throat.

She slips her hand inside my underwear ever so slowly, her fingers inching towards my clit at a glacial pace. All the while, she looks into my eyes, her gaze green and soft, and fuck, I love her so much, because there's so much to love, so much to admire, so much greatness to be around. I know it's because in most ways she's the polar opposite of me and I've always been attracted to that, although I'm also convinced it doesn't necessarily make for a great partnership. None of that matters as her fingertip finally touches down. It slides lower, into my wetness, before scooting back up to circle my clit.

Through the sudden haze of my pleasure, I can see how Marie swallows hard, and the fact that she does, that this might mean something to her as well—the mere fact that I'm even here with her—undoes me more than any touch of her finger ever can.

What would make me come the hardest is if she told me that she was in love with me too, that she'd missed me every single day since she arrived back in Brussels the way that I've missed her. Maybe it's a dangerous game to play, but I imagine her saying it. I imagine her exquisite lips forming the words: *I'm so in love with you, Liv.* Her voice is soft and firm at the same time, because the sentiment is so strong it bears no contesting. Even though I'm just pretending, it is Marie's finger dancing around my clit, applying the most divine pressure, and it's her fingers inside my mouth, and it's her eyes on me, so I come just as hard as if she did really love me.

CHAPTER 33
MARIE

B y the time I wake on Sunday morning, we've barely made it out of my apartment, despite the lovely summer weather. But Olivia seems insatiable, her appetite for me renewed with every orgasm we reach, as though she literally needs to take as much of me as she can get while she's here, and going out would only take away from her time to accomplish that goal. I'm pretty sure that if I asked her, she would tell me something like this. Her brain may work in ways that are mysterious even to me, but I know that much about her. Besides, as she said last night before we fell asleep satiated but exhausted, she didn't come to Brussels for Brussels, she came for the one and only Marie Dievart. It was hard to pretend I wasn't flattered by that, so I didn't.

Having her here has been a throwback to my time in Brittany more than anything, because that's what she represents to me. My time in Bonneau was far from carefree, I had too much stuff to work through while I was there, but Olivia was the ultimate distraction from all of that. She is now as well. When I'm with her, I'm no longer a womanising surgeon—although I haven't practiced my hobby at all since I came home. At first, I believed I had outgrown it, as a person on a long and winding road to self-improvement, but now I'm beginning to think I enjoy sleeping with Olivia, with someone who thinks the world of me and sees me in a different way than everyone else, so much, I can't be bothered with the thrill of the chase any longer.

I roll onto my side and watch her sleeping. She looks so peaceful, so unlike she ever does while she's awake, when she's always worried about something or other. I wish I could root around her brain and fix the area that causes her this constant panic and concern. I wish I could give her more hours when she's the chill version of herself —the version she can be with me.

Her hair is longer than when I last saw her—she's not one for a monthly hairdresser's appointment. Her skin is uncharacteristically smooth for someone her age. It must be all that countryside air and stress-free living she pursues.

I let my fingertips drift along her belly but soon I'm compelled to flatten my hand against the warmth of her skin. Who knew it could be this pleasant to wake up next to another woman? To see them slowly emerge from slumber, stretch their limbs, come back to life.

But Olivia clearly isn't ready to wake up. She's been on her own for the past few weeks. All this conversation—and all this sex—must have worn her out. She doesn't budge when I press myself against her and pull her close. It gives me time to think about what this is. I'm not used to thinking about something like that. The only other time I had to take my feelings into consideration was with Véronique and that never really had the chance to blossom into anything more than a casual fling, despite my growing affection for her. I made sure of that by running away.

Olivia's leaving tomorrow. I'm of half a mind to ask her to stay longer, now that she's here already anyway. I don't think it would be that hard to persuade her—clearly, she still has feelings for me. But I don't want to imply too much and asking her to stay is impossible without also saying something else. Would that be so bad, though? I shake off the thought—something else I'm very skilled at —and kiss her shoulder. She can sleep when she's in Bonneau. Right now, I need her awake and alert, also because then I don't have to pay attention to all these irrational thoughts running through my head.

"You have no mercy." Her voice is croaky, almost hoarse. "I need about double the amount of sleep that you do." She turns on her side, her breasts against mine, and slings her arm along my waist.

"Not this weekend, you don't." I kiss her on the lips. That should wake her up.

"It's Sunday." She closes her eyes again. Maybe she really does need more sleep, despite her easy access to me.

"I'm going to get up. I'll get us some breakfast. You sleep some more."

Olivia just gives a limp nod, then rolls onto her back. Hard as it is to drag myself away from her, I give her the time and space she needs, take a long, hot shower, and head out to the Sunday morning market on the square. Farmers' markets might be all the rage across the Western world these days, but this market has been here for decades. It's properly old school and there's nothing hip or happening about the vendors. Most of them are typical *Bruxellois* and shout at you in both Flemish and French or, even better, the irresistible blend of both that is the local dialect.

I don't buy ingredients for lunch or dinner because I want to take Olivia out. I want her to see my neighbourhood, to inhale the scent of this place, to experience first-hand why I enjoy living here so much. It's a perfect day for it because the sun is out in all its glory, putting everyone in a good mood.

When I approach the bakery stall, I do a double take because one of the people queuing is the spitting image of Véronique. When I see her from up close, I realise it's not her, just a vague lookalike, but it takes my heart a few minutes to find a calmer rhythm again.

I place my order and engage in some banter with the vendor, while, in the back of my mind, I wonder what I would say to Véronique if I bumped into her. Brussels might be a metropolitan city, but it can feel more like a village sometimes—although Olivia would surely argue against that, even though she's barely set foot outside my apartment since she arrived.

When I started back at the hospital last month, Véronique no longer worked in the operating theatre. I inquired about her but all anyone could tell me was that she'd quit. Nurses are in high demand so I'm sure she easily found a job elsewhere. Maybe it's even typical of my vanity to wonder if she switched workplaces because of me. There could be a million other reasons for her to change jobs.

I walk home slowly beside the pond, enjoying the

sunshine on my skin. A jogger rushes past me, making me think of Olivia. Did she pack her running gear? It would bring me great joy to see her running around the pond— now that she has taken to jogging in the great outdoors— from my living room window. I don't know why. Maybe because she'd be in her element and I like to see her in her element. As I approach my building, it's a comforting thought to have her waiting for me upstairs, to have her here with me. Maybe I *will* ask her to stay longer. She can work anywhere, although I'm fairly certain she has a bunch of arguments against that as well. She has one for every last little thing. But I happen to have a counterargument for most. And she does seem to listen to me, although not always. I'm still waiting for a new poem, but I'm pleased she has let her ex acquire the rights to one of her old ones. It's give and take with Olivia. She isn't entirely unwilling to listen to some good old common sense.

To my surprise, she's up and dressed by the time I make it back.

"Oh, no, you're wearing clothes." I pout.

"You keep telling me that no one can see me through those windows, but I'm not sure I believe you."

"You've seen me walk around naked all over this place," I counter.

"Yes, well, you might very well get off on that," she says matter-of-factly. "What with some of the things you enjoy in bed."

I let out a giggle. "I thought you'd still be fast asleep." I drop the bag of pastries on the kitchen counter and pull her close.

"We only have so many more hours together. I can't waste them sleeping."

"My thoughts exactly, unless…" It appears I can't help myself.

"Unless what?" She cocks her head. It makes some of her hair fall in front of her eyes.

"Unless… you stay a little longer."

"Stay here?"

"Where else?"

"You want me to stay here with you longer?"

"Very much so."

"But you'd be working."

"I only have tomorrow off work, so yes. But you could work as well." I nod at my large dining table. "You could sit there or you could use my office. You could even go to a café."

"And have your dinner ready for when you come home."

"Correct." I tighten my grip on her waist. "My perfect little housewife," I joke.

"None of those words make any sense to me."

"You don't have to lift a finger," I assure her.

"Tempting though it sounds, there are two furry creatures who won't be happy with that."

"Can't you ask the woman who's taking care of them to do it for a few days longer?"

"I would need to check with her."

"Of course." She stiffens a little in my embrace as the cogs in her brain start whirring. "Just think about it and know that you are very welcome to stay as long as you like." And god knows when we'll see each other again, I add only in my mind, because I don't want my offer to have the slightest whiff of emotional blackmail about it.

"Aren't you busy? Will I get to see you at all?"

"It's the perfect excuse for me to be less busy. I'll

cancel any social engagements I have this week. But it is true that I don't exactly work nine to five."

"I need to think about it."

"Of course you do." As I look into Olivia's eyes, it hits me that both of us may have more to do than just some thinking.

CHAPTER 34
OLIVIA

It's Tuesday, and I'm still in Brussels. I can hardly believe it myself, yet here I am, in Marie's swanky digs, sipping coffee while peering out of the window. She left at an ungodly hour this morning with the vague promise that she'd call me if she had time. It reminded me of when Sandrine still lived with me and she went to work in the morning, leaving me in peace for the day. And I do need some peace today. To absorb the fact that I'm still here. That all it took for Marie to get me to stay longer in this city, far from my comfort zone and my lonely cats, was ask. Once. As soon as I had confirmation that taking care of Huppert and Deneuve was not an issue, I said yes. Of course I did. That I have to stay in this manic foreign city hardly matters because I get to spend a few more nights with Marie and, at night, everything's different.

After dark, when our limbs are intertwined in bed, and we've said all we've had to say for the day, so much seems possible—until the first light filters through the curtains in the morning. Then I'm reminded that none of this is really anything tangible at all. It's just a bunch of feelings in my heart. Sure, Marie wouldn't have asked me to stay if she didn't care about me, but that's hardly the same as what I feel, which is well beyond smitten.

Another reason why I was happy enough to stay is that I can't imagine saying goodbye to her. It will be different now that I've actually been here, that I've lived part of her life with her. That I've been reminded what it feels like to be so utterly, stupidly in love with another person. How, on the one hand, it erases all the protective measures I've built my life around, and, on the other hand, the sheer delirium of it has me walking around ridiculously pleased with myself all the time.

When we did venture out for a meal over the weekend, I barely felt the usual insecurity that comes with facing the outside world. It was all squashed by the sensation of walking through the streets with Marie's hand in mine. Of simply being with her. Doing the most ordinary things with her. But I also know that the lure of that is dangerous. That none of this will last. That, underneath the gloss of infatuation, I'm still me. Yet, today, I refuse to feel conflicted. I also refuse to go out, apart from the couple of hours that Marie's cleaner stops by. Given the choice between walking around by myself or sitting around awkwardly in someone else's home while a stranger cleans it, I wholeheartedly choose the first option.

Before I go out, I reply to some emails and work on the translation of the lesbian romance novel. I seem to find the correct words more easily now that I'm here, now that I'm under the heavy influence of some romance myself, although romance is perhaps the wrong word. Or is it? What is this if not a romance? It might be short-lived and much more flawed than anything that happens in the book I'm translating. But that's a work of fiction, and this is real life, where people leave you and hurt you and a happy ending is far from always a given.

I'm deeply focused on work when my phone rings. My heart skips a beat when I see it's Marie.

"I don't have much time," she sounds ragged. "But there's a piano recital in the concert hall on the square tonight. Shall we go?"

It's like I'm talking to someone who doesn't know me at all. Maybe this is the version of her she has alluded to before—the surgeon with nerves of steel and a penchant for breaking other women's hearts.

"I'd rather spend time with you."

"We'd be going together. I thought you'd enjoy it because you play the piano yourself." I hear her whisper something to someone in the background.

"I don't want to waste our time together being quiet in a concert hall." If I want to listen to someone playing the piano, I'll just put on Spotify on Marie's state-of-the-art sound system.

"Okay. Sure." Is that a sigh? "I thought I'd ask."

"Thanks for asking. I do appreciate it." I'm just following the common script of politeness now.

"I have to go now. See you tonight."

Before I get the chance to say goodbye, she has already ended the call. I stare at my dark phone screen and wonder what that was. Did she really expect me to go to a concert with her tonight? Would she have derived joy from that? I conclude that she wouldn't have asked if that wasn't what she had expected. This is what people who live here do. They go out, see shows, take part in life. It's not what I do. I live where I live for a reason, because I don't need any of this.

I pace around Marie's place to calm myself. I must have let her down. She didn't sound too pleased on the phone. She barely had time to speak to me. She lives the kind of life my brain finds very hard to fathom. We are so mismatched and it only took one day of her being at work while I'm here for me to see that. I will never be able to adapt to her pace of life, nor will I ever like doing the activities she favours.

Instead of going to a concert, Marie and I should talk. It will be easier for me now that I'm in this frame of mind, when my infatuation is pierced by the sharp knife of reality. Because one thing's for sure: I'm never going down the Sandrine road again. That endlessly slow disintegration of our relationship during which I got blamed for only being partly human and being downright impossible to be around most days. *You're crippled by irrational fear*, Sandrine used to say. *Can't you see that this control over life you're trying to create is one big illusion?* I might have driven her away, but she hurt me beyond the point of no return. She looked me in the eye and told me that I wasn't good enough, that how my brain works is inadequate, that I was no longer a match for her far superior ways.

I gaze out of the window as I begin to regret changing my ticket. If I'd left yesterday the way I had always intended, I would have been sad, but I wouldn't have been feeling so insufficient. Because it's the middle of July, it was bloody expensive to change the date of my return ticket, and I won't be changing it again, although the thought is tempting. But I wouldn't run away from Marie like that. If I did, I would be proving all of Sandrine's points about me and even though she would never even know, that's not a satisfaction I'm willing to give my ex.

———

Marie arrives home much later than the starting time of concert she wanted to attend. I've been waiting for her for hours with no news, but I guess it's hard to text when you're operating on someone's brain. I do get that.

She barely apologises and goes straight to the kitchen to get a bottle of wine out of the fridge.

"The day I've had," she says. She pours herself a glass, blows out some air, then finally looks at me. "How was your day?" Her gaze softens a bit.

I walk up to her and stifle the urge to throw my arms around her. "Good."

"Good?" Lips pursed, she nods. "Okay."

"Are you all right?" It's like someone I barely know just waltzed in.

Without asking, she takes another wine glass from the cupboard and pours me some. She pushes it in my direction. "Sometimes I come home and I need some time to wind down."

"Do you need me to pretend I don't know you, so you can hit on me?" A lame joke feels like the right way to go.

The corners of Marie's mouth tug upward a touch. "It's not you, Liv. I am glad to see you."

"Are you hangry? I didn't make dinner, I'm afraid."

She takes another sip of wine and puts her glass away before walking up to me. "Do you know who I miss?" She pulls me towards her. "The me I was in Bonneau the last two months. I was so relaxed." She rolls her shoulders backwards. "Some days—not all, thank goodness—it's like

I don't know how to cope with the stress of my job any longer. Like something vital in me has broken down and I don't know how to fix it."

I miss that person every day, I think.

"Coming home just now and seeing you here was such a harsh reminder," Marie says. "Of how quickly things can go back to how they were." She shakes her head. "I'm pretty sure that's the last thing I want."

"What *do* you want?"

She gives a small smile. "I guess I wish I could be a bit more like you. A bit more... detached. Because for all the futile things you care too much about, you don't give a toss about what anyone thinks of you and how you live your life. You do your own thing because it makes you happy. You have no idea how much I admire that."

That's a new one. As far as I can remember, no one has ever admired me for my strange, secluded ways. Marie must be in a really bad way to say something like that.

"As far as I'm aware, you're very good at doing your own thing and don't care one iota about what anyone else thinks about you either," I reply.

"I used to be good at it, but now... there are these cracks. When I first returned, it was hard to readjust, but I was happy to be back at it, to do what I do. Being a surgeon is such a vital part of me, so much so that I can't ever imagine not being one. But today... I don't know. Something was different. I was ill at ease. I wasn't feeling it. Everyone has bad days, of course, but as a surgeon, you're meant to shake them off. You're meant to focus on one thing only and that's the patient you're dealing with. That didn't seem to work for me all that much today."

"Because I'm here?"

She exhales deeply and folds her arms all the way

around my waist. "I think having you here while I'm working reminds me of Véronique and what happened when I let myself have feelings for her."

My heart skips another beat—it has done so countless times since I arrived; I may need a doctor soon. I bring my hand to her back and press her against me. "I don't know much about many things, but I do know that it's absolutely possible to have feelings for someone and be an amazing doctor at the same time. The two are not incompatible." I kiss her on the crown of her head. "You're not used to it, that I can easily believe. But that doesn't mean it's not possible."

She nestles her head closer to my chest. "Have I told you how happy I am that you're here?"

"Even though it made you have a lousy day at work?"

"Because I had a lousy day at work. Because…" With Marie pressed so close against me, I can feel her breath hitch in her throat. "You undo something in me and it doesn't suit my life here, whereas it suited me just fine in Bonneau. I enjoyed it. I relished it. But here, at home, I find it hard to reconcile who I was with you in Brittany and who I've always been here." She finally looks up at me. "Does that make sense at all?"

"Of course." It's only a half-lie—at least it's a white lie I can live with. Marie needs my support now rather than my blatant honesty. Although I do understand what it's like to pretend to be someone you're not, to wear a mask when you present yourself to the outside world. But I don't think that's actually what Marie's trying to say. "It's been a rough transition and you're not the same person you were last year. You've gone through something and you've come out the other side with a different perspective."

"Wow." She smiles up at me, although wetness glitters in her eyes. "When did you become so eloquent?"

"I have my moments."

"Liv, um…" She swallows hard, then extricates herself from my embrace. "What I think might also have happened today is that I… it might have hit me that I have more feelings for you than I care to admit."

CHAPTER 35
MARIE

W hy am I saying these things? Who is this person controlling me? It's like I have a bird's eye view of the two of us and I recognise the people I see, but I can't believe what the one who looks exactly like me is saying.

"Would that be so bad?" Olivia reaches for my hand. I can tell she's having trouble suppressing a smile.

"It would be very… complicated."

"Why?"

"Because, you and I, we can't realistically be together." I chuckle at my own audacity. "I'm fifty-six years old and I've never been in a relationship worth the name. What does that say about me?"

"You had other priorities."

"You make it sound so simple. So normal."

"You *are* asking the expert on all things normal."

I have to laugh. I just have to. This is one of the things about Olivia that draw me to her so much. She might be complex and difficult, but she knows exactly who she is and what she wants. She makes no apologies for it and she can crack the occasional dry joke about it.

"Look." She plays with my hands. "We are very different, but maybe, we are also much more alike than we think." She brings a hand to her chest. "In Bonneau, you took a journey inwards. Maybe for the first time in your life, you listened to yourself, because it was all you could do. Your intuition brought you out there, in the middle of winter, when there was nothing else to do on cold, dark nights but listen to yourself. You took a deep, hard look into the depths of your soul. It takes a lot for a person to do that, and you did it day after day…" She slants her head. "Occasionally using me as a distraction, which I didn't mind too much." She curls her fingers tighter around mine. "It's perfectly understandable that you're not the same person and you can't just pick up where you left off. It would be madness if that were the case. Of course, I'm going to be an extra reminder of that, but, maybe when you asked me to stay in Brussels longer, it was your intuition rearing its head again, that thing you got so in touch with amidst the stillness of Bonneau. Because you needed me to. And not only because of my irresistible charms."

"But you…" I start to say. You are the most unlikely woman to have this effect on me, but I can't say that to her. Or can I? Is Olivia the kind of person I can say something like that to? I can be my newer, truest self around? "You're so unlike anyone I've ever been with."

"Maybe that's the point." She narrows her eyes. "Maybe it takes someone unlikely to truly make us see something about ourselves."

I expel a sigh. I did need her to stay, I can see that now. I needed her to say the things she just said to me, and all the things she never says with words, but conveys nonetheless. Olivia often prefers not to speak if someone else is filling the silence with an avalanche of words. She's part of the stillness she referred to that I found in Bonneau. She's the opposite of the flashy loudmouth that I am— and that I'm usually attracted to.

"Remember that itty-bitty thing you told me on my penultimate night in Bonneau?" I ask.

"I told you so many things. You know me. Can't shut up to save my life." Olivia strokes my cheek with the back of her fingers.

"When you said that you were in love with me." I make sure she knows I'm serious, my tone solemn and as level as I can muster.

She gives a slight nod of the head.

"At the time, I didn't feel as though I could reciprocate that feeling, but now… I can. I do." I take her hand and plant a soft kiss on her knuckle. "I'm in love with you too, Liv. Of course, I am."

Olivia's face is as still as the air around us. She looks me straight in eye and it's as though she has trouble catching her breath. Instead of speaking, she cants towards me and kisses me on the lips.

"How did you even know I still had feelings for you?" she asks, after we break from our kiss.

"Because I can read you like an open book." I kiss her again. "Because if you didn't, you wouldn't be here, and you certainly wouldn't have stayed."

"I am in love with you," she whispers in my ear before kissing my neck. "At first, I thought you were way out of my league, but now I'm beginning to think it's the other way around." She follows up with a soft laugh, her breath hot against my skin, before kissing me again.

When my alarm goes off the following morning, it's a rude awakening. I can't tear myself away from Olivia's sleeping body. I want to stay in bed with her. I wish Huppert and Deneuve were here so they could curl up at our feet while we chat and dream up a future we can't really have. Instead, I have to spend my day at the hospital, and the next, and the next, until the weekend, when I can spend all my time with her again. Until I can squeeze out every last second of being with her before she goes back home.

What irks me most is that it's never been this hard to go to work before. And it's not only that. It's knowing that as soon as I walk through the doors of the hospital, I'll get swallowed up by the vastness of my work. By the million little things that make up my job. By the patients' stories and the look of anguish on their families' faces and how I am with my fellow surgeons and the rush of surgery and the feelings afterwards, when it all went well, when I did a stellar job, and I can wipe away some of the agony on the relatives' faces. I used to love every last little thing about it. I loved being able to do what only a very small percentage of people on this planet can do. I loved the looks of admiration it gained me—and not just from other women when I was on the prowl. I loved saving a life that would have been lost if it weren't for my presence. But now, there's this void inside me that can't seem to be filled no matter what I do. It's no longer the effects of the semi-burnout I left for Brittany with. It's as though what used to bring me so much joy and professional pride can no longer fulfil me. Just like going out and putting the moves

on some unsuspecting woman can no longer fulfil me—
not now that I have feelings for Olivia. The two simply
don't compare. While that is understandable as a side-
effect of falling in love, what's happening to me profes-
sionally is much harder to explain. Because do I really
prefer sitting around all day to healing someone's brain?
There's no rhyme or reason to that. Yet, when I think
about the last time I was truly happy, truly content and at
peace, it was when Olivia and I were sitting in my garden
in Bonneau, surrounded by nothing but trees and birdsong
and the cats and each other.

But I am Marie Dievart, neurosurgeon, daughter of
Alice Dievart, retired thoracic surgeon, sister of
Madeleine Dievart, renowned plastic surgeon. Being a
surgeon is as much part of my identity as being a woman,
as being my mother's daughter and my sister's sibling. My
mother gave me my first stethoscope when I was five years
old and it wasn't a plastic toy one—it was the real deal. All
I've ever wanted to be is a surgeon. Not a doctor, but a
surgeon specifically. It's what I do and who I am more
than anything else. Yet why is it leaving me so depleted
now?

I cast one last longing glance at Olivia, who has slept
through my alarm. I'll get back to myself once she's left—
not that I want her to leave. But, for now, it seems she is
one of the causes of my professional malaise. In the
shower, I think about what I said to her last night. That
I'm in love with her. Previously, I would have talked myself
out of such a sentiment easily. But what Véronique set in
motion late last year, Olivia seems to be continuing. Just
maybe, I too want to love someone—and be loved in
return. Really loved, not fondled for a night, or two, a few

weeks at best. I too want to feel like I belong with someone and that same someone belongs with me. The prospect doesn't scare me so much anymore, although that might have something to do with Olivia only being here for a few more days. Perhaps I can only find out how I truly feel once she's gone.

AUGUST

CHAPTER 36

M arie warned me her family would arrive at the house today, so I've been prepared for weeks, yet it feels strange to see people there that are not her. Last summer, any of the Dievarts arriving was but a tiny blip on my radar, something to shrug off. This summer, everything's different. It makes me feel ill at ease to have Marie's family so close by while she's far away. She told me that she has confided in her sister about us and the thought that someone in the house around the corner knows about my existence, and my relation to her sister, makes me walk on eggshells in my own home.

Marie calls me every day now, sometimes more than once, and I make a mental note to ask her about the best way to behave now that her family is here.

I'm sitting outside in my rocking chair, pondering our long-distance relationship, when I hear noises at the front of the house. For a split second, before I launch into my usual panic about unexpected visitors, it reminds me of when Marie stopped by. Towards the end of her stay, I no longer asked her to let me know when she was coming over—I was usually at hers, anyway.

"*Bonsoir*," a woman's voice shouts.

I rush to the front and look straight into Marie's sister's face.

"Special delivery for Olivia Chevalier from Marie Dievart," Madeleine says and hands me a gift-wrapped box. "Don't ask me what's in there." She cocks her head. "In fact, don't tell me what's in there once you've opened it. Knowing my sister, I'm pretty sure I don't want to know."

A blush creeps up my cheeks. Marie's sister is as forward as she is, then. It must run in the family. I wonder what their mother is like.

"Thank you so much." I take the box from her. I guess I should invite her in. I make another mental note to scold Marie for having her sister drop by like this without any word of warning, but it's only a teeny tiny part of me that minds. A much more prevalent part of me is thrilled to get a present from Marie and to come face-to-face with her sister, although it does make me wish Marie were here as well. "Would you like to come in for a drink? I was just having a glass of wine in the garden."

"Oh." Madeleine sounds utterly surprised—maybe Marie warned her that she shouldn't expect me to invite her in. "Yes, of course."

I shake the box about as we walk along the side of the house, but I must keep my curiosity in check because Madeleine is right to suspect her sister of giving me a family-inappropriate present.

"Your garden's gorgeous." Madeleine makes a beeline for the bright pink and purple hydrangeas that bloom wildly in the sunniest part of my garden.

I fetch her a glass of wine from the kitchen and present it to her.

"I'm glad to officially make your acquaintance," Madeleine says. "I'm not sure what you've done to my sister, but she can't seem to shut up about you."

"I find that hard to believe," I say, mostly just to say something.

Madeleine's taller and much blonder than Marie, but their eyes are the same colour and have the same heavy-lidded, melancholy quality to them. She just arches up her eyebrows and nods. "You must come to dinner once we've settled in. *Maman*'s arriving this weekend on the train. She's dying to meet you as well."

What is this? Did I flip through a portal to a different dimension? If Marie told her family about me, surely she also told them that barging into my house and inviting me to dinner is the last thing I want them to do? She might have left out some crucial parts of my personality when she mentioned me. I can hardly blame her for that.

"I'm, uh, quite busy this week finishing a project."

"That's okay. We're here for two weeks. Plenty of time to get to know each other."

Get to know each other? I feel like I should skip town just to avoid them. Maybe I should surprise Marie with an impromptu visit to Brussels.

"I'll check my calendar."

"Oh, yes, of course." Madeleine looks as though she has just remembered what her sister told her about their elusive neighbour in Brittany. "No pressure. Really."

I gesture for her to sit. She exhales deeply before taking a sip of wine.

"It must be heavenly to live here all the time." She scrunches her lips. "Although I was here last winter for a weekend and it wasn't nearly as heavenly then." She sends me a smile.

Marie's sister sitting in the chair Marie used to occupy makes me miss her even more.

"It's very peaceful."

"Did it shake you? To have Marie move in next door for so long? She's not exactly a wallflower."

"Yes. It was an adjustment. Your sister's very persistent." I can't help a small smile from breaking out on my face.

Huppert has decided to approach the stranger in her territory. She sniffs Madeleine's shin for a while, then promptly jumps into her lap. "You must be Huppert." Madeleine catches my gaze. "Marie told me about your adorable cats as well."

Marie certainly has been chatty, but I can hardly blame her for that either. Some days, even I wish I had someone to talk to about this nagging feeling in my gut because she's not here and I'm not in Brussels and we might have both confessed to having strong feelings for each other, but it still ends there.

"In all her fifty-six years, I've never seen Marie like this." Madeleine rubs Huppert's chin.

I guess I won't be seeing much of my cat as long as the Dievarts are in Bonneau. Hold on. What did Madeleine just say?

"How do you mean?"

"Marie's… well, you must know. Save from her very first girlfriend decades ago, and that was more to prove a point than anything else at the time, Marie has never brought anyone home. She never talks about her love interests. Never. I always assumed it was a part of her life she wanted to keep separate from us, from her family, but now I'm beginning to think she never had that much to talk about. Until she returned from Bonneau."

Madeleine's words set something aglow deep inside me. Then we're disturbed by yelling coming from the street.

"*Mamy?* Are you there?" a high-pitched voice cries.

"That's my daughter. She's probably wondering where I am." To my horror, Madeleine doesn't make to get up. To be fair, Huppert isn't letting her. "I'm here, *chérie*," Madeleine calls back.

Before I know it, a girl who is the spitting image of Marie is standing in my back garden. She introduces herself as Elodie. Goodness me, this family. They just do whatever they want.

"Elodie wants to be a neurosurgeon, just like her aunt."

Elodie gives me a thorough once-over in that shameless way Gen Z kids have—not that I'm an expert on the subject of that generation—but luckily she doesn't proceed to give me some sort of quick-fire third degree interrogation. Maybe the news of her aunt and the invisible neighbour from Bonneau hasn't reached her yet.

Thankfully, just then, my phone starts ringing. Hallelujah, saved by the bell. I would have picked up even if it was an unknown number. Anything to avoid this sudden invasion of Dievarts.

"Marie," I say. "You'll never guess who's in my garden right now." Although I try, I can't keep all of the sarcasm out of my voice—it's simply impossible.

"Have they descended on you already? I'm so sorry, darling. I explicitly forbade my sister to just rock up to yours, but she never really listens when I tell her something."

I turn away from Madeleine and Elodie. "Your sister *and* your niece."

Marie chuckles into the phone. "You're going to have to take tomorrow off work to process all that interaction."

She might jest, but it's true.

"I'll make sure none of them make a habit out of it, I promise."

How? I want to ask, but refrain. These women might be strangers to me, but they're also Marie's family. I know I need to open myself up to them a fraction at the very least.

I walk a little further away from my impromptu guests. "I wish it were you that had descended upon me." I feel it again—I always feel it so much more when we're actually talking. That acute need to have her close. To give up some of myself to make more room for her in my life.

"I know. Just a few more weeks." First, she was coming to Bonneau the last week of August, but it's been pushed back twice and now it's looking more like mid-September.

"If you want some Breton summer vibes, best not wait too long." That's all I say in order to get my point across. I don't want to be the long-distance partner who nags her girlfriend every time she gets the chance.

"I'm just trying to make sure I can stay as long as possible. If we hang in there a little longer, we could have three weeks together instead of just two."

"That would be amazing."

"Meanwhile, that package Madeleine gave you should tide you over." I can hear the smile in her voice—and I can easily picture the grin on her face.

"I haven't opened it yet."

"Good. Open it when you're alone." When her voice goes all cheeky like that, I miss her even more. "By the way, I just found out my mother's going to Bonneau as well. Chances are, you might run into her. She's not exactly the quiet type either."

"I wasn't expecting her to be."

"I haven't told her as much about you as I have my sister, but she does know you exist."

Great. I'll be meeting Marie's mother—the formidable retired surgeon I've only heard impressive things about—without Marie by my side then.

"Is that Marie?" Madeleine's voice sounds dangerously close. When I turn around, I find her standing right behind me.

"I think your sister wants to talk to you."

"Don't worry, darling. I'll give her a stern talking-to."

I hand my phone to Madeleine and watch her as she starts an animated conversation with Marie. Elodie has slumped into a chair, huddled over her phone. For an instant, I feel like a stranger on my own property.

My glance cuts to the gift-wrapped box that was the reason for Madeleine's visit and a smile breaks on my face despite the impromptu presence of so many Dievarts in my life.

"Both of my daughters have far exceeded any expecta-tions I ever had for them," Marie's mother says. Is this woman really approaching her eighty-fifth birthday? She doesn't look a day over seventy. "I just want them to be happy, although they wouldn't believe me if I actually told them that." She brings a hand to her chest. "Which is my fault entirely, of course." She narrows her eyes and focuses her gaze on me. "She hasn't told me all that much—that's never been Marie's style—but any fool can see that coming here has changed her. That meeting you has changed her."

All Dievarts have the perfect ability to fill any lull in a conversation. I haven't had to say all that much since Alice arrived at my house, which is how I like it.

"It's also my fault she couldn't talk to me about what happened with the patient who died, and how she felt afterwards. When it comes to certain things, I didn't set the best example." She draws her lips into a tight smile. "I've always had certain ideas of how surgeons should and should not behave when it comes to admitting weakness. How we should always act as though we are above certain things." Alice cocks her head and nearly pierces me with her intense green stare—all three of them have the exact same eyes. "I should really tell her that some day, but, well, Marie isn't always the easiest to talk to." She pauses. "You got through to her in some way, however. I'd like to ask what your secret is, but I know you won't be able to tell me."

"There's no secret." Now that I've got much more acquainted with the Dievarts, the matriarch is easy enough to take a shine to. Besides, it's always intriguing to meet a parent of the person you're in love with.

Alice shrugs. "I knew you'd say that and that's okay." She flashes me a smile. "Anyway, I've been instructed to" —she holds up a finger—"One: not give you a hard time and"—she adds another finger—"Two: not spill the beans on Marie. As if I have any beans on her to spill."

I have to laugh because I can so easily picture Marie telling her mother—this formidably impressive woman— to lay off me. It's like they have confidence instead of blood running through their veins. No wonder that, once in a while, even that kind of supreme confidence, the kind that borders on hubris, gets shaken. In that respect, it's logical that Marie ended up here. What is still far from logical is that she has, somehow and somewhere along the way, fallen for the likes of me.

"I will tell you this, though, Olivia, because I'm her mother and I have an instinct for noticing these kinds of things about my children." She inserts a solemn pause. "Some of Marie's self-assurance receded while she was here. Some of that enormous ego diminished." A hint of a smile. "For reasons I've never fully understood, a lot of people lack self-esteem. This is not an affliction Marie has ever had to deal with. *Au contraire.*" The hint of a smile on her lips morphs into a much wider one. "She got most of that from her late father, by the way."

As far as I can see, she surely got it from her mother as well, but I won't argue with Alice about that—I don't have the necessary self-esteem to steer the conversation that way.

"But what thrills me most of all, is that she found you." She slaps her palm against the armrest of the chair. "I couldn't believe it when she told me about you. I had to come see for myself." She shoots me another smile. "One of the worst mistakes I've made in my life is not showing my daughters that there can be so much more to life than always work-work-work. Because we're all surgeons, we think ourselves so incredibly important, and the work we do has a lot of value, but having a life outside of work also has a lot of value. Marie hasn't always seen it that way, but when she talks about you... I can tell that she has at least noticed." She leans over and gives me a surprising pat on the knee—all Dievarts are also annoyingly tactile people, although in Marie's case I don't mind any longer. "For that alone, I can't thank you enough." She sighs. "I only wish she were here. I wish we could all be on holiday together and I could witness the two of you being together. Because I've never seen Marie with anyone she's been in a romantic relationship with. Can you believe that? I'm her mother."

That makes two of us feverishly wishing Marie were here. "She's working," I state.

Alice scoffs. "Oh, sweet irony."

"Either way, it's very lovely to meet you, Alice. It's very... illuminating."

"I can see why she's so smitten with you, by the way." Alice drinks from the glass of wine I poured her earlier. "It's clear as day to me."

I quirk up my eyebrows, hoping to prompt her to go into more detail, but she doesn't. She finishes her wine and with the gait of a spritely woman in her sixties, heads back to the house around the corner.

SEPTEMBER

CHAPTER 37

MARIE

I'm well aware I'm driving above the speed limit, but those last fifteen minutes before seeing Olivia again are the hardest. Another entirely new sensation to me. It's been quite the year so far for those, and I have an inkling that I'm not done with firsts yet. It's only September. So much can still happen.

I drive straight to her house. I park haphazardly, and the front door swings open, and then there she is. There she bloody well is. I take a moment just to look at her, to relish in the exquisite sensation of having exactly what my heart desires. To be with her. Who knew love could feel this way? I certainly didn't. I never really understood what the fuss was all about, what all those films and novels were about—until now.

It's crystal clear as I open the door of my car and Olivia's impatiently waiting for me to get out. It couldn't be more obvious when I look into her eyes for real, and not into some virtual representation of them on my phone screen, and I inhale her scent, and I conclude that, entirely along expectations, she hasn't dressed up for my arrival at all, because there's no such thing as a dressed-up version of Olivia Chevalier. This is who she is, always. This is the woman I fell in love with—stubborn, immovable, but oh-so delightful. I wouldn't want her any other way.

"Hello, my darling," I say, before I collapse into her arms, and know in my bones that here, right here in her arms, is where I belong more than anywhere else.

She buries her nose in my hair and pulls me close. I dreamed of kissing her, of stripping her naked as soon as I arrived, but now, I just want to stand in her embrace for long minutes, to let the sensation of having come home to her course through me, to let it take me over and erase all the built-up stress of the past few months. I want to let the fatigue of the long drive to get here and the weeks and weeks of missing her flow out of me. Because Olivia can make all of that happen with one single embrace—she has that power over me. She has become that person to me.

I feel something press against my shin and it's possibly the only creature on this planet who can make me drag myself away from its owner for a moment. I crouch down and stroke Huppert's soft little head.

"Hello, you." All the times she kept me company flash through my head. All the times she was just there, doing nothing but being her feline self, which, in Huppert's case, mainly consists of attracting attention, and changed something inside me nonetheless.

She bumps her cheek against my hand, demanding more affection. I pick her up and she starts purring like the smoothest-running engine.

"Next you'll tell me you missed my cat more than me."

Olivia couldn't wipe that smile off her face even if she wanted to—but why would she?

"Three weeks of this," I say on a contented sigh.

"I rearranged my work schedule," Olivia says. "I'm all yours for the full three weeks."

"Maybe you can finally write me a poem, then." Olivia's Instagram has been inactive for months.

"You've just arrived and are already making demands." Olivia raises an eyebrow. "Your mother warned me about your high-maintenance ways, not that I didn't already know all about them."

My mother came back from Bonneau raving about Olivia, urging me to hang on to her—I barely recognised her when she said that. Maybe she was just shocked to have finally met someone I'm in a relationship with, albeit in a frustrating long distance one.

We head inside Olivia's house. We haven't talked about whose house we'll actually be staying at. I had automatically assumed we'd stay at mine because that's where we previously spent most of our time together, but that was then and this is now and I guess the cats are here and Olivia's used to it here and I don't really care where we sleep, as long as it's in each other's arms.

Any past version of myself would roll her eyes right out of her head at the mere thought of that, but now that I've gotten a glimpse of what love feels like, and how it can fundamentally alter something inside you, I take it much more seriously.

Besides, it's about time I spent some prolonged time in Olivia's territory, if only to witness first-hand how she behaves on her own turf—in her own life.

Deneuve comes to have a little sniff before walking off

in a huff. I set Huppert free from my arms so I can wrap them around Olivia again. And then, at last, we kiss. To finally feel her lips on mine again is like waking up from the longest hibernation, from the coldest, darkest winter.

"I'm not sure I can go that long without you again," I say, when we break from our kiss.

"Me neither." Mischief glints in her eyes. "That gift your sister brought is extremely inadequate."

I wish I could have seen Olivia's face when she opened that box and found a personalised vibrator with a picture of me printed on it.

"*Bonjour* Yvette." I send the bar's landlady a bright smile. Who knows, if it hadn't been for her suggestion that I call Olivia on that stormy night I ended up here in February, Olivia might never have made it to my place for dinner—and all that happened after might not have.

"Look what the cat dragged in." Yvette is still her usual charming self. She does smile back, though.

I escort Olivia to a table by the window.

"I can't believe you've never been here." I insisted we come here because, for me, it's part of our history together.

"And I can't believe that knowing me the way you do, you still can't believe that."

We order a bottle of wine from Yvette, who isn't the chatty type despite her chosen profession, and leaves us in peace.

"Just indulge me, darling." I bat my lashes at her ostentatiously.

"Gladly." Olivia's had a perpetual smirk on her lips

since I've arrived. She's been surprisingly easy-going, saying yes to everything I suggest. I might get her to go to Rennes with me for a few days next week. Or maybe even another visit to Paris. But I'm not here for any of those things. I'm here for one reason only and that's to spend time with Olivia. In the end, it doesn't really matter what we do.

"Who would have thought that one day you and I would come here together." I certainly didn't on that night Yvette called Olivia, asking her to pick me up. Maybe the fact that she did, that Olivia managed to drag herself from the comfort of her home, out of her shell, that very night, to do me that one act of kindness, is what tipped the odds in our favour. I'm about to tip the odds a little further because my mind has been churning and I have something to say.

Yvette brings over the bottle and a couple of glasses. She gives me a look, then cuts her gaze to Olivia, before walking off.

"I think you and Yvette would get along swimmingly, by the way."

"We would excel at sitting around saying nothing, that's for sure." Olivia pours us each a glass and we hold them up.

I look deep into her eyes. "To us," I say. "The most unlikely of couples."

"I'll definitely drink to that." Olivia shoots me a quick wink before taking a sip.

"I've been thinking about something." I reach for her hand on the table. To my surprise—because you never know when you're out and about with Olivia—she lets me take it. "About us. Our future."

Her face darkens, as though she's expecting me to ask

the impossible of her—for her to move to Brussels for me. But that would be like asking her to remove a vital part of her. Olivia belongs in the tempestuous landscape of Brittany—she's as much a part of it as it is of her. When I fell for her, I fell for that part of her as well, with how she's so inextricably rooted in her surroundings.

"Don't worry." I give her hand a squeeze. "I'm not asking you to leave Bonneau."

She swallows hard, then takes another sip.

"I want to be with you. I want to try. I want to see what happens when we give this a proper chance."

Olivia nods. "So do I. Very much."

"I'm thinking about taking another leave of absence."

She arches up her eyebrows. "Seriously?"

"When I think of the past few years, perhaps even the last decade, I can't think of anywhere or any time I've been happier than here with you."

"Is this for real?" Her voice breaks a little.

"Yes. It's very real." I hold her gaze. "I like who I am with you. I like that person very much, actually."

"How long a leave of absence are you thinking about?" There's a hint of hope creeping into her tone alongside the hesitation.

"As long as they'll give me." I've thought about resigning outright, but it's too big a step. I can't burn all my bridges just like that. "I'll probably start with six months, then take it from there."

"Can you just do that?"

"Ultimately, what I can and can't do is up to me. If I do decide to go back after six months or even after a year, things will be different. But I'm not too worried about that. There will always be a place somewhere for someone with my level of skill, knowledge, and experience." That is, if I even want to go back.

"But you're a surgeon."

"I was one. A bloody good one at that, but... it hasn't been the same this year. Not because of the woman who died when she wasn't supposed to, although that has played its part. After being here, going back to life as I knew it hasn't really worked out that well. It doesn't give me the same satisfaction any longer and this is not a job you can do when it doesn't fulfil you. It takes everything you've got, all your energy, all your time and focus. And... I'm not that person anymore. I've changed. I can still perform a procedure. I can still go through the motions. But I've lost a lot of my drive, that invisible urge that always pushed me onwards and upwards, without ever looking back."

"Are you saying you need more time before you properly go back?"

"Yes and no. I don't really know, Liv. I don't know what's going to happen or what the future holds for me and it's scary but it's also okay, because I'm no longer alone."

Olivia is holding on to my fingers for dear life, as though she can't believe what she's just heard and I might take it all back if she doesn't react in a certain way.

"I love you," I say. "I want to be with you."

"You make it sound so simple."

I have to smile because, for many, it would be that simple, but not for Olivia, of course. Nothing's ever simple or easy for her.

I give her the time she needs to gather her thoughts. "I love you and I'm over the moon with your plans, but...

you're a surgeon. I'm just a translator. I can do my work anywhere. If anything, I should move to be with you."

I shake my head. "You may be able to do your work anywhere, but you can't just live anywhere. You live here. In this deserted corner of the world that you've made your home. You could never thrive in a city like Brussels, not even if you moved there to be with me—especially not if you moved there for that reason. I appreciate the sentiment, but it wouldn't be right."

"But I don't want you to give up your job for me. That's too much."

"It's not." I shake my head. "It's really not, because it doesn't feel like I'm giving something up. It feels like the opposite. It feels like I'm being given a gift that's entirely new to me." I clear my throat of whatever emotion has lodged itself in the back. "Being a surgeon is a life-defining profession. It's not something you ever do as something on the side. It permeates your being, your life, your ego." I scoff. "For a very long time, I believed I was better than everyone else because of my job. I honestly believed that about myself. I thought I had to, to tell you the truth. I believed it came with the territory. How else can you find the strength to cut open another human being day after day?" I take a breath. "What I've learned from being with you, from being here, from being away from all of that, is that I'm no better than anyone else. Certainly no better than you." I look deep into Olivia's eyes and break into a smile.

"I can't possibly agree with everything you say, but… I think I get the gist of it."

"The gist of it…"—I lean over the table, not caring that a group of gruff-looking men just walked in—"is that you being you, with all your impossible ways and silly rules, has done something to me. You started something and it's still going on and it's not something I can walk away from."

"Has anyone ever told you that you're very wordy? A bit long-winded, even?" Olivia meets me halfway across the table.

"No one would dare," I say, and kiss her on the lips.

CHAPTER 38

OLIVIA

Marie and I have been all over each other for days, but ever since our conversation at Yvette's, my levels of insatiability for her reach new heights by the hour. And there's something I've been meaning to try. Something she, like so many other things, instigated all by herself. Because Marie is not someone who walks into your life without changing it—she hasn't so much walked into my life as gate-crashed it. Like that very first time she showed up at my door. Little did I know that moment, those awkward minutes when all I wanted her to do was leave, would change my life so drastically. Little did I know that I would ever do this. But I've known for a while that the holiday I sent my heart on has ended. All my defences are down. All the carefully constructed brickwork that I laid around my heart has been smashed to smithereens. I'm wholly unprotected but I'm not afraid, because I know that she's worth it—and I didn't have much choice.

"How about," I look into her eyes, "I make your wildest dreams come true?"

"I'm all ears." She smiles up at me. "Although you've already come pretty close."

"I don't think so."

Her eyes narrow. "Don't keep me in suspense."

"Hold on." I tear myself away from her and reach for something in my bedside table. I show her the vibrator with her face on that she gave me. "Marie Dievart fucks Marie Dievart." I'm mightily pleased with myself for coming up with this—it only took me about a month.

Marie erupts into a belly laugh. "Do you really think that is my wildest dream?"

"Oh, yes." There's no doubt in my mind.

"Are you sure it's not *your* wildest dream to have me and an image of me in your bed?"

"As in *nearly* having two of you to play with?"

Marie nods. She's still as unbelievable to me as she's always been. For someone like me, who likes things just so, who is addicted to control and forecasting outcomes, being with someone as unpredictable as Marie should be hard, but it has become the opposite.

"Because I can't get enough of you?" I ask.

"That's why I had that made. Especially for you." She pulls me in for a kiss which I happily return. Only Marie would have no qualms about ordering a sex toy with her likeness printed on it—only she would think of something like that. I didn't have a clue it was even possible, although nothing should surprise me in this day and age.

"I can't thank you enough for your immeasurable kindness," I say when we break from the kiss, which has left me keen to use the toy.

"I only ever aim to please." She draws me to her again and we fall into another kiss that quickly deepens into something more. When the kiss ends, the time for talking has also ended. I want her—again. I need to fit all the love-making that can't happen because we're apart into these three weeks we have together. I need to memorise every last inch of her alabaster skin. I need to etch her post-orgasm grin into my brain so I can use it for comfort when I miss her too much. Because now, because of her, I'm no longer a woman who wants to be alone at all costs. Before Marie, it felt like a small price to pay for being me, but that, too, has changed.

I kiss my way from her lips to her neck, stopping at her breasts. I flick my tongue along her nipples as I make my way down. For now, I put the toy aside. I only want skin-on-skin contact. I want to taste her, feel her, inhale her. This glorious woman who has changed my life because that's what falling in love does. It hasn't forced me to change, but it has made me choose to do it. I've adapted my ways for her; she has done the same for me.

I bestow a slew of kisses on her inner thigh, kissing a path to my final destination. I take a moment to look at her there, between her legs, and wonder how I ever decided to give this up, to consider the lack of this as mere collateral damage to how I wanted to conduct my life. As I sit here, looking at Marie, it seems like such utter madness. But that was the person I was then and this is the person I am now and they are not the same. With her, everything is different. I remember the very first time we did this, when she bowled me over with her charm and confidence and had me spread my legs for her over the course of that short evening. I should have known then, because that was hardly normal behaviour for me either. I also remember how she didn't let me touch her—that, too, is very different now.

Marie brings her hands to the back of my head, delves

her fingertips into my hair. I have learned it's her way of spurring me on. But I take my time. I lick her skin until she squirms underneath me, until I run out of patience and finally sweep my tongue over her clit. She stiffens as I do, her fingertips pressing into my scalp. I circle my tongue around her clit, slide it up and down her sex, until she tilts her hips towards me in the way that I have come to know, alerting me that she's close. But we're doing things a little differently today. Because she was right—no matter how obnoxious, she's always a little bit right—I'm the one who's enthralled with that toy the most. If I could, I would have two of her in my bed—as if one of her isn't enough to deal with already.

I stop licking her and kiss her gently on the thigh. Before she can protest, which I fully expect her to do, I run a finger through her wetness. I slide inside, gasping, as I do every single time, at the exquisite warmth my fingers are greeted with. To be inside her is the greatest gift of all, but that doesn't mean I should ignore the other gift she gave me. I still my fingers inside her and reach for the toy. She looks down at me and I hand it to her.

"Use it on yourself while I fuck you," I whisper, the words barely making it past my throat because I'm too aroused to speak. Maybe I should have asked her to use it on me—but we can do that later. First, I want to see what she does with it.

Marie must be highly aroused as well because she doesn't argue. For once, she does exactly as she's told. She switches on the vibrator and brings the tip to her clit. The sight of it is almost too much for me to bear because I'm also looking at my fingers disappearing inside of her. In the end, the gimmick of having a picture of her face printed onto the vibrator is what has the least effect on me, because my fingers push high inside of her, and the buzzing sound I've come to know so well is drowned out by the strength of her ever-increasing moans. To have a woman like Marie, a woman so glamorous and *of-the-city* not only come for me like this, but have her love me— have her uproot her life for me—is like a dream I never even knew I had coming true a thousand times over. And every time we do this, every single time I witness her giving herself up to me, I love her more.

She cries out loudly as she comes, clenching herself around my fingers so hard I fear I might not be able to play my piano for a few days.

I let her ride out her climax until, spent, she tosses the toy aside without even switching it off. As I slide out of her, for the first time in long months, a line of poetry forms in my head. Maybe that particular dry spell is about to end as well, I think, as she pulls me near and kisses me profusely. No one would be happier about that than Marie.

DECEMBER

CHAPTER 39

MARIE

"*Mon dieu, chérie,*" I say to Olivia as I close the book I've been reading. "This is how you spend your working hours?"

"I've moved on to lesbians now." Olivia looks very much at home in my sofa. It's dark outside but for the city lights glimmering behind her.

"Thank goodness. I don't think I could stand reading another one of these. You were right. Far too many penises." I somehow manage to keep a straight face.

"You don't have to read every book I translate." She barely looks up from the bundle of poetry she's reading— it's the one Sandrine put together and Olivia has a poem in.

"Are you almost ready?" I'm surprised she isn't running around trying to expel her nerves with frantic activity. "*Maman* doesn't like it when we're late."

"*Maman* happens to adore me, so." She cuts her gaze to me.

"True and who can blame her?" I may say that, but

it's astounding how little disapproval my mother has shown at me taking another leave of absence.

I walk over to Olivia and sit next to her, throwing an arm around her shoulders. "Thank you for spending Christmas with me and my family. I know it's not how you prefer to celebrate it."

"I truly don't mind." She puts the book of poetry away. "Your sister's a bit much. She's like you when you first arrived in Brittany multiplied by a hundred, but Nicholas is all right and so is Elodie. And your mother loves me for finally making a proper lady out of you, so what more can I ask for?" She leans her shoulder into me. "And you're moving to Bonneau for me, so it's really the least I can do in the spirit of compromise."

I don't correct her that I'm not exactly moving to Bonneau. I'm taking a leave of absence and spending it in Bonneau—with her. But I guess to her, and if I'm honest, in large part to me as well, it feels as if I *am* moving. Even though I'm keeping this apartment so we can come to Brussels whenever we want—or in case things don't work out.

"But still, I appreciate you being here." I kiss her on the cheek.

"Spending time with you is not a hardship." She draws me near. "I know I shouldn't say this too often, but you're so hot." She cups my cheek and leans in. "Then again, you've known that since long before you met me." She kisses me softly on the lips.

"Just hot?" There used to be a time when I wouldn't be completely joking. When I was simultaneously so full of myself and insecure enough to ask a question like that, but that's not the case with Olivia. I'm not asking her because I have to, because of some undercurrent of unquenchable need inside of me. I'm asking simply because of this tender moment between us. Not to get an answer—she gave me all the answers I needed and then some months ago when she admitted to being in love with me. I know how difficult that was for her, to make herself so vulnerable to me.

"You know I'm only with you because you're so damn hot—for a woman on the cusp of fifty-seven, I mean," Olivia says before kissing me again.

It's only because of the intimacy between us that she can poke such fun at me—and that I can take it. Because I see now that my ego used to be so fragile, I had to inflate it all the time—by chasing women, mostly, but also by relentlessly showing everyone around me what I was worth. By not giving myself enough time to sleep and rest. By pretending I was still in my thirties long after I'd turned fifty. By staying up half the night even though I had back-to-back surgeries the day after.

All of that is in the past now—all of that changed after my self-imposed exile to Bonneau. When I left for Brittany on the first of January, I didn't really know what I set out to achieve. I just left because I couldn't stay in the same place where everything had so suddenly gone wrong, hoping to feel better after a while. And I did. And now I also have Olivia.

"I might be fifty-seven soon, but I'm still a little afraid of my mother." I tear myself away from her lips. "Or are you going to explain to her we're late because you couldn't keep your hands off me?"

"It's worth a try just to see if she still likes me so much after saying that," Olivia deadpans.

During the past year, especially the first few months of knowing her, there have been many moments that I believed Olivia wasn't worth the trouble, yet she always proved me wrong. I stuck around and she was always there. And here we are now. As implausible as it sometimes still seems that I'm in a relationship with a woman who basically slammed the door in my face the first time we met—a woman so cranky, with such negative energy emanating from her, I had no desire to ever see her again.

"Come on." I pull her out of the sofa. "Time for Christmas carols around the tree with the Dievarts."

Olivia laughs because she knows very well my family would do no such thing for Christmas. Then again, it wouldn't be the first time a Dievart has surprised her.

CHAPTER 40
OLIVIA

I hate having all eyes on me at the best of times, but especially when I'm opening a present. I'm already practicing my reaction, even though I have no idea what's inside this package. Of course, the tape is too sticky and I can't pry it loose so I end up tearing at the paper. Inside is a grey sweatshirt. I turn it around and, on the front, printed in stark black letters, it says: *Je ne décroche pour personne.* I don't pick up the phone for anyone.

When I look up, I see Marie snickering. She would think this is funny. I can kind of see the joke myself, especially because it's a throwback to how I would always ignore her calls those first few months she was staying in Bonneau.

"How lovely," I say with plenty of sarcasm in my voice.

"I knew you'd love it, darling," Marie says. "Now you don't have to say it out loud anymore." She walks over to me and wraps her arms around me. "It was a toss-up between that line and your other favourite 'I can't really explain'," she whispers in my ear.

"I'm just surprised it doesn't have a picture of you on it." In my head, I high-five myself.

"I can easily have one of those made." Marie gives me a quick kiss on the cheek and continues distributing presents to her family members. She is a generous giver of gifts, bombarding everyone with multiple whimsical small presents and at least one outrageously luxurious one. Mine is one of those ultra-smart watches with which I can track the most detailed piece of data when I go for a run outside —which I do more of now, even in winter. Not everything has to be so controlled anymore. I can now handle a modest amount of curveballs in my day—being with Marie has trained me to catch them.

I had Marie handle most of the gift-giving from me to her family, although I do have a surprise gift for Alice, who has really taken a shine to me, for reasons I'm not sure actually have all that much to do with me personally. I think she genuinely just wants her daughter to be happy, as she confided in me last summer in Bonneau.

Heart beating in my throat, I hand Marie's mother a rectangular package.

"*Pour moi?*" Alice clutches a hand to her chest—it's not hard to see where Marie gets all her dramatic airs and graces from.

I nod and momentarily feel like fleeing the room, until I let the smidgen of pride that lurks somewhere in the depths of my consciousness take over. Because the biggest gift of being with Marie is that I no longer let fear rule my entire life. I can let go more. The best example is that I'm here with her family instead of alone with my cats in Bonneau celebrating Christmas, which is what I've done since Sandrine left.

Alice unwraps her present and displays the olive-green cover of the poetry collection Sandrine has put together.

"Huh," Marie says to me. "I had no idea you were giving her that."

"I'm so glad I can still surprise you."

"You've surprised me every single day since I met you," Marie says to me, then turns to her mother. "Olivia's one of the poets," she says, as I knew she would.

"Really?" Alice looks at me as though she admires me even more, while all I've done is finally take her forever-single daughter off the shelf. She thumbs through the book. "I can't wait to get you all out of here so I can read it in peace." She sends us a smile, letting us know she doesn't mean that in the slightest. Alice loves having her two daughters and their families here—I'm part of the family now.

"Just be happy Liv didn't give you the last book she translated," Marie says.

She and her mother banter back and forth and Madeleine soon joins in. I sit and look at them, happy for the few connections I've allowed myself to make this year. I might have been content on my own, but being here, with the Dievarts, isn't half bad either.

JANUARY

CHAPTER 41
MARIE

When I kill the engine and glance at my house, all I feel is warmth, despite it being below zero outside.

"Is this a significant moment for you?" Olivia, who's in the passenger seat, asks. "Because my furry babies are waiting for me."

I look at her and I can't help but smile. "I would never ask you to choose between me and your cats."

"It's not a choice." She leans towards me. "We're all here together." She gazes into my eyes before kissing me on the lips. "Come on. Let's go inside. The cats can wait a little longer." She opens the car door and gets out. I remain seated a few more moments, remembering the same day exactly one year ago, when I arrived here and everything was so bleak and dark and depressing. When I set out to find myself underneath the mess I'd made of my life. When I first spotted Olivia's house through the barren branches of the trees.

So many years of my life have passed me by as though they were nothing, as though they were just time to get through while I had people to see and heal and, at times, offend. While I lived at a speed so fast, I outran myself. The past year has been the opposite of that. Because everything slowed down when I arrived here. This house is the symbol of that—this house, this place, and the woman waiting for me to get out of the car. If there's one thing Olivia has in spades it's patience. And time. And all the other things I didn't know I was looking for a year ago. Because she may think she won the most extraordinary women's lottery when I fell for her—admittedly, she kind of did—but, in return, she has given me so much more than I could ever have imagined.

I get out of the car and instead of unloading my suitcases I take her hand. I unlock the front door and we walk in together and I feel like I've come home, simply because she's here with me. I think of all the women I've known while I look at the one I've ended up with—coming home here with Olivia by my side does feel like I've reached the final destination of a long journey.

The last thing on earth I want to do is ever hurt Olivia. There are never any guarantees, but in the past, when I waltzed into some poor woman's life, it was usually with the ferocious energy of a wrecking ball—my affair with Véronique the perfect, destructive example of that.

I pull Olivia towards me so I can kiss her. It's a relief to no longer be on the look-out for a new pair of lips to kiss—to come home to the same woman time and time again. I wonder what it will be like, now that I'm here. Now that I've come back, for myself and for her. I won't be working and Olivia will need her space, I know that much. We will be living next to each other but not with each other, although we'll spend plenty of time together.

I'll cook for her. I'll entertain Huppert. Maybe I'll even

get Deneuve to like me more. I'll walk and walk and stop at Yvette's and do all the things I used to this time last year, yet everything will be different. Because a year later, that cranky woman next door is crazy about me.

If that's possible, then I know anything is.

THE RAIN

OLIVIA CHEVALIER

The rain outside reminds me
    of when you were still here

Of those long days of just us
    when you and I would disappear

When our separate souls would vanish
    into thin air—inside this palace
    built of our new skin's veneer

The rain's still here
    but you've long gone
    you've disappeared without me
    and my soul's been torn apart.

ACKNOWLEDGMENTS

Dear Reader,

This was such a difficult book to write, I almost didn't write it at all. About halfway through, I was ready to chuck it in the bin and never give it another thought. But, of course, then, I couldn't stop thinking about it.

For the longest time, this book went by the working title of *Difficult Women*. Being a self-declared (and proud) difficult woman, I know a thing or two about them, yet the level of personal confrontation this book made me go through was a bit much at times—hence the dramatic bin-chucking.

I might as well have hung my soul out to dry, for all the world to see, that's how much of myself is portrayed in the character of Olivia. Why, oh why I set her up with *French Kissing* villain Marie Dievart may forever remain a mystery. All I can tell you is that I got the idea on a trip back from Brittany and it stuck. I had to write it. I was always going to write about Olivia, who I qualified in my notes as 'a woman on her journey to unapologetically become herself'. As you may remember from *French Kissing*, Marie Dievart's never been big on apologies either. Yet writing about her is what, ultimately, saved the book. Because it was such a delight to contrast Marie's borderline arrogance with Olivia's profound inwardness.

Some books I can't let go. And I'm glad that, after a long break during which I wrote *About That Kiss*, I returned to this one; that I persisted, and finished it.

Even though it's one of those books that's too revealing and private to become a true reader favourite (although I know some of you will really take it to heart), it has really become my own personal favourite. Thank you for giving it a chance—for giving *me* a chance.

A million thank-yous to my wife, Caroline (who is nothing like Marie Dievart, FYI.) We're coming up on 21 years together and it hasn't always been plain sailing but, so far, we've had the greatest adventures—and we're about to embark on the next one. There's no one I'd rather move to the Breton countryside with than my Mrs.

My editor, Cheyenne Blue, could easily fashion a stand-up show out of the one-liners she leaves in the track changes of my manuscripts. And that's definitely not the only reason I haven't worked with another editor for years.

Claire Jarrett, my trusty proofreader, always gives my books one last, ultra-thorough polish.

I don't have a huge team of beta-readers, but I do have Carrie Camp, who has been giving me her gut reactions on my books for many years—and has developed the uncanny ability to reliably predict how a book will fare once it's out there.

Because this book is so close to my heart, I did ask for one more outside opinion, and boy did I get one from lesfic reader extraordinaire Sophie Lennox! Her passionate feedback took away most of my doubts about baring my soul (once again) and I can't thank her enough for that early and much-needed encouragement.

The members of my Facebook Group go through all my writerly highs and lows with me and for someone quite averse to social media, my Facebook Group has really become my own personal safe space. I can be as pompous, long-winded and dramatic (some would say 'difficult') as I want and no one bats a virtual eyelid. Thank you for your every-day support. It's so lovely to have a place to turn to for (over-)sharing just about everything.

The members of my Launch Team are equally supportive and always help my books off to such a brilliant start.

And, as always, thank *you*, Dear Reader, for sticking with me on the mad rollercoaster ride of light-hearted and more profound books I tend to write. I just saw this survey that said readers tend to move on from a writer after having read 7 of their books. That may very well be the case, but I know that some of you have read all 34 of my books, and are already looking forward to the next. Thank you for that from the bottom of my heart.

Harper xo

GET THREE E-BOOKS FOR FREE

Building a relationship with my readers is the very best thing about writing. I occasionally send newsletters with details on new releases, special offers and giveaways.

And if you sign up to my mailing list I'll send you all this free stuff:

1. An e-book of *Few Hearts Survive*, a Pink Bean Series novella that is ONLY available to my mailing list subscribers.
2. A free e-book of *Hired Help*, my very first (and therefore very special to me) lesbian erotic romance story.
3. A free e-book of my first 'longer' work, my highly romantic novella *Summer's End*, set on an exotic beach in Thailand.

You can get *Few Hearts Survive* (a Pink Bean Series novella), *Hired Help* (a spicy F/F novelette) and *Summer's End* (a deeply romantic lesfic novella) **for free** by signing up at www.harperbliss.com/freebook/ or scanning the QR code below

ABOUT THE AUTHOR

Harper Bliss is a best-selling lesbian romance author. Among her most-loved books are the highly dramatic French Kissing and the often thought-provoking Pink Bean series.

Harper lived in Hong Kong for seven years, travelled the world for a bit, and has now settled in Brussels (Belgium) with her wife and photogenic cat, Dolly Purrton.

Together with her wife, she hosts a weekly podcast called Harper Bliss & Her Mrs.

Harper loves hearing from readers and you can reach her at the email address below.

www.harperbliss.com
harper@harperbliss.com